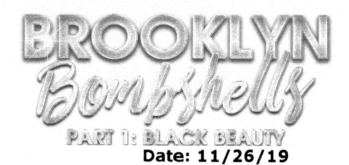

BROOKLYN Bombshells

PART 1: BLACK BEAUTY

Melodrama Publishing
www.MelodramaPublishing.com

FOLLOW
ERICA HILTON

FACEBOOK.COM/THEREALERICAHILTON

TWITTER.COM/MS_ERICA_HILTON

Order online at
bn.com, amazon.com, and
MelodramaPublishing.com

www.melodramapublishing.com

Library of Congress Control Number:1620781005
ISBN-13: 978-1620781005

First Edition: January 2019

BROOKLYN
Bombshells
PART 1: BLACK BEAUTY

Erica Hilton

Prologue

Jamaica Estates, Queens

It was Christmas Day, and the swanky house at the end of the block in Jamaica Estates was decorated with a dazzling array of lights. The home represented affluence at its finest with a Mercedes Benz and a Lexus parked in the driveway. A marked squad car pulled up to the place and came to a stop. Two officers climbed out and were met by a concerned neighbor who stood outside the front door waiting for the police to arrive. The Johnsons were a pleasant and social couple, and every Christmas morning, they would invite neighbors and family over to have breakfast and share gifts. It had been a routine of theirs for ten years. But today, their house sat in silence and was absent of any cheerful activity. The entire place looked bleak and almost dark, except for the Christmas lights.

"Something's wrong, officers. I know it," the neighbor lady told them.

"When was the last time you heard from them?" asked the senior cop.

"Two days ago. But every Christmas, this place is lit up with family and friends over for breakfast and gift giving. The Johnsons are that kind of couple—always giving and having folks over for a good time. They always open their doors to everyone," she said.

She filled them in on the couple. Malik was a corporate lawyer and Liasha ran a successful online business as an SEO consultant and web designer.

"Okay, we'll check it out," said the partner.

One of the officers jiggled the doorknob and found the door to be open. Seeing that, the neighbor immediately became worried. The cops slowly entered the home on alert with their hands against their holstered weapons, and they started to call out the residents' names, Liasha and Malik Johnson. But there was no response. Right away, the officers noticed the disturbance inside. The home had been completely ransacked. Both men being veterans on the force, they instantly knew it was a home invasion.

They carefully went through the house, and each room was the same—items wildly scattered everywhere, furniture turned over, and cabinets and drawers open and looking rummaged through. Inside the master bedroom was where they found the real horror. The couple was gagged and bound on their king size bed in their underwear, and they had both been shot in the head at close range. Their bodies were stiffened by their violent deaths and were reaching rigor mortis stages, meaning that they had been dead for a couple of hours now. The officers gazed at the scene in wide-eyed horror.

"Shit! Call it in," said the senior cop.

When the neighbor heard about the tragedy, she immediately burst into tears. She couldn't believe it. Not the Johnsons—and not on Christmas Day. Word of their ghastly murders started to spread through the affluent community, and their families were notified. It was heartbreak all around—tragic news that thrust everyone into profound grief over the horrific murders of their favorite neighbors.

Chapter One

A shirtless Butch Brown sang a slurred rendition of "Jingle Bells" and danced around the project apartment to music that wasn't playing. He took another healthy swig from the half-finished bottle of Hennessy he clutched and continued to sing.

". . . laughin' all za wayyy—ha ha ha! It's Christmas in Brooklyn!" he continued.

Butch was a forty-year-old alcoholic and a part-time mechanic. He was a skinny man with reddish brown skin, freckles, hazel eyes, and flaming red hair. He consumed most of his meals from liquor bottles.

He staggered to the window and peered outside at the projects on a sunny, but cold Christmas afternoon. He was already full-blown drunk, and it was only 1 p.m. But a drunk Butch was a friendly Butch. It was when he was sober that everyone had to worry. He became vile and angry, and no one liked to be around him and his quick temper. He would go crazy and lay hands on his girls, including his wife, Bernice. At times it got so bad that the cops were called to the apartment, and Butch had spent plenty of nights in jail. Although everyone knew he should be in rehab, they would encourage him to drink or buy him a bottle because a sober Butch was unbearable in the household.

"Look at Daddy. He's actin' all exalting and everything," Butch's seventeen-year-old daughter Claire said with a giggle. She sat on the couch with an English textbook in her hands, staring and laughing at her father, who had distracted her from reading with his drunken antics.

"Daddy, you know what you are right now? Jolly and inebriated. But that's fine—we need some contempt in this house, and some agitation too," she added.

Exalting? Contempt and agitation? What the fuck? the youngest daughter, Chanel, thought to herself. She gave Claire a peculiar look. Claire was known to use big words wrong, but no one in the family except Chanel knew the meaning of the words she used. Claire was heading to college in the fall, and everyone was proud of her.

Chanel didn't say anything. If she spoke up and corrected Claire, World War III would break out inside the apartment. Instead, Chanel coolly lifted herself from the couch and left for the bedroom to be alone.

"Daddy, you so stupid," Claire added, laughing. "Bacardi, you need to come in here and get your husband."

With her reddish brown skin, freckles, hazel eyes, and red hair like her intoxicated father's, Claire Brown sat there on the raggedy living room couch trying to look high-class in the ghetto apartment while her mother cooked neck bones, collard greens, and white rice in the kitchen. There was a sickly and sparsely decorated Christmas tree in the corner with no gifts under it.

Butch continued to sing, drink, and dance around the living room like he was getting paid to put on a show for everyone, and he would occasionally stare out the window. It was Christmas Day, and he had the perfect gift in his hand—liquor.

"Butch, you need to go sit your fuckin' ass down somewhere," Bacardi hollered at her husband. "It's too damn early for this shit!"

Butch turned around and smiled at his wife. He then outstretched his arms and jovially exclaimed, "Come dance wit' me, baby! C'mon, let's get our groove on . . . oh yeah."

Butch started to do a hilarious late-eighties Michael Jackson routine by the window. His shoulders shifted up and down in a robot-like move, and then he spun around on his heels and roared with laughter.

Bacardi shook her head at her husband like he was crazy. She wasn't in the mood to dance. "You're a damn fool, Butch. Sit your silly ass down before you end up hurting yourself. We ain't got time to take your ass to no fuckin' hospital on Christmas." She went back into the kitchen to check on her neck bones cooking.

Bernice Brown, AKA Bacardi, was a weathered looking forty-year-old with a foul-mouth, dark chocolate skin, a straight nose, and thick permed hair. As her name suggested, Bacardi drank and smoked weed regularly. She had a nice shape back in the day, but now she was thick with a wide butt, matching wide hips, and a protruding gut. Bacardi was proud of two things—her job with the city at ACS that she hated but was grateful to have, and the three-bedroom apartment in the Glenwood Houses she shared with her husband and three daughters. She believed their apartment was luxury because the Glenwood Houses were one of the better projects in Brooklyn with less violence, but mostly because they lived next door to a white family.

Bacardi was in a foul mood this Christmas Day. She was dead broke and pissed off about it. She had put $500 to the side to get her daughters some gifts for Christmas, but she had gone to her best friend Keisha's apartment to play cards a few nights earlier. Drinking heavily and winning more than losing, Bacardi got trashed during the card game and passed out on Keisha's couch. She woke up the next morning to discover that someone had stolen the $500 she had stashed in her bra. As expected, Bacardi became enraged and ready to turn violent. It was all the money she had. Immediately, she blamed Keisha.

"Bitch, who fuckin' stole my money?!" Bacardi had growled at her friend.

Keisha was completely dumbfounded. She had no idea who took the money, but it was Keisha's place and Bacardi held her responsible. Bacardi wasn't leaving without her money. The two ladies came to a compromise, and Bacardi gave Keisha two weeks to replace her money or else trouble would rain down on Keisha, best friend or not. The clock was ticking down on the deadline.

Butch took another mouthful of Hennessy and continued with his erratic behavior. The bottle was nearly depleted.

"It's fuckin' Christmas, bitches!" he shouted. He wildly spun around with the bottle and accidentally spilled some of his brown juice onto the couch and some onto Claire and her textbook.

Claire sighed and frowned, suddenly not finding her father's behavior amusing. But it could be worse. He could be sober and cruel—cursing everyone out and carrying on. His drinking was the lesser of two evils.

Somewhat upset, Claire said, "I'll be in the bathroom." She shot up from the couch with her textbook in her hand and marched to the back.

While Butch, Bacardi, and Claire occupied the living room, kitchen, and bathroom, Chanel locked herself in the bedroom she shared with Claire. Her oldest sister Charlie had her own room whenever she was home, but she had been gone for two days now.

Chanel sat by the window and gazed aimlessly outside at the chilly streets from four stories up. Christmas Day in the projects, and everything seemed quiet; there wasn't a crackhead in sight. Chanel didn't want any part of her family's foolish activity in the next room. She didn't feel wanted—never had.

Chanel was sixteen years old, considered awkward, and she was the black sheep of the family. She wasn't close with either of her sisters and not even her mother. Her dark complexion and dark brown eyes were the utter opposite of her two older sisters. With her straight nose, full lips, and long, jet black hair that she forever styled in two braids or two ponytails—simple—some said she looked like a young Naomi Campbell. Her natural hair was wavy like her mother's, but her mother and sisters were always telling her she needed a perm and constantly saying to her, "With your nappy hair."

A deep sigh emanated from Chanel's mouth. Outside her window, she noticed a black Jeep come to a stop and park across the street on Ralph Avenue. Chanel watched the doors open, and exiting the vehicle were Charlie and her boyfriend, Godfrey—God for short. Chanel felt no excitement seeing her sister coming home after being gone for two days. The only thing she felt was more drama arriving into the apartment. It was the last thing she needed. Nonchalant, Chanel removed herself from the window and plopped face-down on her bed. *Why me?*

Hearing knocking at the door, Bacardi ran toward the door like a child expecting Santa Claus to show up. She was all smiles seeing Charlie arrive with God. They came bearing gifts, carrying large black garbage bags full of surprises. Charlie came marching into the apartment wearing a brand new auburn mink coat that swept the floor when she walked. The coat looked a little too big for her, but who cared? It was a mink coat. Bacardi was wide-eyed and in awe.

"Shit, bitch! Who the fuck did you rob?" Bacardi joked.

"You know I couldn't let Christmas go by without showin' my family some love," said Charlie with a wide smile.

Bacardi hugged her daughter and God. "Where's Fingers at? How's he doing?" she asked, referring to God's friend.

"That nigga home wit' his peoples playin' Santa. He good, though," God replied.

Bacardi wasn't the only one excited about Charlie and God showing up. Butch was all smiles, and Claire was happy to see her big sister too—

especially when she saw the bags filled with gifts. It was officially Christmas Day for the family.

Charlie was eighteen years old and she was her parents' pride and joy. Like Claire, she had reddish brown skin, freckles, hazel eyes, and curly red hair. Charlie was the hustler of the family. She got money, and that was what mattered most to the family.

Reluctantly, Chanel exited the bedroom and joined the others in the living room where Charlie and God stood clutching the garbage bags like Santa's toy bags. The family was like wide-eyed children anticipating what Charlie had brought them.

"C'mon, Charlie! Let's get this party started. I'm overwrought and ready to see what I implemented this Christmas," said Claire excitedly, once again misusing her big words.

Chanel rolled her eyes and shook her head—and Claire was supposed to be the smart one. *Yeah, right*, she thought to herself.

Charlie started to dig in each garbage bag and hand out the goods. The first to get a gift was Bacardi. Charlie tossed her mother a Valentino bag and a leather shearling coat, which was a little too tight on her, but Bacardi didn't care. She also received some Christian Louboutin shoes—which were a half-size too big—and an Apple watch. There were plenty of *oooohs* and *aaaahs* at the start, and it escalated to excited yelling getting louder with each gift presented. Bacardi was over-the-moon. It was becoming the best Christmas ever!

Butch received Christian Louboutin men's hard bottoms, which fit him perfectly, along with old school Adidas and Puma sweat suits, a cashmere sweater, slacks, and Beats by Dre headphones. Butch right away kicked off his smelly sneakers and put on the expensive shoes, the cashmere sweater, and headphones. He started to slide across the floor trying to balance himself, swirling around like he was a skilled dancer.

"Damn, look at me," he hollered. "Ooooh watch out now!"

Butch started to dance like he was one of The Temptations, entertaining his family. Even God had to laugh at Butch's silly antics. Butch behaved like he was a man in his sixties, but everyone loved seeing him this way, funny and affable—because an inebriated Butch was a tolerable Butch.

With her parents' gifts out of the way, Claire was thirsty to see what her big sis had brought her. She eyed her mother's red bottoms because she wore a 40 too, and she wanted those same shoes. Claire soon got her wish. Charlie reached into the bag, pulled out the nicest boots Claire had ever seen, and tossed them at her. Claire was flabbergasted. She clutched the boots tightly to her chest and started to scream and run around the house like she had no sense. Joy filled her eyes to the brim.

"Ohmygod, Ohmygod, Ohmygod, I love 'em! Oh shit! I got fuckin' red bottoms, bitches! I can't wait to see these hoes start to hate on me out there when they see me rockin' these," Claire breathlessly exclaimed.

Everyone laughed. They loved the moment.

Charlie continued with her benevolent nature toward her family. She continued to remove gifts from the bags, handing Claire a mid-length tan mink coat. You would have thought Claire had won the lottery for a billion dollars. She started screaming at the top of her lungs again and shedding tears of joy at the same time. She snatched the coat so quickly from Charlie's hands that even the Flash couldn't keep up with her. Claire tried on the coat, and it was a little too big for her, but that was nothing a thick sweater couldn't fix.

As Claire pranced around the living room in her new coat, Charlie had one demand for her. "I get to wear it when I want, Claire. And I don't wanna hear any shit from you, or else I'll keep it for myself."

Claire didn't like the ultimatum, but she agreed to it, for now.

Bacardi started to feel some kind of way. Unable to restrain herself, she spewed, "And where the fuck is my mink coat? I'm the fuckin' one that gave birth to you."

Charlie glared at her mother. "Damn, didn't I give you enough, Bacardi? You got a leather shearling. Why you gotta be such a greedy bitch?"

"I'm sayin'—a mink is always nice to have," Bacardi retorted.

"Bitch, I just gave you some damn near two-thousand-dollar shoes and then some!"

"But I always wanted a mink."

"These coats can't fit you, Bacardi. Damn! Stop being fuckin' greedy! If one coulda fit you then I woulda blessed you wit' it."

And just like that, an argument erupted between Charlie and Bacardi—dysfunctional family at its finest. While the two argued, Chanel stood on the sidelines still waiting her turn to see what her big sister had brought her for Christmas. But leave it to Bacardi to ruin everything.

It took Claire to get between the two ladies before the situation escalated. She shouted, "Can we just all chill and have a nice Christmas for once?"

In the meantime, Butch sat on the couch entertaining himself with his gifts, tuning everything out for the moment.

Bacardi and Charlie fell back from each other and their argument ended, but something Charlie had said caught Claire's attention. She pivoted toward her sister and asked, "And what do you mean, Charlie? Where did these coats come from? Y'all didn't buy them for us?"

Charlie frowned. "What's wit' the third fuckin' degree? Y'all some ungrateful muthafuckas in this apartment! Don't be askin' me any stupid fuckin' shit like that! And y'all can either keep the fuckin' gifts or give 'em the fuck back! Fo' real."

While Charlie and Claire went at it, Bacardi took it upon herself to try and squeeze into Claire's mink coat. Seeing this, Claire immediately attacked her mother and tried to wrestle the coat away from her hands and it ignited a brief tug of war between them.

Bacardi growled, "I just wanted to try it on. Don't be a selfish fuckin' bitch, Claire!"

"It won't fuckin' fit you! And you gonna ruin it before I can even get to flaunt it outside," screamed Claire.

Meanwhile, Chanel noticed that two bags were already empty and the last bag almost was. She was going to be last, like always. But Chanel didn't gripe; she patiently waited her turn to see what Charlie would bless her with this Christmas Day.

Charlie turned to look at Chanel with disgust and reached into the garbage bag and handed her an Amazon Echo Dot and a used laptop. That was it—nothing else came out of the bag. It was the only thing left she had to give Chanel. Chanel stood there feeling her eyes welling up, but she refused to cry. She didn't want to give Charlie and everyone else that satisfaction. Everyone received fabulous gifts that made them over-the-moon, and she got two less expensive items, and one looked used. Graciously, Chanel said, "Thank you," to her big sister and decided to excuse herself, leaving the items in the living room.

Charlie grimaced. "Oh, so your black ass just gonna walk out the fuckin' room and not be fuckin' grateful for what I got you? And I know you don't got ya fuckin' lips poked out, bitch. You lucky you got that shit!" Charlie barked at her sister. She was upset that Chanel hadn't screamed at the top of her lungs in delight like Claire, Bacardi, and Butch had.

Chanel stopped walking and spun around. "I said 'thank you,' Charlie. What more do you want me to say?"

Charlie snatched the Echo Dot and laptop from the table and gave them away to Claire. Claire had no problems taking them. It was more gifts for her, and more was great. No one else found her behavior wrong.

"That's one jealous-hearted, miserable child I done gave birth to," Bacardi commented as if Chanel wasn't standing in front of her. "She think her shit don't stink walkin' 'round here like she the Queen of Sheba or some shit. Charlie, you shoulda smashed her fuckin' teeth down her throat and made her eat that fuckin' laptop!"

"That's y'all fault. You and Butch spoiled her li'l ugly ass." Charlie gave a delusional explanation, which everyone accepted.

Chanel quietly retreated to her bedroom, closed the door, and cried her eyes out. It was turning out to be one of the worst Christmases ever. Her life was hard because of her family, but Chanel saw herself as a survivor. She was the black Cinderella in a family that hated her. She wondered where her Prince Charming was. Where was that tall, dark, and handsome man to sweep her off her feet and take her away from her hell? She wanted a man who could protect—provide her security from anything. She had the most precious thing a woman could give a man, something her sisters could no longer give—her virginity.

"Fuck that bitch!" Charlie said about her own sister.

It was the standard behavior with the family. Chanel got the crumbs while everyone else feasted on a fine meal.

Happy with their gifts, the rest of the family enjoyed a good meal that Bacardi put together, then God sparked up a joint and they all smoked some high grade weed and drank hard liquor. The family was happy and they couldn't wait to show off their gifts—*wait until the neighbors see all this new shit.*

Charlie boasted her Christmas gifts the best, taking off her new fur coat and showing off a diamond necklace and a gold Rolex watch. Bacardi and Claire were floored—in complete awe at the gleaming jewelry she had on. Bacardi had never been so proud. She beamed. Her daughter had gotten with the right nigga. Bacardi loved God like he was her own son.

Unbeknownst to everyone, the perpetrators of the gruesome home invasion and double homicide in Jamaica Estates of Liasha and Malik Johnson were Godfrey "God" Williams, Frederick "Fingers" Avery, and Charlie Brown.

Chapter Two

The temperature outside dropped to a freezing 19 degrees, making it the coldest day of the month so far. The nasty chill outside matched the chill Chanel felt in her heart that early morning. She woke up with an attitude. Everyone had really nice Christmas presents except for her, and no one saw anything wrong with it.

Chanel was the only one awake in the apartment. Claire was still sound asleep in the twin bed opposite Chanel's, Butch was passed out on the living room couch with a half-empty liquor bottle still clutched in his hand, her mother was asleep in her bedroom, and Charlie and God were passed out in Charlie's bedroom. Her folks didn't have a problem with a nigga laid up with a teenager.

Chanel got out of her bed, donned a long robe and some slippers, and left her bedroom for the kitchen. The entire apartment was left a wreck. The trashcan was overflowing with garbage, the living room was cluttered with junk and remnants of drug paraphernalia, and the sink was piled with dishes. No one had attempted to clean up anything. Chanel was adamant that she wasn't going to clean up shit. She looked at the hurricane of untidiness and sighed heavily. Her family was the worst.

The knocking at the door made her pivot and walk to the foyer. Chanel looked through the peephole and saw her friend, Landy, standing in the hallway.

"Girl, I know you see me standing out here and shit. Hurry and open da' door," Landy hollered.

Chanel gladly opened the front door and let Landy inside.

"Hey bitch, what's good wit' you?" Landy spoke in her urban tone.

"I just got up," said Chanel.

Landy was a young white girl one would call a wigga. She dressed and spoke more urban than Chanel. Landy's long, brown hair was styled in cornrows under the dark blue Yankees fitted skewed atop her head. She had tattoos and several piercings, including a nose ring. Dressed in a white sweatshirt, a gold cross around her neck, navy basketball shorts with leggings underneath, and a new pair of Air Jordans, Landy bopped inside the Browns' home.

"So, you the only one up, huh?" Landy said, eyeing Chanel's drunk pops on the couch.

"Yup! They won't be up no time soon."

"Lazy fucks."

"But them Jordans are nice. I really like those joints."

"Thanks—one of my Christmas gifts from my bitch-ass father. At least he did somethin' right, know what I'm sayin?" said Landy. "And what you get fo' Christmas?"

Chanel shook her head and frowned.

"Yo, they ain't get you shit, Chanel?" Landy said.

"Not one thing. But everyone else got some nice shit."

Landy sighed. "Yo, that's fucked up."

"Tell me about it."

Landy hated the Browns for the way they treated Chanel. Chanel was cool and innocent, and she was a good friend. There were plenty of times Landy wanted to go off on the Brown family for fucking with Chanel. She could and would fight anyone in a heartbeat. But out of respect for Chanel, Landy kept the peace with Chanel's sisters and the parents.

"You want breakfast?" asked Chanel.

"Yo, that would be cool. I'm fuckin' starvin' out this bitch, fo' real."

Chanel and Landy made their way into the kitchen. Chanel washed out a few pans and went to work on making some bacon and scrambled eggs for breakfast. While she worked her magic over the stove, Landy pulled out the latest iPhone, and Chanel's mouth dropped.

"Oh shit, you got the new iPhone? Get the fuck outta here—that's what I wanted for Christmas."

"Yo, this fuckin' phone is dope, Chanel. Shit got wireless charging, it's water and dust resistant, a fuckin' ill-ass camera an' shit. It's on point, ya feel me?"

"That shit is nice. What else did you get?"

"A couple of hundred-dollar gift cards, a Fire Stick, and a new bedroom set."

Chanel was happy Landy had a better Christmas than she had. At least someone got what they wanted. Landy took a seat at the rickety table and slouched in the chair. She eyed the messy kitchen that matched the messy apartment and shook her head in disgust.

"Damn, your peoples don't clean?"

"They don't do shit around here," Chanel replied.

"So what happened yesterday?"

Chanel turned to her friend with a look that said, *Bitch, too fuckin' much*. She made sure not to speak too loud while talking to Landy, nearly whispering her troubles to her friend.

"Charlie came by with her boyfriend God with three big ol' garbage bags of gifts, and she hooked everyone up. I'm talking about red bottoms and mink coats and a Valentino bag for my mother, a cashmere sweater for my father. She was just spilling out nice shit for everyone, and she was even rocking a fuckin' diamond necklace and a Rolex for herself."

Landy asked, "Damn, where she get that kind of money?"

"That's what I want to know. But she out here actin' like she won the lottery. And then she gonna give me my gift last, handing me some old-ass laptop and some Echo Dot, and she wanted me to kiss her ass for it."

"Wow, that's crazy, yo."

"I know. I gave her that shit right back."

"I woulda whooped that bitch's ass!"

"It's all good."

"Nah, it's not all good, Chanel. They need to stop treatin' you like shit! You don't deserve it. You one of da coolest peoples I know, and if I gotta pop off on ya family, then bitch, let me do it," Landy said.

Chanel smiled. She knew that her sisters would beat the brakes off of Landy and Bacardi would pulverize her. "Thanks. You're a good friend."

"You my bitch, Chanel. I got your back."

"It's just odd, Landy. I don't understand why they hate me so much." Chanel sulked. "I guess it's because I'm the black and ugly one."

Landy was confused. "Y'all are all black, or am I missing something? If it's us four in a car who do you think is not getting racially profiled?"

"We're all black but not the *same* black. My sisters are that lighter, whiter black with red, curly hair—it's too much to explain. If you were African-American you would get it. I'm the ugly one."

"Ugly? You really believe dat?"

Chanel shrugged. "Landy, you're more of a sister to me than my own blood, so I feel like I can keep it one-hundred with you. You know some black parents love their kids to be bright white with that good hair like Charlie and Claire. Charlie and Claire walk around here talking about how their freckles are like Meghan Markle and how niggas love their red pussy hair. They're so revolting! And they're constantly talking about how I'm not a redbone like them."

Landy smirked. "Girl, bye wit' all that dumb shit. I would kill for your complexion. I look like a jar of mayonnaise."

Chanel chuckled. "You do not."

"Let's just say I don't run from the sun but I'm cool wit' that. I use my complexion to my advantage 'cause I understand the politics of it all, and you need to get down wit' that."

Chanel had no idea what Landy was referring to. "How do I use my black skin to my advantage, Landy? There is no such thing as black privilege. You're talking foolishness."

"You're not red like your sisters 'cause God wanted you to be darker. Stop comparing yourself to them and be happy in your own skin. Look in the mirror and see the black beauty and watch how differently Charlie and Claire start to treat you. If you know you're pretty too, shit gon' change. All these beautiful black women didn't pave the way for you to be walking wit' your head down. You need a role model—Oprah Winfrey, Naomi Campbell, Viola Davis, Serena Williams, that beautiful Lupita chick. I shouldn't have to tell you dis shit."

"You don't get it."

"But, I do, though. You want a pity party. Bacardi really got you fucked up, yo. You're one of the prettiest females I know, and that's no homo. In fact, you're beautiful—like model–pretty, but your low self-esteem will be your downfall. If you fall in the hands of the wrong nigga you're done. Hasta la vista done."

"You're being dramatic. I don't even have a man." Chanel paused for a beat, "And, Landy, you my bitch, but you don't get to say the N-word."

"My b."

Things got quiet in the small, messy kitchen as the girls processed their conversation.

Landy continued with, "Check this, Bacardi pits y'all against each other and runs a divisive household. It's manipulation 101. As long as you don't feel worthy enough for her love you will always clean out the shitty toilets, wash the dirty dishes, and take whatever abuse Bacardi dishes out.

How she treats you is her issue not yours, yo. I would start cursing her fat ass out."

"I can't disrespect my moms, Landy. She'd fuck me up."

"Well then I would go hard on them two red bitches. I would be callin' them hoes fire crotches and soulless gingers. Let them know all those freckles ain't cute. It's a fuckin' connect-the-dots puzzle on their face! Start speaking up for yourself."

Chanel laughed. She appreciated that Landy was trying to cheer her up. She also knew she had some good points. It was hard to take advice about self-esteem and colorism from a white girl who wanted to be black, though. Landy was book-smart—she had a 4.0 GPA—but she too was suffering from image issues. Maybe that was how she was able to recognize Chanel's insecurities.

Chanel finished making breakfast. The bacon and scrambled eggs mixed with green peppers and onions were the bomb. Landy praised Chanel on her cooking. The two sat at the table and shared a few laughs. But their enjoyable moment together was short lived. A few minutes at the table and Bacardi entered the kitchen scowling at the two girls.

"Hello, Mrs. Brown," Landy greeted with a smirk.

Bacardi completely ignored Landy. Her focus was on Chanel. She had smelled the food cooking and desperately needed something in her stomach to soak up the alcohol she'd consumed last night. She took one look at the empty pan on the stove and went off.

"Oh, you selfish bitch," she started. "You cook you and your friend some fuckin' breakfast and don't make any for anybody else?"

"Y'all were all 'sleep," said Chanel.

"So! That's your damn excuse? After your sister done hooked you up wit' some nice shit yesterday, you can only think about yourself. And why the fuck this house ain't clean?"

Chanel could feel her face getting hot. Her mother was always a crass woman, and now she was embarrassing her in front of her company. Landy sat right by Chanel's side frowning and trying to keep herself from going off on Mrs. Brown in her own home.

"You need to tell your company to leave and you need to make us some fuckin' breakfast too. And clean up this damn place! Shit! I work hard every day, and your lazy ass just eats, sleeps, and shits!" Bacardi griped.

Landy stood up. "I'll see you later, Chanel," said Landy coolly with her plate of breakfast in her hands.

Bacardi quickly vetoed the idea of Landy taking food out of her home. She snatched the plate out of Landy's hand. "You ain't pay for shit in this fuckin' house to take home wit' you." Like a barbaric bitch, Bacardi sat down at the table and started to gobble down the meal.

Landy clenched her fists with a hard stare aimed at Bacardi that expressed, *Oh, no this bitch didn't just snatch shit out my fuckin' hands.*

Chanel looked at her friend and her eyes pleaded for Landy to chill. She didn't need any drama and problems right now.

For Chanel's sake, Landy excused the incident. "Yo, I'll see ya around, Chanel."

She pivoted and marched toward the door. Once she was gone, Bacardi berated, "You always got that white bitch in this fuckin' apartment. Her fuckin' wanna-be-black ass. She wanna be a fuckin' nigga, then I'm gonna start treatin' her like a fuckin' nigga!"

Chanel kept silent. Her mother was in an extra foul mood this morning. Chanel just stood there coyly, not wanting to escalate the situation. She sighed lightly. Bacardi wasn't done with her yet. Still stuffing her face with eggs and bacon, Bacardi exclaimed, "You need to make some more breakfast and take your sisters a plate too. You know they gonna be hungry when they wake up."

Chanel grudgingly did what she was told. She cooked up some more of her specialty eggs and bacon and took the plates of food to her sisters, including God, because Bacardi considered him family too. Afterwards, she cleaned the entire apartment alone. Once again, Chanel felt like a ghetto adaptation of Cinderella—but there was no fairy godmother, and most certainly no Prince Charming.

After devouring her breakfast, Bacardi lifted herself from the table and marched to her bedroom. She closed her bedroom door, went into her dresser drawer, removed a pack of Newports, lit one up, inhaled and exhaled, and then took a seat at the foot of her bed. From where she sat, she could see her disheveled image in the bedroom mirror. Her glory days of beauty and fitness were becoming a faraway memory for her.

Bacardi had lived a hard life and she carried a lot of burden and guilt on her shoulders. She sighed profoundly with her eyes still fixed on her dark image—her murky soul gazing right back at her. She thought about Chanel and the animosity she carried toward her youngest. She would never admit to herself or anyone else that she hated Chanel. It wasn't because Chanel was her darkest child out of the three girls or that Chanel looked like her in her younger years—when Bacardi had the finest shape and beauty like a runway model. She held a profound hatred for Chanel because she knew that Chanel wasn't Butch's biological daughter. Bacardi didn't know who the father was until Chanel had gotten older.

When Bacardi was a bartender at a Harlem bar, she had an affair with a man named Leroy, a smooth and handsome hustler with the gift of gab. Night after night, Leroy captivated Bacardi with his charm. It didn't take long before she fell deep for his sweet, big black dick that would thrust deep into her after her shift ended at the bar every night. She became infatuated by him. He made her feel good. He made her feel like a woman, and the sex was amazing. Then she became pregnant—and Chanel came into her world.

By the time Charlie and Claire were six and seven years old, they started to tease Chanel about her dark skin and say she wasn't their sister.

Bacardi never stopped them. In fact, she was the most divisive one. Bacardi would treat Charlie and Claire like queens and Chanel like trash, and her daughters treated Chanel accordingly.

Whenever Bacardi would look at Chanel, she saw Leroy all over again—the man who rocked her world with great sex, the man who'd made promises to take care of her and love her forever. But Leroy soon became the man to break her heart, suddenly leaving her with no explanation, a protruding belly, and no idea if the baby she was carrying was his or her husband's.

"Damn, your sister can burn in the kitchen. These eggs are fuckin' good," God said as he munched on the breakfast Chanel had cooked.

Charlie twisted her face at the compliment. "She a'ight. Don't be sweatin' her cooking."

"I'm just sayin', that bitch did us nice wit' this breakfast. A nigga was fuckin' starvin' this morning," said God.

They were both seated at the foot of the queen size bed in Charlie's bedroom. Charlie was dressed in her panties and bra, and God was shirtless and in his boxers. His physique was manly—tattoos, battle scars, and muscles. He rocked a low haircut and a long, thick beard and mustache. He was twenty-three years old and a monster on the streets—everyone's worst nightmare. He was known to be ruthless and coldblooded. He had been killing people since he was thirteen years old and he once lived in Miami's Pork 'n' Bean projects. It was his gang initiation. When he was seventeen, he moved to New York City with his mother in search of a better life, but his criminal life only advanced in the Big Apple.

"I can give you sumthin' better to eat," Charlie said with a flirtatious smile.

God laughed. "I bet you can, shorty."

God's cell phone rang on the bed beside him. The caller ID indicated that it was Fingers calling him. God answered. "What's up, my nigga?"

"Yo, turn to the news on channel five right now," Fingers quickly said.

God wasted no time picking up the remote and powering on the flat screen TV. He turned to Fox News and there it was, their horrendous job displayed across the television screen. He turned the volume up to listen to the anchorwoman.

"What was supposed to be a joyous and celebrated holiday for this family on Christmas Day turned out to be a nightmare. A couple was found brutally murdered in their home after an apparent home invasion," announced the female field anchor.

The lavish house in Jamaica Estates was broadcasted for everyone to see. The area was flooded with police. The camera panned right to show distraught neighbors lingering in the background, and then it showed friends and family members pulling up the crime scene and folks consoling one another after hearing the news. Some were completely inconsolable. They cut to a middle-aged female neighbor who had nothing but nice things to say about the Johnsons.

"They loved each other so much, and they loved life, and they loved people. This is so horrible. I can't imagine how anyone could do such an atrocious thing to such wonderful people," the neighbor lady proclaimed.

Charlie munched on her bacon and God stared intently at the news. He was watching and listening to find out if they had any suspects or if there was a break in the case. But he knew the police didn't have any suspects. God was a very cautious criminal. He had been doing home invasions for over five years and had never been caught. To him, robbing and killing became simple—always wear latex gloves and black, know everything about your targets, always strike after midnight, and never leave any witnesses behind. To God, it was less risky than robbing hustlers or dealing drugs.

God and Charlie felt no remorse for the deadly home invasion—not when they'd struck payday. Liasha and Malik Johnson had lots of nice things—a closet full of pricey clothing and furs, diamonds, watches, electronics, and, of course, money. It was a beautiful score for the robbing and murderous trio. Fingers walked away with fur coats too—one for his girl and one for himself. God wasn't into wearing mink coats—too effeminate for his reputation, but he took one anyway. Free was free.

After the story of the deadly home invasion ended, Charlie turned to God and uttered, "Let's fuck! I'm horny."

She didn't care that her parents were home. They both let Charlie do whatever she wanted, including have sex with a twenty-three-year-old man in her bedroom.

God smiled. She stole the moment to yank his boxers down and used her forefinger and thumb to tease his dick and stir up a huge erection from him. She straddled him, rubbing her dripping pussy over his hard dick and moaning when he bumped her clit. She worked his dick into her nice and slow. She moaned when he thrust into her—almost going animalistic on her—hungry for every square inch of her naked and natural frame. God was a beast. And she was on fire with need.

"Oh baby, fuck me! *Fuck me!*" she groaned.

She panted as he pushed himself farther in. His erection was hard like concrete inside of her. She wrapped her arms around him, clutching him affectionately, and their bodies became entangled in sexual bliss. Their mouths opened and they kissed fervently. She continued to grind her naked bottom into his lap, wanting to explode with fire.

God moaned and groaned. "You're so fuckin' tight!" he cried out.

Charlie rode him like a professional. She reached behind her and started to massage his balls. God was her rock, and there was never a boring moment with him. He provided her with whatever she needed—money, material things, and security.

"Oh shit . . . you 'bout to make me come, shorty!" God cried out, his breath hard and hot.

Both conveniently forgot about the Christmas Day massacre.

Chapter Three

Bacardi waltzed into the ACS office proudly wearing Claire's mink coat without her permission. Despite the cold, she had to keep the coat open since it wouldn't close around her, and she had to wear two pairs of socks with the red bottoms she strutted in. She also carried her new Valentino bag and sported her new Apple watch. It was hardly appropriate clothing for her job. She was a walking fashion disaster—a mismatched heap of ill-fitting designer clothes that looked a mess on her overweight frame, but no one could tell her she wasn't fierce.

It was early Tuesday morning, and it was her first day back to work from their short Christmas break. Bacardi paraded through the office with her tight mink coat and designer bag and started to chitchat with her coworkers so they could see the new items that her wonderful and beautiful daughter had bought her for the holidays. Some coworkers complimented her coat, but many ignored her and the coat, bag, watch, and shoes altogether. Some even snickered at the outfit she had on behind her back, even uttering the words, "Ghetto trash."

Bacardi just knew she was the shit, though. She wanted folks to hate on her. Everything she had on was expensive and stylish.

She went to her cubicle to start her day as an ACS caseworker. The office was busy with cases, and Bacardi had a backlog of work to do. In the past year alone, the agency had received over seventy thousand abuse reports. Most times she felt overworked and underpaid, but it was a city job with benefits that she truly needed.

Before Bacardi sat down at her cubicle, she noticed her friend Keisha coming in to work. Bacardi was about to take off her coat and start her day, but she decided to keep it on for just a bit longer so Keisha could see her in it. Not only were they best friends, but they had been coworkers for many years now. Every chance she got, Bacardi would brag about her beautiful daughter Charlie and her amazing boyfriend God to whoever would listen—especially to Keisha.

Keisha walked toward Bacardi and stared at the ill-fitting coat and the red bottoms with the thick socks, and she immediately knew that her friend was wearing her daughter's clothes. But she smiled brightly at her friend, gave Bacardi a friendly hug, and said, "Damn, girl, that coat is gorgeous. And shoot, you got red bottoms too?"

Bacardi beamed. It was exactly what she wanted to hear. She absorbed the compliments pompously and then, with the snap of a finger, she went completely dark. Her smile transformed into a hard frown aimed at Keisha. "You got my muthafuckin' money?" she asked in a low tone.

Keisha didn't want to discuss it at the moment, especially at work, but Bacardi wasn't going to let her off the hook. "I'm putting it together right now, Bernice. But I thought you gave me two weeks, and you know I didn't get paid yet. We both get paid on the same day."

"Keisha, don't be tryin' to play me. You fucked up my kids' Christmas!"

"I told you before, I didn't steal your money. But I'll get you your money. Show you how good a friend I am."

Bacardi frowned. She hated to wait, especially for something that belonged to her in the first place. But Keisha was a good friend and she always kept her word, so Bacardi didn't push the issue. Instead, she decided to change the subject.

"Anyway, how was your Christmas?" Bacardi asked her.

"It was okay."

"Well, you know my Christmas was fabulous, as you can tell," boasted Bacardi as she did a twirl with her arms extended so Keisha could take everything in.

"I see."

"Charlie came through for us on Christmas Day. She and her man came through with a boatload of gifts for everyone. I love my firstborn."

Keisha smiled while Bacardi continued to brag about all the magnificent gifts her family received. Not once did she mention Chanel. Keisha knew they treated Chanel like shit. She slightly tilted her head and raised her eyebrow.

"Damn, y'all came off lovely this year, but where would Charlie and God get the money to buy so much nice stuff? And what did Chanel get?"

Bacardi didn't like the questions. She quickly spewed, "I got work to do," and then she turned her back to Keisha and sat down at her cubicle—conversation over.

Keisha shrugged. She knew her friend and her family like Mayweather knows boxing. Keisha pivoted and started to walk to her cubicle. On her way, she overheard one coworker say to another, "Bernice is a hot damn mess walking into work looking like that. She thinks she cute!"

"I know, right?"

They laughed at Bacardi's expense. Keisha didn't respond to the insult. She minded her business and went to work.

The first day back to work felt long and dragged out. Phones rang constantly with reports of abuse during the Christmas holidays, and supervisors and caseworkers were running around like chickens with their heads cut off. There were too many neglected, abused, and dysfunctional families in New York City to count. It was one horror story after another. Caseworkers were working feverishly to prevent another Nixzmary Brown. After the little girl's death in 2006, the department made some changes to the system, and the last thing they needed was another child's death on their watch.

Thirty minutes before quitting time, Bacardi and Keisha were given a removal assignment in the Bronx to place three children in protective custody. Bacardi was tired. It had been a long day. Her feet were hurting because of the too-high shoes she wore, and the mink coat was strangling her arms. She was becoming highly aggravated, and she wanted to go home on time, soak in a nice hot bath, smoke weed, and drink some Hennessy.

Her job as a caseworker for ACS wasn't easy. The hours were grueling and the supervisors were overbearing. The pay was decent, but it wasn't life changing. The worst part was going out in the field to handle the reported cases of child neglect, endangerment, and abuse—sometimes dealing with hostile parents and an unwelcoming environment.

Keisha was ready to go, but Bacardi was hesitant.

"Let's just try and beat the traffic into the Bronx," said Keisha.

Bacardi sighed and grumbled. "You think I want to go to the Bronx at this hour and deal with this case?"

"It's our job, Bernice. These children need to be removed by day's end."

Bacardi sighed heavily. The office was nearly empty. She coolly looked around her surroundings and came up with an idea. She looked at Keisha and suggested, "Look, why don't we just drive to the home and sit for a moment in your car, and then note that the mother wasn't present during our visitation? We can follow up on the case another day. If we do this knock for a removal, we might be there for hours. I'm fuckin' tired, Keisha."

It was a good idea, Bacardi felt, since caseworkers' phones had tracking and the supervisors were known to do call checks. However, Keisha was against it. She flat-out refused to go along with the plan.

"We can't do that, Bernice. Plus, I need the overtime. Did you forget? I got to pay you your money back, right?"

Bacardi grumbled and sighed again. Keisha wasn't going to budge, and she did need her $500 back. Bacardi dragged herself away from the cubicle with her mink coat in hand and her feet on fire. Her toes ached so badly, she was ready to walk out in the street barefoot. She didn't care if it was cold outside.

The traffic going into the Bronx seemed longer than the Great Wall of China. The roadways were a parking lot, with brake lights stretching for miles and miles. Every minute Bacardi sat in the traffic was a minute closer to her boiling point. She blew air out of her mouth and frowned.

"We're almost there, Bernice," Keisha said.

"We should have *been* fuckin' there. I swear, this city is a fuckin' mess! I hate this fuckin' city!"

"We're just doing our jobs."

"I fuckin' hate this job too!" she griped.

Keisha decided to keep quiet and just drive. Bacardi was bitter. Keisha felt it was best not to say anything else to piss her off.

The five-story brick building on Jerome Avenue looked like a mountain of trouble. Their assigned removal was on the top floor. There was no elevator, so they had to take the stairs, which agitated Bacardi even more. Her dogs were barking like the mailman was outside. She grimaced and cursed every step and every floor. When they finally reached apartment 5D, Bacardi said to Keisha, "This bitch better not give me any problems."

Bacardi knocked several times on the apartment door. She could hear music playing and the kids inside, sounding loud and disorderly. It was taking a while for the occupant of the apartment to answer the door and Bacardi was growing impatient. What made it worse was the fact that she could smell weed burning from inside and she couldn't take a hit of it when she needed it the most right now. Bacardi clenched her fist and once again rammed the bottom of it against the door.

"I got a bad feeling about this. Maybe we should wait for our police liaison," Keisha said.

Bacardi looked at her like she was crazy. Waiting for an escort meant more time, and it was time she didn't want to waste. She wanted to get the shit over with. Protocol was that every caseworker would be required to seek entry orders when denied access to a home of a child suspected to be at risk of neglect or abuse. But this was an immediate removal, and every minute was valuable.

Finally, the old, brown door was swung open by the children's mother. She stood barefoot in front of Bacardi and Keisha looking a ghetto mess in tight blue pum pum shorts, a tattered bra, a red scarf covering her head, and a serrated knife in her hand. Both of her arms and chest were swathed with tattoos. She scowled at the caseworkers and placed her hand on her hip, looking at them like, *Bitch what?* "Y'all fuckin' bitches ain't coming up in here takin' any of my fuckin' kids!"

Her unruly kids were behind her, running around the messy and foul smelling apartment. They were 10, 14, and 16. There had been reports of the ten– and fourteen-year-old girls being physically and sexually abused by the mother's boyfriend, who also lived in the home. The sixteen-year-old daughter was a known Blood gang member in the neighborhood, and it was alleged that she was pregnant by a man old enough to be her father. It was total chaos inside the two-bedroom apartment.

"Y'all bitches need to get the fuck away from my fuckin' door! I ain't fuckin' playin'. I will fuckin' cut and kill y'all muthafuckas if you try to step foot in this apartment and disrespect me and my fuckin' kids!" shouted the mother.

It didn't take long for her kids to join her at the door and emulate their mother. They too started to curse and threaten the caseworkers.

Keisha immediately took a few steps back from the apartment door. She didn't want that kind of trouble, so she got on the horn to call for backup.

Bacardi was livid. She thought, *The audacity of this bitch pulling a knife out on me!* Her hateful scowl matched the threatening mother and her kids. Bacardi was a bitch from the block, and a dumb ghetto thot with a kitchen knife didn't intimidate her.

"You need to fall the fuck back, bitch, or get fucked up," Bacardi retorted.

"You stupid lookin' big bitch, fuck off!" the mother shouted, while wildly waving the knife around in the air.

The shouting echoed through the hallway. A few neighbors opened their doors with inquisitiveness.

The oldest daughter was up in Bacardi's face too, furiously wagging her finger and threatening to have both ladies fucked up by her peoples. The mother egged her daughter on. They were two peas in a pod, and they were ready to tag team Bacardi. It soon became a shoving match at the doorway, and Bacardi saw her moment and abruptly charged at the mother with two rapid punches to her face, somewhat dazing her and catching her off guard. Then Bacardi grabbed the arm that carried the knife and she made sure it was flung from the woman's hand. Bacardi outweighed the lady by fifty or sixty pounds. A violent fist fight between them ensued inside the apartment. The sixteen-year-old daughter jumped in and tried to protect her mother from the pit bull of a caseworker.

"You dumb fuckin' bitch!" screamed Bacardi as she strongly clutched a handful of the mother's hair and nearly dragged her around her own apartment like a ragdoll.

The daughter started punching Bacardi on her back, and Bacardi elbowed the young girl in her face, spewing blood. Keisha stood in the background in absolute shock. It was chaos. It wasn't supposed to go down like this. The two younger daughters were crying, and a few neighbors had gathered at the doorway to observe the violent fight inside the apartment.

Bacardi had lost it. She repeatedly punched the mother in her face and tossed her around the living room something serious. The daughter was no match for Bacardi either. They were giving it their all, but Bacardi was a beast, giving them both hell. Those bitches had pushed her buttons, and that violent street thug came out of her.

Finally, two uniformed cops arrived at the scene. They charged into the apartment and broke up the fight before they killed each other. The mother was highly upset and shaken. She screamed at Bacardi, "Yo, arrest that bitch! She came into my fuckin' home and assaulted me!"

"You lying fuckin' cunt! Fuck you, bitch!" Bacardi retorted.

The mother looked like she had gone some rounds with Floyd Mayweather—a bloody face, a torn weave, and a bruised eye. The daughter was in a similar condition. Bacardi was breathing heavily. The situation had turned into a disaster and a nightmare all in one. Seeing the police in the room taking statements from people, Bacardi knew she'd fucked up. She had lost her cool and reacted. She mouthed to herself, "Shit!"

She looked at Keisha, who stood in the apartment looking dumbfounded by everything. It happened so fast. Bacardi expected Keisha to have her back and say that the mother and oldest daughter had jumped on her and started the fight. Bacardi didn't want to lose her job over the incident.

However, Keisha was on the fence as to whether she would lie for her friend. She'd warned Bacardi to follow protocol and wait for a police escort. Keisha needed her job and her pension.

Word spread of the violent incident in the Bronx, and Bacardi was immediately placed on suspension pending an investigation.

Bacardi was heated when she walked into her apartment. It was possibly the worst day of her life. Her believed best friend, Keisha, had hidden behind the supervisor and stayed at work to write up her paperwork, so Bacardi had to take the subway home.

The moment Bacardi walked through her front door, looking like she'd been to hell and back, Claire charged toward her and practically tried to rip the mink coat off her back.

"Why you wearing my new coat!"

Bacardi was in no mood to fuss with her daughter, but Claire was being an asshole. For a moment she forgot that Claire was her flesh and bone and she attacked. A scuffle ensued between them, but Butch immediately broke it up.

Bacardi screamed at Claire, "Try me, bitch! I'm not in the fuckin' mood!"

Claire replied, "You look so fuckin' stupid in my coat! It don't even fit you! Damn, why would you ride the dirty train in my mink coat! I fuckin' hate you!"

"Hate me then, you stupid, ungrateful bitch! I don't care!"

Chanel sat in the background watching the brief melee with her family. Her mother was taking it easy on Claire after her sister damn near attacked her at the door. She couldn't help herself. She mumbled, "Shit, if that had been me trying to snatch off the coat, I would have gotten my ass whooped."

Bacardi heard the smart comment and pivoted in Chanel's direction. She stampeded and raised her fists and started pounding on Chanel madly. Chanel cried out and tried her best to defend herself, but her mother had become a raging machine.

"Your mouth is too fuckin' grown and you never know how to fuckin' mind your fuckin' business!" Bacardi exclaimed.

Chanel hollered while Claire stood there and egged it on. She even said, "You shoulda shut up, Chanel. Always instigating somethin'—so asinine and wildish!"

"I'm sorry!" Chanel hollered.

But it was too late for sorry. Bacardi beat her youngest daughter like she stole something. Butch didn't intervene this time. He sat there and watched—almost proudly. After the beating, Chanel ran into her room with tears streaming down her face. She slammed the door and Bacardi warned, "Don't be slamming no fuckin' doors in this house, or I'll give you worse than that, bitch!"

Bacardi marched into her bedroom and slammed her own door. She wanted to be alone. She had been in a fight, nearly arrested, and she was suspended from her job. The only thing she wanted to do was take a long hot bath, smoke some weed, and get some sleep—and she dared anyone to bother her again.

Meanwhile, Chanel was spread out across her bed crying her eyes out. *It's not fair!* she thought. Claire could almost get away with attacking their mother, but she simply uttered one sly remark and havoc erupted inside the living room. Chanel wanted to run away and never come back. Why did her family hate her so much? She laid there on her stomach with her face pressed into the pillow, and her tears seemed never-ending. The room was dark and quiet, apart from her crying. Then suddenly, the bedroom door opened and Claire entered the room. She flicked on the lights, interrupting Chanel's darkness and her emotional solitude.

Claire stared at her sister with apathy and then laughed. "You look so pathetic and insignificant," she exclaimed. "If you picked up a book and read how to strategize like Tsu Zu or Greene's *48 Laws of Power* you'd know how to beat Bacardi at her own game. You too stupid to learn about cognitive dissonance and the philosophies of great thinkers. You'd know that your cognitive mind keeps you distant from your own mother."

Chanel ignored her. She would bet her last dollar that Claire was using the definition of cognitive dissonance incorrectly, but she kept her face buried into her pillow and didn't mumble a word.

"Anyway, I need the room to study," said Claire.

She shook her head and went toward her bookshelf and pulled out a book. She loved being the smart one in the family and spoke to everyone like they were dumb. She had them believing that they were dumb too by using her big, fancy words.

Claire sat at the foot of her bed with a text book in her hand. But she didn't start to read yet. She looked Chanel's way and once again shook her head. She said, "So, you just gonna lie in bed all day looking obtuse?"

Chanel turned over and shouted, "Just leave me alone!"

"Yo, don't be yelling at me. Who you think you are?"

Chanel glared at her sister—enough was enough. Claire was relentless with her insults, calling Chanel ugly and telling her that she was adopted and how she wished she would go live with her real family. Hearing enough of the verbal abuse, Chanel snatched her cell phone off the night stand and stormed out of the bedroom. Claire sat there and smirked. Getting under Chanel's skin was fun for her.

Chanel stormed into the bathroom and closed the door. Right away she dialed her friend, Mecca, who lived in Harlem, hoping and praying that she could go there to escape the abuse and insanity at home—if only temporarily. Mecca used to live in the same building as Chanel, but she moved uptown last year when her mother found a better job and a more suitable place to live.

Mecca answered her phone, and Chanel was relieved.

"Hey, you busy?" she asked.

"No. I'm just home chilling," said Mecca.

"Can I come over? I can't take it over here anymore."

"Yeah, sure. How long?"

"I'm leaving my place now," said Chanel.

Chanel quietly and hurriedly gathered a few of her things and left the apartment to sneak onto the C train to Harlem.

Chapter Four

The two speakers in the corner of the living room were somewhat small, but they were loud and clear, and they boomed old school R&B jams from artists such as Prince, Chaka Khan, Mary J. Blige, Keith Sweat, D'Angelo, and many more. It was a full-blown New Year's Eve party in the Browns' three-bedroom project apartment. The apartment was packed with revelers, young and old. The guests were mostly men, all vying to get a look, glance, or a quick feel of a round ass or perky tit brushing up against them from one of Bacardi's exotic looking daughters, Charlie and Claire. The girls were prime real estate, but the project guys were too broke to pay the mortgage. They could only fantasize and gawk at the Brooklyn bombshells.

"I'd give my left nut for a slice of Charlie's red velvet cake. I'd eat that shit out ev'ry fuckin' day. That's my word, my nigga," one goon stated.

"Nah, it's Claire that got the goodies I want. She the smart one going places and will be able to take care of a nigga. I'd lick her strawberry shortcake from the rooter to the tooter," another loser, who was five years older than Butch, remarked.

Another thug added, "Y'all buggin'. Both them ruby red bitches could get this dick. Why I gotta choose?"

The men all laughed.

Fried chicken, baked chicken, macaroni and cheese, collard greens, and fried fish were being sold for $7 per plate. BBQ ribs, potato salad, and collard greens were a bit more at $8 per plate. Hennessy and Patrón were being sold for $5 per cup and beer for $3. There was a pitty pat game going in the kitchen, and the house got a cut of all the winnings. All the cash was being stuffed into Bacardi's big bra. She was making a small fortune from the party.

"Bacardi!" a woman named Candy hollered from across the room. "You need to come over here and get your damn husband! He messing wit' the liquor, and I done told him a few times to get from over here."

Bacardi turned and shot her eyes in Butch's direction. He was lingering by the impromptu bar near the kitchen with a plastic cup in his hand. She hollered, "Butch, get the fuck away from my profits. I'll be damned if you fuck up my money tonight!"

Butch smiled at Bacardi before he downed what was left in his cup and staggered toward her. He was in a cheery frame of mind and entertaining everyone at the party. He went up to Bacardi and did a few two-step dance moves to Mary J. Blige's "You Remind Me." He spun around with laughter and tried to take his wife by the hand. "C'mon, baby, let's show these no-how's how to really dance."

Bacardi was in no mood to dance. "Butch, I ain't got no time to be dancing wit' you. Get out my face!"

She shoved him to the side and went into the kitchen to check on the food. She was about her business and making a quick buck. She had to keep an eye on things, knowing there were lots of thieves and cheats attending her party.

It was a lively affair; everyone was laughing, eating, and drinking. They were leaving the old year behind, partying like it was 1999, and bringing in the New Year with a bang. Every room had people inside of it, except for Bacardi's bedroom. Chanel had her own company.

Charlie and God came through all smiles with more liquor to sell and nearly an ounce of weed to smoke. It was a time to celebrate. The entire apartment was ablaze with different varieties of marijuana—OG Kush, Silver Haze, Raspberry Cough, Zombie, Gelato, Hawaiian Punch, and more. It was a smorgasbord of pot inside the apartment. Everyone looked at God and Charlie like they were celebrities—like they were gods. Charlie pranced around the party dressed in a pair of tight jeans and an asymmetrical halter top under her new coat. Her jewelry was dazzling like her hazel eyes. God looked a thuggish goon wearing dark jeans with his matching construction Timberlands and a dark brown hoodie under his leather coat. His diamond watch peeked from his sleeve, and his diamond earrings gleamed.

Bacardi couldn't stop smiling at Charlie. She was so proud of her for hooking up with a good man like God. He provided her and her family with whatever they needed, and he was highly respected and feared throughout the hood. Bacardi couldn't imagine Charlie with a bitch-ass nigga—or some working-ass sucker who couldn't afford to hold her daughter down. Charlie needed a real man—a fuckin' goon to love, and God was it. Shit, most times Bacardi wished she had a man like God.

It was nearing midnight, and the party was in full throttle with no signs of slowing down anytime soon. Fingers came through dressed in his best to join in on the fun. He and God politicked in the hallway for a moment, smoking weed and discussing their next lick before heading back into the apartment. Fingers wanted to get down with a few ladies that caught his eye.

"Do your thang, my nigga," said God.

Claire walked around the party with a book in her hand, but it was more for show than to learn. She figured a room full of folks was the perfect opportunity to boast her intelligence. She sat in a folding chair in the packed room and pretended to read.

Some of the young girls in the room started to whisper and snicker to themselves, even called her a wannabe bougie bitch. Claire heard their remarks and cut her eyes at the three young girls huddled in the corner and staring at her. She quickly stood up and marched their way, book still in her hand.

"Y'all bitches need to fuckin' go!" she said.

"Bitch, who is you?" one of the girls responded.

"A modish bitch that's gonna kick you out the door or throw y'all out the damn window. Y'all choose," Claire exclaimed.

"I'd like to see you try it!"

The tension grew thick between them, but before things escalated, Charlie made her way over and intervened.

"Is there a problem here?" Charlie asked coolly.

The girls didn't want any problems with Charlie, so they relented. "Nah, no problem, Charlie. We were just about to leave."

The girls made their way toward the exit, and Charlie shot an angry look at her sister. "You fuckin' up our money by kickin' people out. You shouldn't be reading a fuckin' book at a party anyway! Why can't you leave studying alone for one day?"

Claire sucked her teeth and simply walked away. She didn't want to hear her sister's rants. Charlie found God in the crowd and decided to do a little dirty dancing with her man.

The DJ got the crowd hyped when he played Childish Gambino's "This is America." It was like setting off a bomb. Everyone began doing the Wobble, Shmoney dance, Stanky Leg, and a host of others. Charlie backed her ass up against God, twerking and grinding her body against his. His hands were all over her like an octopus. They left nothing to the imagination—dirty dancing at almost a pornographic level.

Bacardi stood there and observed Charlie's wild behavior with her man at the party and slightly grinned. A bitch should keep her man happy by any means necessary. She almost wished she could trade places with her daughter. God was a fine man.

The music continued to blare inside the project apartment like it was a nightclub, and Bacardi's bra shrouded close to four hundred dollars in profits. It wasn't a bad take for a New Year's Eve party in Brooklyn. Bacardi had something to smile about.

Once again, a drunk Butch approached her for a dance, and this time she gave in. After seeing Charlie dance with her man, she decided to get her own groove on. Besides, it was a party. Butch pulled his wife into his arms and thrust his pelvis against her backside. Bacardi happily moved with her man to Earth, Wind & Fire's "September."

Butch continued his dance and started singing in her ear—out of tune of course. His hand reached up to cup her right breast and she allowed the fondling. It was cute how he touched her in public, not caring who was watching them. In fact, the fondling kind of turned her on. It was a peculiar sight to see mother and daughter both dancing passionately with their men.

Keisha arrived a half-hour before the countdown to the New Year was to begin. Dressed fashionably in a red lace dress that hugged her thick frame and red shoes to match, Keisha had all the boys eyeing her goodies.

Bacardi saw her and gave her the cold shoulder and continued dancing with her husband. She felt ambivalent about Keisha showing up. Her supposed best friend already had two strikes against her—owing her money and not having her back at the apartment when those bitches tried to jump her.

It took a moment for Bacardi to corner Keisha in a private area to finally ask her what she told their supervisors about the incident. Bacardi needed to know. She wanted to believe that Keisha had her back and her best interest at heart. She couldn't afford to lose her job—not now.

"What's good, Keisha? What did you tell them?" she asked seriously.

Keisha could only lock eyes with her friend and confess the truth. She knew that Bacardi would eventually read the deposition about the incident and find out.

"I told the truth, Bernice," said Keisha.

Bacardi was baffled by the statement. "The truth? What you mean you told the truth? What the fuck does that mean? You had my back, right?"

"I just told them what happened."

"You know what happened, them bitches tried to jump me—and that dumb bitch pulled out a knife on us."

"Look, I couldn't lie for you, Bernice. I told you to chill and just follow protocol. You did overreact somewhat," Keisha said.

"Are you serious, bitch? That bitch pulled out a knife on us and you wanna fuckin' blame me! You shoulda fucked that bitch up too!"

"I just can't lose my job over some foolishness," replied Keisha.

"Lose your job!" Bacardi shouted. "Bitch, you supposed to be my best friend! I thought you had my back on this!"

Bacardi stepped closer to Keisha. Her angry voice was starting to boom over the music.

"Bernice, get out my face like that," Keisha warned.

"Or what, bitch? What the fuck you gonna do!" Bacardi replied.

"You know what, bitch? Fuck you!" Keisha shouted.

Those two words—"Fuck you"—were fighting words for Bacardi. Folks were watching, anticipating a fight. And that's exactly what they got. Without warning, Bacardi swung first, striking Keisha in the face. As expected, Keisha reacted, and a full-scale fistfight ensued. Bacardi and Keisha thumped like animals in the wild, and for a split moment it was pound-for-pound. But that soon changed. Bacardi, who was drunk and short-winded, was having a hard time. Keisha had her backed into a corner and was hammering on her like a prize fighter going for the knockout and shouting, "Fuckin' dumb bitch! I'm sick of your shit!"

Seeing this, Charlie and Claire immediately jumped in on their mother's behalf. It was almost like a reverse replay of Bacardi's fight with the mother in the Bronx. Now Keisha was outnumbered and being attacked from both sides. She felt her real hair almost being pulled out from its roots, and fists were banging into her from left to right, front and back. She went down from the series of punches and now she felt strong kicks slamming into her ribs and face. Her sexy red outfit was being torn to shreds, her breasts were becoming exposed, and she could feel the blood coating her face. She hollered and pleaded for help—but there was no help coming her way. Bacardi, Charlie, and Claire were like a pack of wild hyenas tearing into meaty flesh with their razor sharp teeth. Keisha didn't stand a chance against the three of them.

"Fuckin' bitch!" Bacardi screamed, followed by a hard kick to Keisha's face.

It almost knocked Keisha unconscious, but she managed to stay awake out of fear for her life. Somehow, a man—a stranger—came between them, and it was the split-second Keisha needed. She hurried out the front door bloody, exposed, and badly beaten. She screamed at the top of her lungs and ran fast, fearing for her life. Bacardi had snapped and it felt like she was going to kill her. In fact, she knew they were going to kill her. She barely made it out the apartment alive. Just as the front door slammed, the countdown to a New Year started—5, 4, 3, 2, 1—HAPPY NEW YEAR! And the party continued.

Meanwhile, Chanel had locked herself in the bedroom with her friends, Landy and Mecca. The girls could hear the music from the party thumping through the apartment. They knew better than to leave the bedroom and chance running into the many perverts Chanel's parents had over.

They were having their own private party in the bedroom. Chanel adored her friends' company, and it wasn't every day that Mecca came back to the projects. The three girls were devouring snacks, drinking sodas, and talking about the things they would do, the places they would go, and the men they would date if they were celebrities.

"Girl, I would date Idris Elba with his fine fuckin' ass," Mecca proclaimed.

Chanel wagged her finger Mutombo style. "Uh-uh, you can't be taking my man like that. We gonna get married in Barbados, and I'm gonna give him the best honeymoon he's ever had and some of the cutest babies. You know I'm saving myself for him," she replied in jest.

"Well, we gonna have to fight for him, cuz you know I likes me a dark skin and tall, fine-ass man . . . and I would suck his dick," Mecca lightheartedly replied.

They both couldn't help but to laugh and roll around on Chanel's twin bed.

"Girl, you're so silly. I bet you would too," said Chanel.

"Damn right I would."

Landy wrinkled her nose at the thought of fucking an old man like Idris. "Y'all bitches insane. I would shoot my shot wit' 6ix9ine or Lil Yachty."

"Ewwwww!" Both Chanel and Mecca screamed at Landy's choices.

Mecca continued with, "Those tats on 6ix9ine's face and those braids and beads on Yachty make my skin crawl. Neither could ever get this tight pussy!"

The girls went from talking about Idris Elba and other celebrity men, to talking about colleges. Chanel couldn't wait to get away from her family. She got decent grades and she wanted to go to college in North Carolina— maybe Wake Forest, Duke, or the University of North Carolina. She wanted Landy and Mecca to attend a college in North Carolina too, so they could be close to each other. The girls were sixteen and had two years to plan for college.

As they talked and finished off another liter of Pepsi, it was then that they heard the ruckus in the living room. The music stopped, and they heard a series of thumps coming from the living room.

Landy jumped up and ran to the door and said, "Shit, I think they fightin' out there."

Chanel sucked her teeth and shook her head. There was always some kind of drama happening in her home.

"Don't open the door, Landy," Mecca warned.

Landy put her ear to the door to try to hear what was going on. "I'm not."

"Just let them fight. I'm not trying to get involved in their mess," Chanel said.

In the living room, the party went on like the Keisha incident had never happened. The music was loud, the drinking became heavier, thick weed smoke permeated the air, and Bacardi licked her wounds and praised her daughters for having her back. But all that was soon going to come to an end.

At first, the banging on the front door went unnoticed, but eventually, someone heard it and opened the door. Four uniformed cops marched into the apartment with their guns drawn and immediately flexed their authority inside the apartment. With them was a shaken and badly beaten Keisha. Instead of going to the hospital to treat her injuries, she wanted to exact revenge on Bacardi and her family and have all of them arrested.

"Turn the music off!" one of the cops shouted with weight in his voice.

The music ended and all eyes were on the officers and Keisha, who looked like she was going to fall apart and pass out. Everyone sobered up—cops were bad news. It wasn't even a full hour into the New Year, and the drama had already started.

"Is there a problem, officer?" one of the guests asked.

"Yes, there is a problem. A woman was assaulted at this party," Officer Krokowsi replied.

Keisha pointed them out for the cops—Bacardi, Claire, Charlie—the three culprits she believed tried to kill her. They were standing near the window, angry that Keisha had brought the police into their home.

The officers approached them.

Bacardi could only glare at her friend in disgust and shout the words, "Fuckin' snitching-ass bitch!"

"Bernice Brown, you're under arrest for aggravated assault and attempted murder," said Officer Krokowsi.

Bacardi was livid. She hated the police. "Y'all ain't got no fuckin' right to be in my fuckin' house!"

"Place your arms behind your back," Officer Myles demanded.

Bacardi didn't relent. The officers grabbed her arms and spun her around, pushed her against the wall, and threw on the handcuffs. Claire and Charlie protested their mother's arrest and were ready to throw down again, but they too were read their rights. The girls weren't going down silently, though. Every foul word they could think of spewed from out their mouths.

"Fuckin' nasty-ass pigs! Y'all some bitch-ass muthafuckas!"

"Black lives matter, you stupid fuckin' assholes! Fuck you and your cunt of a mother that fuckin' gave birth to you," Charlie shouted. "Go fuck yourself!"

The crowd could only stand around and watch, hoping that it ended with the three girls being arrested. The place was a melting pot of drugs and liquor, and Keisha had become enemy number-one by involving the police and bringing unwanted drama to a lively party where everyone wanted to have a good time.

"I need for everyone to back up!" shouted Officer Krokowsi.

The weed smoke was so thick inside the apartment that the four officers were catching a contact high. Looking at the faces of a few guests, they saw possible warrants and potential overtime.

The ladies were escorted into the hallway, where their foul mouths continued to spew hatred and resentment at the cops.

"Yo Charlie, just chill and be quiet, a'ight? I got y'all. I'm gonna get y'all out," God said to them.

"Fuck these niggas, God! I hate bitch-ass police!" Charlie continued to carry on.

God and Fingers were dirty, along with a few other individuals inside the apartment. Fingers had a pistol on him, and God had a gram of cocaine. The last thing they needed was a criminal charge. They wanted the girls to shut their mouths and go quietly, but it wasn't happening. The girls' spiteful rants echoed throughout the hallway non-stop.

Bacardi screamed, "I'ma fuck that bitch up again!"

"Keep talking!" shouted Officer Krokowsi.

The insults were starting to anger the cops. Officer Duke, who wanted to get promoted to detective, had the brilliant idea to interrogate the other folks inside the apartment and implement random searches to see what kind of goodies they came up with.

"Call in for a paddy wagon," he said to the others.

Officer Duke wanted to search anyone who looked to be under the influence of an illegal substance or suspicious with a warrant. But the other three officers started to look nervous; there were too many people in the small environment, and they didn't have absolute control of the area. They wanted to make their arrest and leave.

"You sure about this?" asked Officer Fletcher.

Officer Duke intensely stared at the others and repeated, "I said call it in!"

Officer Duke then turned to the crowd and yelled at them, "Okay, I want everyone to get against the wall and stay there."

"We ain't do nothing," shouted someone from within the crowd.

"Keisha, you done fucked up everybody's shmood, bitch!" someone else yelled.

"Let's not make this difficult, people!" retorted Officer Duke.

"Y'all making this shit difficult!" exclaimed another voice from the crowd.

"Yo fuck you, cop!" a voice roared from the other side of the room.

The rumbling of complaints and anger started to rise, and Officers Myles, Fletcher, and Krokowsi were growing concerned. They had their hands on their weapons and their heads were on a swivel. They were in enemy territory, and backup wouldn't be able to come fast enough.

Officer Duke continued to be an asshole, shouting, "I said let's not make this shit difficult, people!" He was already in defense mode, ready to react if or when things got ugly.

But cooperation with the crowd wasn't going to come easy. In fact, the hordes of folks started to grow antsy, and before the officers could get a handle on the situation, all hell broke loose. The entire crowd charged toward the officers, pushing and shoving by them and hurrying out the exit, down the hallway, and down the stairway. God and Fingers ran too. Three of the cops gave chase while Fletcher stayed with the three perps in handcuffs.

Within a minute, rapid gunshots rang out from the stairway—*Bak! Bak! Bak! Bak!* And chaos continued to ensue.

Hearing the gunfire finally made Chanel, Landy, and Mecca emerge from the bedroom. It was pandemonium inside the apartment. Trash and furniture were everywhere. Chanel saw her mother and sisters handcuffed and detained in the hallway where there was a nervous cop watching over them.

"Ohmygod, what's going on?" Chanel asked.

"Get back inside!" Officer Fletcher shouted with his gun pointed at the teenage girls. They were wide-eyed with terror on their faces.

Fletcher was already on his radio calling for backup and he was too afraid to leave his position to see what happened. He knew an officer was involved in the shooting. Then it happened. He heard crackling through his two-way radio. "10-13, officer down! Officer down!"

Oh shit!

"Get the fuck back in the apartment!" Officer Fletcher screamed again at Chanel, Landy, and Mecca.

The girls complied. They were scared and shocked. Chanel's home was turning into a war zone. Officer Duke finally emerged from the stairway looking torn down. He was angry. They all became angry and to feel like men, they began slamming and roughing up the handcuffed Bacardi, Charlie, and Claire. The girls were thrown to the floor, shouted at, and cursed. Question was, who shot a cop?

Chaos swept everywhere in less than an hour—from the Browns' apartment, into the stairwell, and outside the project building. The SWAT team and dozens of police cars flooded the area, and homicide detectives and brass converged inside the building where it was confirmed. A cop was shot dead in the stairwell. The gloves were off, and the police shut down the Glenwood Houses—no foot traffic in or out of the place.

Butch was dragged out of his bed by several NYPD officers. He had slept through the commotion. Groggily, he stared up at a half-dozen cops glaring down at him—ready to beat him to a pulp simply because a cop was dead. Landy, Chanel, and Mecca were being treated like criminals, cursed out, and spoken to disparagingly. They too were placed in handcuffs and made to sit on the floor in the apartment while it was thoroughly searched. Unfortunately for the cops, they didn't find anything except for two blunts—nothing to make a significant arrest. A few cops still wanted to arrest Butch, Landy, Chanel, and Mecca with a hard-on to thrust them into the system—maybe fuck 'em up. But an impartial captain overruled their racist desire.

The handcuffs were finally off, but Chanel couldn't shake the feeling of being disrespected and treated like a criminal when she wasn't. Landy decided she would stay far away from the Browns from here on out. They were too much drama, and murder was going too far. Even if it was a pig.

Mecca hugged her friend, but she too was in shock. She wanted to call her parents, but the police continued to treat them as if they were under arrest. Butch, now sober, was furious and he threatened to sue the NYPD. Everyone was upset. They all felt humiliated, and their wrists felt swollen because of the handcuffs being on for such a long time.

Camped outside the building were numerous reporters and news cameras. A cop being killed in the projects was big time news—if it bleeds then it leads. Locals were hounded by the reporters, and hovering above the projects were several police and media helicopters with a bird's eye view of the commotion below.

When the house was finally cleared out and quiet, all Chanel thought was, *Who shot the cop?*

Chapter Five

Bacardi, Charlie, and Claire were attached to the chain gang and led into the Brooklyn precinct. They weren't cursing out cops anymore, but they continued to seethe. They'd fucked up. They knew it, and it showed on their faces. New Year's Day was going to be spent in jail, and due to the holiday, it was going to take a full forty-eight hours before they would go before a judge. They already had a strike against them with the NYPD—a cop was killed because of them. Each cop they came across at the precinct glared at them with hatred and disgust.

"Fuckin' bitches!" one uniformed officer said. "If you ask me, the entire family needs to be put down."

The girls heard the comment but kept quiet. It would behoove them to keep their cool, unlike a few hours ago when they were madwomen ranting obscenities at the police. They were now in enemy territory, and they truly did fear for their lives. Once a cop was killed, the gloves came off.

All three were placed in separate interrogation rooms, where the detectives questioned them about the shooting. The detectives started with Claire and they grilled her for hours, asking about guests at the party and details about what had taken place. She was a hot mess. She tried to speak with some intelligence, but nervousness overcame her and she ended up sounding like a bumbling idiot.

Charlie was next. She held her own and was adamant that she had nothing to do with the shooting and she wasn't there. Bacardi frowned at the detectives and growled the same thing. She didn't know who killed the cop. She and her daughters were cuffed when it went down.

The detectives wanted a shooter, but each of them separately said that they were nowhere near the crime scene. They were already under arrest and being detained in the hallway when it happened. Their statements angered the detectives, but there wasn't anything they could do.

Inside Central Booking, they all had their mug shots taken, they were fingerprinted, and the guards conducted a full body search.

Once they were all together again in the holding cell, Bacardi immediately asked them, "What did y'all say to the police?"

"I ain't say shit because I don't know shit," Charlie replied.

"I don't know nothing either," said Claire.

Bacardi whispered, "So who you think killed that cop?" She looked at Charlie.

Charlie knew what she was hinting at. "God ain't do it!"

"What about Fingers?" Claire asked.

"I don't know. We don't know shit!"

"You think God will get us out of here?" Bacardi asked Charlie.

"He will, believe me. My nigga is a man of his word. He ain't gonna let me rot in here—y'all either. We just gotta keep cool and wait."

Bacardi didn't want to spend two days in jail, but she didn't have a choice. She knew that this was serious shit and they were going to be constantly harassed because of the cop shooting. She was already on thin ice with her job—now this. *Fuck me!* she thought.

The holding cell was growing packed with female inmates, but the Brown girls sat on the bench against the wall and kept to themselves. They weren't worried about any trouble coming their way, but they would have each other's back if it did come. Bacardi felt if some stupid bitch started trouble, she would be in for a rude awakening. She felt ready to kill someone.

The judge set their bail at twenty thousand dollars each—sixty thousand in total. Their arraignment wasn't pretty. They were charged with assault and battery, and resisting arrest. They were also hit with a restraining order to stay at least 100 feet away from Keisha. The authorities couldn't pin the cop's murder on them, which was disappointing for the NYPD. The judge brought the gavel down, displeased that he couldn't do more for the fallen officer. The girls were escorted back to the bullpen under the courts to wait for their bail to be paid.

God lit a cigarette and took a few drags. He sat alone in the idling Ford Taurus parked across the street from the Kings County Criminal Court in Downtown Brooklyn. The area was bustling with people and police—too much police for his comfort. His girl was finally being released after two days. He had paid the girls' bail via a bondsman and had to come up with six thousand dollars total. It was a small setback, but he couldn't leave his baby in lockup.

"What the fuck is taking them so long?" he griped to himself.

His head was on a constant swivel. He was vulnerable not to just the police, but to anyone that didn't like him. He had enemies. He didn't have a pistol or weed on him, and the Ford was legit. The last thing he needed was police fucking with him.

Two days after it happened, the shooting was still major headlines. The slain officer Krokowsi had three young daughters, and his distraught widow seemed inconsolable. His colleagues, friends, and family repeatedly proclaimed to the media that he was a wonderful officer and an excellent human being who cared about everyone. But God didn't care. To him, the only good cop was a dead cop.

He sighed heavily and continued to wait. His cigarette was dwindling with every drag. He eyed civilians and cops coming and going from the building. He hated to sit in one spot for too long. His cell phone rang and it was Fingers calling him.

"Yo, what's good?"

"They out yet?" Fingers asked.

"Nah, I'm still parked in this bitch and waiting."

"A'ight, then. Holla at me when they get out. We need to talk."

"A'ight, my nigga. One!"

"One."

Their call ended. After a few more pulls from the cigarette, God turned to his left and saw Charlie and her family coming out looking a hot mess—their hair was in disarray and their clothes disheveled. God climbed out of the car and approached Charlie with concern.

The minute Charlie saw him she beamed and ran toward him. "Baby!" she cried out. Her arms wrapped around him tight, and they kissed passionately in public. "Thank you for getting us out."

"You know I got your back," he said. "C'mon, let's get the fuck outta here. You know I don't like police."

"Fo' real," Charlie agreed.

Everyone piled into the car, and God couldn't leave the area fast enough. He didn't look back.

"I just want to go home and wash up. Ohmygod, I never stank so badly," griped Charlie.

"You got another cigarette?" Bacardi asked him.

God handed her the Newports, and each girl removed a cigarette from the pack and lit up, needing a smoke after their tiresome ordeal in lockup. The smoke was flavorsome and the one good thing they had to enjoy in the last 48 hours.

Bacardi exhaled. She had questions. She stared at God and asked, "What the fuck happened at my apartment?"

God was silent, driving and looking ahead. His expression was deadpan. The traffic in downtown Brooklyn was gruesome in the early morning, and he wanted to get far away from the area.

"You know who shot that cop?" asked Bacardi.

"It was Fingers," said God.

"Fingers!" Charlie voiced with worry.

"Yo, he ain't had no choice. That cop was on us and he was going after Fingers for some reason. Fuckin' Fingers spun around and put a bullet in his chest. He was vested up and fell back—tried to reach for his gun. But Fingers went up to him and shot him three times in the head," God said.

"Good for that muthafucka!" Charlie beamed. "Break up our party by bringing that dumb bitch to the apartment."

"Fuck his racist ass!" chimed Bacardi.

Claire was the only one who didn't celebrate the cop's death. "We need to think undoubtedly about this and not look too inept and assertive, y'all. It's gonna get crazy. Let's not gloat too much right now," she proclaimed, trying to start with her articulate talk.

Bacardi cut her eyes at her daughter and shouted, "Claire, shut the fuck up! I'm not in the mood to hear any of your reasoning. That muthafucka got what he deserved."

"I'm just sayin'—"

God quickly interrupted them, glancing through his rearview mirror. "Yo, I think we're being followed."

The girls all turned around to look out the back window to see a black Crown Vic behind them.

"Shit!" God muttered.

"You clean, right?" asked Charlie.

"Yeah! I ain't no fuckin' fool. I knew these muthafuckas was gonna be on us," he said. "Y'all got ya seatbelts on, right?"

They did.

"Is this car clean?" Bacardi asked him.

"Yeah. We good."

As they predicted, the police lights started to flash behind them, and a loud *whoop-whoop* blared from the Crown Vic, indicating for them to pull the vehicle over and stop.

"Here we go wit' this bullshit," God griped.

He slowly pulled the Ford to the side of the road and put it in park but kept the engine on. Not to take any chances, everyone inside the car placed their hands outside the window. Claire, thinking quickly, made sure God turned on his cell phone to record the entire incident. He left the phone hidden in the seat.

Two Caucasian plainclothes detectives climbed out of the Vic and cautiously approached the Ford. They flanked the car on both sides, with their hands on their holstered weapons.

"Turn off the car!" said the detective by the driver's side.

God did so slowly. "What's the problem, officer? Why did you pull us over?"

"We ask the questions, you understand? License and registration."

Both detectives looked inside the vehicle, fixing their eyes on the three females who'd just left lockup. Everyone inside the car remained silent.

God handed them the information they requested and said, "This is a friend's car."

"Everyone slowly step out of the vehicle, and do so calmly," the detective demanded.

"Seriously?" Charlie protested.

"You wanna make this difficult?" said the detective on the passenger side.

Both of them were ready to be assholes and exercise their authority to the fullest. Not having a choice, all four occupants slowly climbed out of the car and were forced to stand by the trunk. One detective started to thoroughly search the vehicle while his partner did an impromptu interrogation in public.

"Godfrey Williams, huh?" he stated while looking at God's identification.

God stood there deadpan. He didn't respond. What he wanted to do was kill that pig right where he stood, but it would be suicide.

"Where are y'all coming from?" asked the detective.

God frowned. "You know where we're coming from."

"Don't get cute, Godfrey. I can make this a good stop or a bad stop for you. Your choice."

"The courthouse, sir!"

"Any drugs or weapons in the car?"

"Nah, nothing," God replied dryly.

"And who are these bitches? Your hoes?"

The remark made Bacardi's face tighten with anger. She wanted to go off on the detective and knock his head off. *White-ass honky*, she wanted to scream.

"They family," God said.

The detective continued to be an asshole to everyone and he took delight in doing so. It was a cold day in January and the girls were freezing, but the detective didn't care. His partner was taking his sweet-ass time searching the car. To embarrass God even more, the detective patted him down and made him unbutton his shirt to see if he was hiding any contraband. He wasn't. But it was only to put on a show, to harass and humiliate God. They felt that he was connected to the murder of Officer Krokowsi, but they didn't have any proof. The stairwell didn't have any cameras, and well over two dozen people fled the party.

"Anything, partner?" the detective asked the man searching the car.

He retreated from the interior of the vehicle and replied, "It's clean. Nothing."

"I guess this is your lucky day." He tossed God his ID and stared him down. "But you won't get too many of those, I'll bet."

"Can we go?" God asked with a scowl.

"Yeah. You're free to go—your hoes too."

God pivoted and got back in the car. Bacardi and her daughters followed suit. God was so mad he wanted to put the car in reverse and run over both detectives several times. And he wasn't the only one. Bacardi and Charlie gritted their teeth in anger, feeling the two cops had no right to do what they had to them.

"I swear, if I see them two pigs again, I'm gonna fuck 'em up," God said as he started the ignition and drove off.

The two detectives had gotten what they wanted—the name of the driver and to let them know who was in charge and that they were being closely watched.

Fingers finished off the cigarette he smoked and extinguished it in the ashtray next to him. Once again he got up from the chair, walked toward the window, and gazed outside. Nothing. Everything was the same. There was no SWAT team there to kick in his front door and fuck him up. He tried not to be paranoid, but he had just killed a cop and there was no coming back from that. He wasn't going back to jail either. It was him or the cop.

He paced around the room and picked up his cell phone and attempted to dial God again. But he needed to keep his cool. He looked at the gun on the dresser and he shook his head, knowing it was a mistake to keep the weapon he'd used to shoot three slugs into the cop's head. It was overkill, but he hated the police. He needed to get rid of the weapon before it came back to haunt him.

Shirtless and slim with curly twists, Fingers didn't have the look of a killer—but he was one. He was twenty-two years old, and he'd had his nickname since he was a child. His hair looked like small fingers when he was a little boy, so for humor, his friends started to call him Fingers.

Fingers had a scar across his cheek and right lip from a razor that'd opened his face up during a fight in the juvenile detention center. The scar came from a young punk named Crooks. Crooks was a mean muthafucka who picked on those he deemed weaker than him. Fingers defended himself inside, but it came with a cost—his scar.

It took a few years for Fingers to carry out his revenge. He ran into Crooks by chance at a Miami nightclub, and the nigga looked the same after three years. Seeing his opportunity, Fingers followed him to his car and shot Crooks eight times while the man was seated in the front seat. It was his first kill, and it was personal. Once Fingers began killing people, it was rumored that his nickname came from being quick to pull the trigger.

Fingers wiped the gun clean and placed it in a brown bag. He then got into his Accord and jumped onto I-87 northbound. He drove an hour and a half away from the city, near a small town called Middletown, and came across an arched bridge with a river underneath it. With no one around, he tossed the murder weapon into the river and watched the river carry it away. He sighed with relief and then lit a cigarette. He felt that if the cops hadn't come for him already, they weren't coming. But for sure, it felt good killing that cop.

Chapter Six

With her mom and sisters locked up for two days, it was up to Chanel to clean up the ransacked apartment and take care of her father. The last task was nearly impossible. Mostly, Butch just drank and stayed in his bedroom either passed out or drinking and watching TV. He barely ate, but Chanel would leave his plate by the door and knock. She figured he would either take it or not. Mostly he didn't. Butch would rather drink than eat. She still cooked for him when she knew he despised her. *Why, though?* What had she ever done for her father to hate her so much?

For two days, Chanel had repeatedly tried to call Mecca to see if she was okay, but Mecca didn't return her calls. She understood that her friend was upset. It was fucked up how they were treated, and Mecca wanted to sue the NYPD for harassment and abuse. Landy had unequivocally told her that they could no longer be friends because her parents were spooked by the cop being shot and wouldn't allow Landy over at the Browns'.

The only good thing that came from the chaos was that the apartment was somewhat peaceful. There was no Bacardi to abuse her, and no sisters to talk shit to her or call her black and ugly. Her father kept to himself, and she didn't bother him, except to bring him the meals he didn't eat.

But that bizarre and beautiful solitude soon came to an end.

Chanel brought Butch a plate of breakfast, gently tapped on the door, and turned to leave as she usually did.

"Stop banging on the gotdamn door, Chanel," Butch yelled from his bedroom. "You fucking wit' me too early in the morning."

Chanel rolled her eyes. She knew that voice. It was the voice of a sober Butch.

She ran to the kitchen cupboard, and sure enough, all the liquor from the party was gone, which meant that Bacardi needed to get home soon or else. Chanel began washing the dishes, and within minutes her father appeared.

"What the fuck I tell you!" Chanel stared at Butch—a long look. He looked terrible, worse than his normal wear and tear. His body was a bony frame that appeared malnourished. His narrow face was gaunt, his eyes bulged, and his naturally red skin tone had a yellow tint to it. His jeans held on for dear life by a thick leather belt that could have been wrapped around his tiny waist twice. He was irate because his body was going through withdrawals. It usually took a full day before Butch *needed* a drink. Now, just under ten hours had passed, and his body was going through the signs of detox.

"Clean up this mess, Chanel. Your mother should be home soon!" His shifty eyes darted back and forth at the almost spotless apartment.

"What do you think I'm doing?"

"What's that shit over there?" Butch pointed toward the folded laundry, but had to lower his arm because it was shaking uncontrollably. In fact, his whole body had the shakes, and that infuriated him. He was embarrassed that he couldn't control his movement. He continued with, "You need to put all that shit away!"

"And you need to stop drinking before you die!"

Butch was still the man of the house, and nobody spoke disrespectfully to him. He went after Chanel quickly. She dropped the glass she was washing and took flight. Her father's strong, bony fingers stretched out and grabbed a fistful of her hair and yanked her toward him.

"Oooowwww," she screamed and tried to wiggle free.

His free hand punched her head and face several times until her lips split open and blood gushed out. He then tossed her up against the wall like a ragdoll. She felt a sharp pain in her ribs. He hovered over her like he was about to go in for the finisher.

"Daddy, no!" She cowered in the corner covering her vital lady parts. "Please! I'm sorry! I just love you . . ."

Butch was about to deliver more harsh blows, but truthfully he was already winded. He wasn't steady on his feet like he used to be, and the shakes weren't helping the matter. When Butch tossed Chanel up against the wall, he nearly came tumbling down behind her. He knew he needed to stop drinking, but the alcohol had a hold over him. He had an addictive gene, and if he had to choose life, his wife and kids, or the booze, sadly his addiction would win.

"Now stop fucking around and do what I say."

"Yes, Daddy."

Butch began walking back to his bedroom but suddenly stopped. "Hey, you got five dollars?"

Chanel just shook her head and continued to weep quietly.

Butch snorted. "Just like I thought. Good for nothing!"

Chanel was in her bedroom when she heard the front door open and slam shut. Immediately she heard the ruckus. She heard her mother's fearsome voice and Charlie's complaints. They were ranting about the NYPD and the mistreatment they'd endured earlier.

"I fuckin' hate cops!" shouted Charlie.

"I swear, all them muthafuckas can go to hell!" Bacardi added.

She then heard Claire's voice. The entire gang was back home. God had dropped them off and left. It was too hot at their place. There were cops everywhere. They were maintaining a strong presence at the projects, and they planned on harassing folks until whoever was responsible for killing a cop was brought to justice. The Brown girls were going to be enemy number-one.

Chanel sighed and walked out of her bedroom to sadly greet them, looking like an obedient dog. She wanted to be praised and thanked for her efforts in cleaning up the outrageous mess that was left behind. It took a lot of hard work and elbow grease, but Chanel had the apartment looking spectacular—almost brand new. Most importantly, she wanted Bacardi to see what Butch had done to her face. But of course, she received the exact opposite. They ignored her and her bruised face and busted lip. It was like she wasn't even standing in the room.

"I need a fuckin' shower," said Bacardi as she placed a couple bottles of hard liquor on the counter.

"Me first," Claire said.

"I need a fuckin' drink," Charlie chimed.

They didn't even look at Chanel. In fact, Charlie removed her coat and just tossed it aside, and the other two started to remove their clothing and leave things scattered everywhere in the living room, disrupting the tidiness of the place.

"We need to talk about this shit before we do anything," Bacardi said.

"About what? I'm tired, Bacardi. I just want to shower and get some sleep," Charlie said.

Bacardi finally shot a hard glance at Chanel. "Claire, you and Charlie come to my room so we can talk." They marched down the hallway to her bedroom and closed the door, leaving Chanel in the living room alone. She went into the kitchen.

Inside the bedroom, Bacardi and her girls went over the events. Butch was finally passed out on the bed and didn't look like he was waking up anytime soon.

"Look, this shit is serious," Bacardi said to Charlie and Claire.

"We know that," Charlie said.

"The cops are going to keep fuckin' wit' us because of that dead cop. So from now on, no more ounces of weed on us, or in this apartment. We smoke that shit and keep it moving. And Charlie, don't ride wit' God when he's dirty."

While they were talking in the bedroom about what to do, Chanel knocked on the door. She wanted to let them know that she'd made some food for them, thinking that they might be hungry after such a horrendous ordeal. But instead of a "Thank you," Chanel was instantly met with hostility. Bacardi cursed her out for interrupting them and shouted, "Bitch, don't knock on my fuckin' door again."

Chanel sulked and walked away, but Bacardi quickly called her back. *Did she have a change of heart?* Chanel wondered. Instead, Bacardi barked at her daughter, "In fact, bring us all a plate of food. And bring me a cup of Bacardi. I need a drink. And hurry the fuck up! I need to calm my fuckin' nerves."

Chanel complied.

Chapter Seven

The alarm shattered the stillness of the early morning. Bacardi grumbled and dragged herself from bed. A deep sigh spewed from her mouth. She felt like it was going to be a long day. All the shit that had gone down since late last year was going to have an effect on her future.

She zombie-walked into the bathroom and started to prepare herself for work. She took a shower and did her hair and makeup. She took her time to ready herself. She wanted to look professional and not like a ghetto mess. She decided to dress in a gray pantsuit that fit modestly and some shoes that she could actually walk in. For a while, Bacardi stared at her image in the bedroom mirror. She looked somewhat decent—a professional woman for once. There was no mink coat or red bottoms. It was a New Year, and that meant a new life and new things—better things, she hoped. While everyone was either in school or sleeping, Bacardi trotted off to work.

The train ride was uncomfortable. It was packed with people and she couldn't find a seat, so she had to stand for nearly forty minutes on the local C train. The morning was a cold 29 degrees, and she had to walk three blocks to her job. It was a life she hated—up early, living paycheck to paycheck, and dealing with coworkers she despised, but it was how she provided for her family and herself. It didn't stop her from bragging to all her non-working neighbors about her position with the city, though.

Bacardi walked into work and it felt like a bad dream. It was like she'd arrived to work naked and everyone was staring at her. The looks she received were discouraging and judgmental. She took it that her coworkers had heard about the big fight with Keisha and a cop being killed in her building. They stared at her with contempt and disappointment. Bacardi wanted to shout, "What the fuck y'all looking at?" But she didn't. She kept her cool and continued walking to her cubicle. Bacardi found herself the black sheep at her place of employment. No one wanted to talk to her. There were no "good mornings" uttered to her—just silence and foul looks.

She took a seat at her station, sighed heavily, and sat there for a moment. There was no sign of Keisha around, which was a good thing for Bacardi. She couldn't be within 100 feet of Keisha. She looked around the office, and the tension she sensed almost felt like she was going to be attacked herself. Bacardi was bracing herself for something. She had no idea what, but it was coming sooner than later. Bacardi wasn't at her workstation for five minutes before Barron approached her. She looked up at him with a quizzical stare.

He said, "Mr. Richards wants to see you right away."

"What's this about, Barron?"

"I don't know. But he wants to see you now," said Barron.

Bacardi nodded. This wasn't good. She picked herself up from her chair and headed toward the supervisor's office. It was a dreadful walk. It felt like she was marching toward the gas chambers—to her own death. She knew it wasn't going to be anything good. In the past month she had been overloaded with cases and there were some complaints filed against her. She stood at the door to Mr. Richards' office and lingered for a moment, trying to delay the inevitable. Finally, she knocked and stepped into her supervisor's office. He sat behind his cluttered desk looking egotistical, and the look he gave Bacardi was nerve-wracking.

"Close the door and have a seat, Bernice," Mr. Richards said coolly.

Ten minutes later, Bacardi stepped out of her supervisor's office to find two security guards waiting to escort her to her cubicle to pack her things. She had been fired. Like she was a prisoner, the guards flanked Bacardi and shepherded her to her workstation. They were there to make sure her departure went smoothly.

She was humiliated. She wanted to act out and go berserk, but she had a case lingering and she did not want to get locked up again under any circumstances. So, she bit her tongue, kept her cool, and packed all of her belongings into one box. She left the office with dignity, her head held high with all eyes on her. God, she wanted to scream and curse so badly. She wanted to go out with a fuckin' bang! The only good thing about the day was that Keisha wasn't there to see her departure. That bitch was still out on sick leave after her ass-whipping.

Charlie heard the faint sound of a door slamming. Someone was there. It was an hour before noon, and both of her sisters were in school and Butch was in the bedroom doing whatever. Charlie figured her mom was still at work. She stopped sucking dick and sprung up from the bed.

"Someone's here," she said to God.

"What? What the fuck you talkin' 'bout?"

"I just heard the door close."

God wanted her to finish, but Charlie looked somewhat spooked. After the incident with the police, she felt the urge to be careful. She donned a robe and marched out of the bedroom. God hurriedly put his boxers back on and followed her. In the living room she saw her mother returning home from work.

"What happened?" Charlie asked her.

Bacardi looked like she was going through it. It almost looked like she had been crying.

"They fired me today," said Bacardi.

"Oh shit. Why?"

"Why the fuck you think? Because of all the shit that happened! And Keisha ain't make the shit better," Bacardi snapped.

"I'm sorry," Charlie said.

"Fuck it! It's just a fuckin' job, right? I ain't like it anyway," Bacardi said. "I need me a fuckin' drink."

"I'll get you something," God said.

Bacardi expressed a faint smile toward God. She was happy he was around, especially now that she was unemployed. Seeing Charlie in her robe and God in his boxers, Bacardi knew what they were doing before she arrived. Hey, whatever to keep God happy, because now they needed some extra income.

"I'll be in the bedroom," Bacardi said sadly.

She walked off down the hallway. Once she was in her bedroom, the full weight of her circumstances hit her. She was forty years old and unemployed. She didn't have a job anymore, and she didn't have any money saved. She had to take a seat at the foot of the bed, where Butch was still sleeping like he was dead to the world. She had a lot to think about—or worry about.

She had taken the civil servants test seven years back and scored reasonably high, but there was a hiring freeze. They'd called her four years ago, and things had turned around for the Brown household. Bacardi found herself bringing in more money weekly, and she had health insurance for herself and her family, and she kept on bragging about how much her pension would be worth by the time she retired. She figured if she worked for ACS from when she was thirty-six and retired around sixty-seven or seventy, she would have a healthy package for her retirement. She and

Butch could move to Florida; her dream. But now things done changed.

Before she started working for ACS, Bacardi was a bartender at local bars, but being a bartender in her thirties became a tiresome gig, and it was a young girl's hustle. The young bitches with butt implants, breast implants, and beat faces squeezed out an old pro like her. Tips and jobs became scarce, and it was hard making ends meet taking care of three girls and a husband. It was Keisha who had forced her to take the test years back. Shit, Keisha even woke her up and drove her there.

Now, their relationship was estranged and she was jobless.

A few hours later, Charlie opened her mother's bedroom door to find her passed out on the bed alongside Butch. On the floor was an empty bottle of Hennessy. The room was dark with an odor. Charlie didn't judge her mother or say a word. She understood that Bacardi was going through a difficult time.

Bacardi was coming unhinged. The weeks following the killing of the cop, she sunk into a deep depression and started to drink more with her husband. Now the girls would come home and find both of their parents drunk. But the drinking wasn't the only thing the girls had to worry about with Bacardi. Sometimes after downing half a bottle of Hennessy, Bacardi 151, E&J, or Jack Daniels, Bacardi found herself worked up and angry. She would sloppily get dressed and march toward the front door with a knife in hand. When either Charlie or Claire would confront her, she would curse them out and shout, "Get the fuck out my way, bitch! I'm gonna fuck that bitch up! She cost me my fuckin' job, and that bitch still owes me five hundred dollars!"

"No, you can't go over there, Ma! You need to fuckin' chill out!" Charlie would shout at her.

Charlie would sometimes have to wrestle her mother away from the front door. They couldn't afford to make things worse for themselves, especially with a criminal case still pending in the courts.

With Bacardi unable to take out her anger and frustration on Keisha, she went to the next best thing. Chanel. The more depressed Bacardi got, the more she took it out on Chanel. She would burst into her youngest daughter's room at random and throw venomous threats and insults at Chanel. But it didn't stop with words. Sometimes she came at Chanel with a belt, a shoe, or whatever she could get her hands on and tried to beat the black off her. She would call her daughter black and ugly even though they were the same complexion.

Today was a day that Chanel decided to take Landy's advice and defend herself against Bacardi's unrelenting foul mouth. It all started over a Twinkie.

"Who drank the last of my Pepsi?" Bacardi asked as she stared into the almost empty refrigerator.

From the living room, Chanel rolled her eyes and said, "I did."

Bacardi snorted and slammed the refrigerator shut before sauntering over to the cupboard looking for something sweet. She reached for the Twinkies, only to grab an empty box. She looked inside, shook it, and then turned the box over as if it was a magic trick and a Twinkie would magically drop to the floor. The rage began as a slow, simmering emotion slowly coursing through her body. Just as Chanel placed the last Twinkie bite into her mouth, she could see her mother looming over her from her peripheral vision.

"You ate my muthafuckin' Twinkie?" Her voice was an unwavering, accusatory growl.

Wide-eyed and frightened, Chanel stopped licking the cream from her fingers. She swallowed hard and simply said, "Yes."

Bacardi's rage was still on pause. She knew that if she pressed play she might kill her daughter in there. She continued with, "What . . . the . . . fuck . . . I tell your greedy ass 'bout touching my personal shit?"

"You didn't even buy the Twinkies; Charlie did. So, technically, the food belongs to my sister."

"Oh, so you Claire now? You think you're a smart bitch?"

"I'm only playing the game you started."

Bacardi placed the palm of her hand to her forehead and simply breathed in and out to calm her nerves. There was always one child that gave each parent hell, and Chanel was it.

"Chanel, tread muthafuckin' lightly. I'm tryin' to be nice here, bitch, 'cause I'm on my menstrual. But if you ever eat my fuckin' Twinkies I will break ya fuckin' neck. Do your ugly li'l black ass—"

"You black and ugly too then!" Chanel hollered. "Look in the mirror, Ma! We're twins!"

That remark stopped Bacardi dead in her tracks. Her? Ugly? In her day she had her choice of the biggest ballers in Brooklyn. Everyone lusted after Bernice. And she was hardly black. In Bacardi's eyes she was 'brown-skinned'—imaginary shades lighter than her daughter.

Bacardi let out an egotistical snicker. "Chanel, I'm gonna keep it one-hundred wit' you 'cause you too stupid to see the truth wit' your own eyes. I don't know where you came from. I think you got switched at birth like that other li'l black child on the news. You don't look like me, and you damn sure don't look like your father. There's some other family out there missing a troll 'cause my pussy only pushes out dime pieces and that, you're not!"

"My black is beautiful, Bacardi, and if you don't think so then your mind is still stuck on a plantation! You Uncle Tom turd!" Chanel had been doing her homework. She was ready.

When Bacardi heard "Uncle Tom," she finally lost it. Her strong fists beat mercilessly across Chanel's arms, head, and back. The punches were solid, quick, and unforgiving. She pulled globs of hair from her daughter's head—just ripped out bundles of hair from the roots. Chanel refused to cry out and got some slaps and punches in too.

"Eat my Twinkie again, bitch!" Bacardi continued to yell as she wailed on her third-born. She needed to make this about the Twinkie, then skin color.

Chanel broke free and ran into the kitchen with Bacardi right on her heels. A butter knife was the only weapon she could grab. She missed the serrated steak knife by an inch.

Chanel wildly swung the knife at her mother as Bacardi blocked each blow with her forearms. The dull butter knife only left scratches and long welts, but the message was sent. Chanel was no longer easy prey.

A drunken Butch was able to pull the two apart. But things were growing so ugly in the Brown household, Chanel thought there were only two ways for her to escape it—run away or commit suicide.

Chapter Eight

It was late March and the weather was looking warm and breezy. The trees in the neighborhood were gradually going from a mess of unruly branches to greenery dotted with buds. It was a sunlit morning, and the sky held a soft blue glow. There were flowers blossoming, and the days were becoming longer because of daylight savings. Everyone welcomed the fresh new season—a needed change from a cold and brutal winter.

Bacardi, Charlie, and Claire were all dressed in their finest attire. It was an important day for them. They had a court date to appear in front of a judge to find out their fate. With the help of one of the best criminal attorneys in Brooklyn, all three ladies felt optimistic about the outcome. With God's help, they were able to afford the lawyer fee, and since January, criminal attorney Wendell Gilliam put in work to either have their charges dismissed or reduced to disorderly conduct.

For once, Bacardi was sober and looked decent in her long skirt and blouse. She stood by the door and shouted, "C'mon, let's fuckin' go! It's getting late and our cab is waiting outside."

Charlie and Claire rushed from their bedrooms looking like schoolgirls. Each girl wore a pastel dress and looked like the epitome of innocent and educated. They hurried downstairs and piled into the idling cab.

All three ladies were nervous. They met their attorney at the courthouse to go over today's proceedings. Wendell Gilliam stood in front of his clients dressed sharply in a dark blue Brooks Brothers suit. His black skin was smooth and flawless, and he had salt-and-pepper hair with a matching goatee. He was a handsome and distinguished black man in his late forties, witty and charismatic. Bacardi found him to be perfect. In fact, she wanted to fuck the man if he would have her—Claire too. But Wendell made it crystal clear that he was a happily married man and he was only about business with his clients.

The group stood at the steps of the courthouse. Before entering, Bacardi uttered to everyone, "Let us pray first."

It took everyone by surprise. Pray? They never went to church or spoke of or practiced any religion. But now Bacardi wanted to say a small prayer before they went before the judge. Bacardi gathered everyone closer, and they held hands in a small circle and lowered their heads.

Bacardi began with, "Dear Lord, we pray to you today to help us with this case. We are good people, we've done no wrong, and we pray you end this injustice against my family, and I'll owe you one, dear Lord. Amen."

It was a tacky prayer, but Bacardi felt proud and confident about it. She was sober and ready to get this over with. Together with her daughters, she waltzed into the courtroom with her head held high and feeling like she was ready for anything.

Two hours later, Bacardi emerged from the courtroom ecstatic. The charges against Charlie and Claire were dropped. Keisha didn't testify. Bacardi had to plead no contest and was sentenced to six months of probation. If she didn't get into any trouble, then the case would be fully closed. Their lawyer did an exceptional job. It had been a long two months. Finally, everyone could breathe again.

Bacardi, beaming with joy, exclaimed, "I need to get high, high, and high! And thank you, God!"

Tonight, they planned on celebrating—nothing too crazy, just a few drinks and some weed. Bacardi needed to remind herself that she was on probation for six months.

"Chanel, wake up. Wake up," Mecca said gently, nudging Chanel in her side and trying to wake her friend up as she slept in her comfortable bed.

Chanel was sound asleep and looked very peaceful.

"C'mon, Chanel, get up. It's getting late," continued Mecca.

Chanel finally opened her eyes to see Mecca looking down at her. She rose up and uttered, "Oh shit, what time is it?"

"It's almost eight."

"At night?"

"You're a heavy sleeper," Mecca said.

"Shit, Mecca, I didn't mean to sleep all day in your bed."

"Nah, you cool. I understand."

Chanel couldn't believe she'd slept for so long. She remembered lying across Mecca's comfortable bed and simply closing her eyes, and that was around noon. Now it was eight at night. Chanel knew it was time to take her ass home, even though she didn't want to. Bacardi, Charlie, and Claire were insufferable, but Chanel didn't want to wear out her welcome at Mecca's place. For the past three weeks, she had been coming by almost every day and spending hours and hours there. Her friend's room was cozy and comfortable. It was neat, entertaining, and with Mecca being the only child, there was some needed solitude. Chanel wished she had a bedroom like her friend's. Shit, she wished she had a warm home like Mecca's and a doting mother too. But it was wishful thinking.

"I'm about to go," Chanel said.

"I'll walk you to the subway station."

"Mecca, you don't have to."

"Yes, I do. You're my friend and I wanna make sure you good. And it's getting late."

Chanel smiled. Mecca was good peoples, and Chanel knew she could count on her. Chanel gathered the few belongings she brought over and placed them into her book bag. It was dusk outside, and Chanel could hear Harlem alive and buzzing on a beautiful spring evening from Mecca's second-floor window. The neighborhood had become her stomping grounds away from home. It was a beautiful melting pot of culture and diversity, and in Harlem, Chanel felt like she could breathe again. Not to take anything away from her Brooklyn roots—but Chanel desperately needed a change in environment.

The two teenage girls walked out of the apartment and decided to take the elevator instead of the stairs, though it was only two flights.

"Thanks again for having me over," Chanel said.

"C'mon, Chanel, you're welcome here anytime. You're family. I know it be hectic at your crib. Shit, I seen that shit with my own eyes."

"I swear, Mecca, I just wanna pack my shit and go somewhere far away and never come back. I hate it there."

"It's just jealousy, Chanel," Mecca added. "Look at them and look at you. You're pretty and fly, and hateful bitches always try to knock someone down to make themselves feel good."

Chanel sighed. "I'm just trying to be strong and not make any more trouble for myself."

"Well, you can spend next weekend with me. My mother's going out of town. It's not a problem. We can sit back, eat popcorn, and watch my husband on *Luther* and *The Wire*."

"I appreciate that."

They stepped out of the elevator and strolled through the lobby with their conversation still flowing. Chanel zipped up her spring jacket and they exited the lobby. Chanel wanted to take her time and not hurry toward the subway. She wasn't in any rush to get home. Home was hell.

As the girls walked down the pathway from the building toward the street, Chanel noticed a pearl white Range Rover parked on the curb in front of Mecca's building with rap music bumping. It was a beautiful vehicle sitting on chrome rims. Seated in the passenger seat was a handsome Latino male who looked to be in his early twenties. Chanel noticed the New England Patriots logo cut into his fresh low haircut. From a distance, he seemed intriguing. In the driver's seat was another Latino male dressed urban with a low haircut.

As she and Mecca walked and talked, the passenger quickly locked eyes with Chanel. Though it was a fleeting gaze, he took in Chanel's long, black ponytail and her clothing. Chanel was cleanly dressed in black jeans that somewhat hugged her curves and highlighted her booty and white Nikes and her purple-and-white spring jacket. She looked cute and sexy, and there was nothing trashy about her.

Chanel couldn't help but to flash a quick smile at the passenger. *Damn, he's cute*, she said to herself. She and Mecca continued to walk right by the Range Rover toward the nearest intersection.

The passenger, a man named Mateo, was immediately drawn to Chanel. He climbed out of the vehicle and approached her with a wide smile.

"Excuse me, ladies!" he politely hollered at the two girls. "Can I get your attention?"

Chanel turned around to gaze at Mateo approaching her. Mecca wanted to keep walking, but she had no choice but to stop and wait for Chanel because she wanted to stop at some nigga's catcall.

"Ohmygod, you're exquisite," said Mateo.

Chanel chuckled at the word. "Exquisite . . . now that's something new," she replied.

"But you are. What's your name, if you don't mind me asking?

"Chanel."

"Hello, Chanel. I'm Mateo," he said, extending his hand. Chanel shook his hand. "I couldn't help it, Chanel; you definitely caught my attention."

"Oh, really? And what about me caught your attention?"

"Your swag."

She grinned. "Swag? Me?"

"Oh, absolutely. I never saw you around here before."

Chanel shoved her hands into her pockets. "That's because I'm from Brooklyn."

"Damn, Chanel. Don't tell this nigga your entire life story. You don't know him," Mecca chimed.

"I'm not trying to create any conflict. I'm just trying to have a nice conversation with a beautiful woman, that's all," said Mateo.

Mecca rolled her eyes and sucked her teeth, but Chanel smiled. She couldn't help but to blush in front of the male stranger.

"So, where y'all going?" Mateo asked.

"I'm on my way home."

"Oh, that's sad. I thought maybe we could hang out, maybe get something to eat—"

"We're not hungry!" Mecca blurted.

"And it's getting late," Chanel said.

"I understand. How old are you anyway?"

Chanel didn't want to tell him her real age, but she didn't want to lie to him either. Her smile was innocent. She kept her attention on him and said, "I'm sixteen."

"Sixteen! Wow, you're young."

"I know. And how old are you, Mateo?"

He grinned. "I'm twenty."

"Damn, you're old," Mecca blurted.

Mateo laughed. "I'm old, huh?"

"Yeah! What, you're into young girls? You some kind of pervert?"

"No. I'm into gorgeous women, like Chanel," he smoothly countered.

The remark made Chanel smile more, but her glorious moment of compliments and flattery was short-lived when Mateo said, "Well, it was nice meeting y'all ladies. Y'all have a nice evening."

His gaze lingered on Chanel and then he pivoted and walked back to the Range Rover. Chanel felt like a balloon that had been abruptly deflated. Just like that, he left without taking her number or giving her his. She was disappointed.

"You scared him off, Mecca."

"He was too old for you anyway, girl."

"What, you're my keeper now?"

"No, but I know his type. He just wanted some pussy, that's all. And his friend didn't even get out of the truck," Mecca said.

"Ah, are you jealous," Chanel joked.

Mecca laughed. "I did it to save you. You were looking thirsty, girl."

"Oh, I was looking thirsty?"

"Yes. You should have seen your face—you just went Forrest Gump on us."

"Oh, shut up." Chanel laughed.

"For real girl, you was."

"You got to admit it, though. He was fine, right?"

Mecca didn't reply right away, and then she burst out, "Yeah, he definitely was."

Chanel sighed. "I wonder if I'm gonna ever see him again."

"Don't even think about him, girl. He probably has like four or five women anyway, and maybe a few baby mamas," Mecca said. "You probably didn't need the headache in your life."

Chanel hadn't thought about that. That sudden moment with Mateo was a spark for her, and it felt like it was still burning. She had him on her mind and he was going to stay there for a while.

The girls continued their walk toward the subway. Chanel sighed with delight. He'd called her exquisite, gorgeous, and beautiful. Harlem was the bomb.

Chapter Nine

God stood by the bedroom window smoking a cigarette. He stared at the locals coming and going like he was the apex predator and they were all prey. Charlie was in the shower, and the place was quiet. He had permanently moved in with Charlie without asking permission since he'd been evicted from his own place. He had been walking around the apartment like it was his castle and undermining everyone. Chanel hated that he was living there, but Bacardi and Butch didn't mind. They treated him like he was their son.

God had to think. He was contemplating his future—their future. It had been months since they'd hit a lick. Things were too hot, and the police had been on them like white on rice. Shit was dry. Between the lawyer fees and Bacardi not working, money was really tight. God needed another come-up, and he needed one right away.

Fingers had left town for a while to escape the fire of shooting a cop, but with the city coming alive because of the warm weather, God knew the time was now to get back into action—back to getting paid again.

Charlie entered the bedroom wrapped in a white towel. She had just finished her shower, and seeing her man smoking by the window raised some concerns for her.

"Baby, you okay?" she asked him.

God turned and looked at her. "Yeah, I'm good."

"You sure? You look like you stressin'."

"I said I'm fuckin' a'ight!" he barked.

"Shit, nigga, you ain't gotta catch no attitude wit' me. I was just checkin' to see if my man was good," Charlie retorted. "But fuck you!"

God took one last pull from the cigarette and flicked it out the window. Charlie was frowning at him, her arms folded across her chest. He had no right to snap at her after she gave him a place to stay and pussy on demand.

"Look, I ain't tryin' to fight wit' you. I just got a lot of shit on my mind, a'ight?"

"And I don't? What the fuck, nigga?"

"We need to find another lick," he said.

"I know that. I've been on a mission lookin' for muthafuckas to get got, and I think I have the perfect mark," she lied. Charlie had been looking, but she hadn't come up with anything concrete yet.

"Who?"

"Can you get in contact with Fingers?"

"I'm always in contact with him," he said.

"Cool. With the heat finally dying down, it's time for us to get back to business and shit. We need to get paid again."

"That's what I'm talkin' about, baby. Now that's my bitch talking business," said God with a smile.

"You know me, baby—doing whatever to make us happy and get this money," she said.

God was pleased that Charlie had found another victim. In fact, she found the majority of their targets, scoping out potential victims to transform into a payday. Leaving a trail of bodies behind didn't bother her. The thrill of robbing and killing had become an addiction for her. Just thinking about potential money stirred up Charlie's sexual desire. She wanted some dick now. She opened the towel around her body and let it drop to the floor. She was hungry for her man.

"You need to fuckin' apologize to me, nigga," she said.

"Oh, you want me to apologize, huh?"

She nodded. "Yup. And I don't want a weak fuckin' apology. I want an apology from you that will put a damn smile on my face."

God grinned, knowing what she was hinting at. Charlie positioned herself on her bed and spread her legs for God.

"Come eat, baby," she said.

Chapter Ten

O hmygod, I can't believe my baby is graduating today and she's going to Harvard on a partial scholarship. You always were the smart one," Bacardi said to Claire.

It was graduation day, and Claire was beaming with joy. Today was her day. In a few short hours, she would be walking across the stage in her cap and gown to accept her high school diploma.

She was the talk of the town—a local girl accepted into Harvard—*how the fuck did that happen?* And the main one scratching her head over her sister's acceptance into an Ivy League school was Chanel. What was more astonishing was that she actually had a partial scholarship. Chanel wanted to ask questions. How did Claire pull it off? She even wondered who Claire fucked in high school to gain such achievements. But Chanel was happy for her sister—at least she would be out of the house and in a different state.

The family treated Claire like she was baby Jesus on Christmas morning. They raved and celebrated Claire every minute, but there was one problem Chanel had with it all—it was her birthday. Today, she turned seventeen, but it had been forgotten and overshadowed by Claire's festivities. What a coincidence. What a shock—no one gave a damn about Chanel. However, Chanel kept quiet about it and went along with the program.

"After all we fuckin' been through this year, it's good to see something wonderful happening with this damn family," Bacardi proclaimed.

"Fo' sure, fo' sure! Let's get it on today," Butch chimed cheerily, the liquor already in his system.

"Butch, don't fuckin' embarrass this family today," Bacardi warned him.

"My baby girl is graduating high school today, so we gonna party. No better day than today to drink and celebrate," Butch replied, followed by a quick two-step. He took a swig from the flask he carried.

Bacardi frowned at her husband.

The family was dressed and ready for the main event at Brooklyn College. For once, they looked like a normal family, but looks could be deceiving. Bacardi was all smiles and almost looked brand new in the blue maxi dress she wore. Charlie and God looked like a loving and generous couple. Charlie wore a blue A-line dress, and God wore jeans and a button-down. Claire was glowing in her cap and gown, and Chanel played things simple in a polka dot skirt, a white camisole under a jean jacket, and a pair of high heels. She felt uncomfortable around God. His eyes lingered on her for far too long, and he was the only one that complimented her attire, saying, "You look really nice, Chanel."

She replied with a dry, "Thank you."

The family piled into a cab, but God and Charlie drove to the college in his Jeep. At Brooklyn College, hundreds of people waited to see the seniors graduate and accept their high school diplomas. It was a joyous day for everyone. The day was sunny and warm, with a blue sky that stretched for miles.

Chanel sat quietly through the graduation ceremony with the long-winded speeches and awards. She had a few things on her mind, like Mateo. It'd been three months since that night she met him and she never ran into him again on her trips back to Harlem to hang out with Mecca.

She wondered why she couldn't stop thinking about him. They met once. It was brief, but that brief moment made a big impression on her.

Finally, after what felt like a lifetime of waiting, Claire's name was called and she strutted across the stage to accept her diploma. The family went crazy with cheers, clapping, and hollering.

"You go girl! That's my fuckin' sister!" Charlie screamed.

"I fuckin' gave birth to a Harvard girl!" Bacardi shouted.

The Browns looked ghetto fabulous and they were loud enough to wake the dead. It was like they were at a sports game. They drew enough attention on themselves that Chanel had to shake her head and sigh. After the graduation, the family went out to eat.

Claire was their spotlight, but she had a problem. Although she had a partial scholarship to Harvard, it was still too expensive. Unless she came up with the money, she wouldn't be able to attend the school in the fall. Since she was their only student accepted to Harvard, Claire's high school had contacted the local papers. Within days, her story being about hard work and dedication was in the papers. "From housing projects to higher education" was the topic.

They all wanted to help Claire, and they bragged about how she had gotten into Harvard. The entire family believed that she was smart enough to get into the school. She was always reading and studying, and she was always using those big words. To them, Claire was impressive and ambitious.

Chanel was happy for her sister—a bit skeptical, but still, she was happy. She felt the urge to do something nice for Claire, despite constantly being treated like she had the plague. Chanel thought if she could help raise the money, maybe Claire wouldn't be such an asshole toward her anymore.

Chanel went online and started a GoFundMe page to help Claire raise the tuition money. Chanel kept the page a secret from everyone because she wanted it to be a surprise. The page was skillfully put together. She wrote about how her sister was a poor project girl who had graduated high school with honors and was now in danger of missing out on the opportunity of a lifetime—a Harvard education. Chanel expressed sadness and guilt on the page, and she reached out to everyone. The campaign was created the day after Claire's graduation, and by mid-July, Chanel was able to raise $30,000.

Feeling excited about the money she'd raised, Chanel felt that it was finally time to share the good news with her sister. It was early afternoon and the house was quiet. Claire was in the living room supposedly reading. Chanel took a deep breath and with Claire's laptop in her hands, she approached her with a smile on her face.

"Claire, can I talk to you for a minute?" Chanel asked.

Claire looked up at her sister deadpan. "What do you want, Chanel?" It was clear that she didn't want to be bothered.

"I want to show you something."

"Like what?"

Chanel took a seat right next to her big sister and opened the laptop. Claire looked like she was ready to become upset, but she took the time to listen to what Chanel was going to tell her. Chanel went to the GoFundMe page and proudly announced, "I got you the money you needed."

"You got me what?" Claire asked, her face a picture of confusion and shock.

"I was able to raise thirty thousand dollars for you to attend Harvard this fall. I set up a GoFundMe page and lots of people wanted to help you out with your education."

Claire's mouth remained open. "You raised thirty thousand dollars?"

"Yes. And I'm turning the account over to you."

"Wow!"

At first, Chanel thought Claire was proud of what she'd accomplished. But then Claire went on to say, "So you think you're better than me?"

A look of incomprehension decorated Chanel's face. "Huh?"

"You think I'm some fuckin' charity case, Chanel?" Claire asked.

"I just wanted to help you out."

"*You* help *me*? Do I look like I need your help?"

Claire felt some kind of way that she hadn't thought of the idea. Then Claire uttered the unthinkable when she said to Chanel, "Thirty thousand dollars, huh? You sure you ain't steal any of it? How do I know you didn't raise more and spend it?"

Chanel was befuddled by the accusation. Now Claire was accusing her of stealing?

When Charlie heard about the idea, she was upset that she hadn't raised the money. She was supposed to be the hustler of the family. The fundraiser completely turned against Chanel, and her family looked at her foul and showed absolute ungratefulness for what she did to help Claire out.

The only thing Chanel could do was cry and hide in her bedroom. What was an act of kindness turned into bitterness and hatred against her. After her tears and disappointment dried up, it hit her. She'd had enough.

"Fuck this!" she said to herself.

She called Mecca and asked if she could stay with her for a while. Chanel wanted to spend the rest of her summer in Harlem, and when Mecca's parents said it was okay, Chanel packed her things and left the apartment that evening without anyone noticing.

Chanel exhaled and smiled. It felt like a new day. Sleeping at Mecca's place was like a whole new world—absolute peace and tranquility and no bullshit from her family. Last night, she and Mecca laughed and talked for hours and snacked on pizza, chips, and candy and played games. It was the perfect sleepover.

Chanel wanted to thank Mecca for having her over, and she felt that the perfect way to thank her friend was to cook breakfast. The one thing Chanel knew how to do well was cook. She went into the kitchen to make an omelet, but the one ingredient she needed to make her omelets was missing—eggs.

"Mecca, you don't have any eggs in your fridge," Chanel said.

"I know. We need to get some."

"I'll go to the store," Chanel volunteered.

"You sure?"

"Yeah! I got this, girl. I'm about to make us the bomb-ass breakfast," Chanel said cheerfully.

Chanel quickly got dressed. It was a beautiful summer day, and the only thing she needed to wear outside was her cream shorts, a tank top, and her clean white sneakers. Of course, her long hair was styled into a ponytail. With a five-dollar bill from Mecca, Chanel left the apartment and walked toward the nearest bodega. She smiled the entire way, enjoying the bright sun in her face and taking in the busy sounds of Harlem—the people, the culture, the boys, and the atmosphere. She did not want to go back to Brooklyn anytime soon.

Inside the bodega Chanel bought a dozen eggs and a couple of sweet peppers to season the omelets. Her family always took her for granted, but her friends cherished her talents in the kitchen and it made Chanel feel special for once.

"Gracias," she said to the Spanish man behind the counter.

He smiled at the young girl. She was cute.

Chanel turned and made her way outside, but once she stepped foot onto the sidewalk, her entire world lit up and a wide smile grew on her face. She couldn't believe it. Her heart fluttered and her eyes became fixed on him.

"Hey, I'm seventeen now," she called out to Mateo.

He was standing near a black Tahoe and talking on his cell phone. Mateo turned around to see Chanel gazing at him with admiration, and her wide smile caused him to smile wide too. He curtailed his phone conversation and focused his attention on Chanel. He laughed at her comment.

"Seventeen, huh? Well, happy belated birthday," he said.

"Thank you." She moved closer to him. "It's good to see you again."

"Likewise."

Chanel couldn't stop staring at him. He was fine—extraordinary. He had on a pair of beige cargo shorts, a stylish T-shirt that fit his frame, fresh new Nikes, and that Patriots logo designed into his haircut.

"You know that logo in your haircut's gonna piss off some Giants fans," she said.

He laughed. "So, let 'em be pissed. I'm proud of my team."

"So you're from New England?"

He smiled, taken aback. "You watch football?"

"A little . . . not much, though."

"Impressive."

"I haven't seen you around lately," she said.

"I've been busy. Why, you missed me?"

She chuckled. Of course she did, but she wasn't about to tell him that. "How can I miss someone I don't know?"

"You're witty. I like that."

Chanel continued to smile brightly. Mateo couldn't take his eyes off the pretty, young girl. There was something special about her. He told himself that seventeen was better than sixteen. Still, he was twenty years old, and the last thing he needed was a statutory rape case against him. But

Chanel was compelling, and staring at her beauty was almost hypnotizing.

"You have a very pretty smile," he said, mesmerized by her pink lips against her bright white teeth and her deep dimples.

Everything about her was pulling him in.

"Thank you," said Chanel.

Though their conversation was brief, it was engaging. Chanel wanted to ask him so many questions. She wanted to get to know his world, and she wanted to tell him about hers. But they were still strangers simply encountering each other in passing. How could she involve herself in his life?

Mateo's cell phone started to ring and he glanced at it. By the expression on his face, it seemed like an important call that he needed to take. He looked at Chanel and said, "Well, anyway, it was nice seeing you again, beautiful. You take care, a'ight?"

He was about to leave. No! Chanel didn't want Mateo to leave and let another four months go by before they saw each other again. She had to say something.

He turned with his cell phone to his ear and was about to walk back to his vehicle. Chanel took a deep breath and said loudly, "Can I get your number?"

He turned to look at her. He said to the caller in the phone, "Yo, hold on one minute." He then asked Chanel, "You want my number?"

She nodded. She could hardly believe it herself, but he was too cute and he was so nice to her. At first, she felt embarrassed that she had to ask. She didn't want to appear thirsty or desperate, and by the way he looked at her, she wasn't sure if it was a bright idea to blurt it out. But then he smiled. "I'll give you my number only if I can get yours in return."

Ohmygod! Chanel exhaled with relief of finally breaking that ice between them. They exchanged numbers right there and he said, "Call me."

"I will. Maybe today," she said.

Mateo grinned. "I'll be looking forward to speaking with you." He walked back to his truck and resumed his phone conversation.

Chanel stood there feeling a mixture of shock, bewilderment, and excitement. It was the happiest day of her life. She couldn't wait to run back to Mecca's place and tell her the wonderful news.

Chanel hurried into the apartment screaming, "Mecca, Ohmygod! Ohmygod! I can't believe it!"

Mecca came flying out the bedroom in her panties and bra, thinking something was wrong. She shouted, "Chanel, what happened?"

"I saw him again! I ran into him again!"

"Who? Who did you run into?"

"Mateo. I saw him when I went to the store, and guess what? We exchanged numbers!"

"Damn, Chanel, you had me thinking someone was trying to murder you in here. Shit! You scared the shit out of me."

"I'm sorry, Mecca. I'm just so excited. We talked and laughed, and it felt so good seeing him again."

"Damn, you go to the store for some eggs and come back like you're ready to get engaged."

"I really like him, Mecca."

"Chanel, you hardly know that man."

"But there's something so special about him. It's like we connect so easily," said Chanel.

"Wow. Y'all ain't even fuck yet and he already got your virgin ass sprung," she joked.

"Yup!" she happily admitted.

It felt like nothing could ruin Chanel's day. Her time in Harlem was already beginning to look great. She wanted to call Mateo right away, but she had to fight the urge. She didn't want to look too desperate.

Three hours later, Chanel called him. She couldn't wait any longer. She wanted to hear his voice. She locked herself in the bathroom with the cell phone glued to her ear and heard his phone ring several times before he picked up.

"Hello?" he answered.

Chanel's heart skipped a beat. "It's me, Chanel."

"Hey, beautiful," he replied.

"I was just calling you because I wanted to talk."

"It's good to hear your voice," he said.

"Yours too."

"So, you live in Harlem now?"

"Not really. I'm from Brooklyn, but Harlem is my second home. And you?" she said.

"You already know. You saw the Patriots logo carved into my haircut. I'm from Boston, but I moved to New York when I was nine."

"I never been to Boston."

"It's nice. I go back once or twice a year," he said.

Talking to him was a fresh of breath air for Chanel, but their conversation was brief. Mateo was a busy man, but the chat left Chanel with some hope that she would see him again, maybe sooner than later.

It took a week for Mateo to call her back. It had been a week too long, and Chanel was about to lose hope in seeing him again. But hearing his voice again, she became excited.

"I wanna take you out. Is that cool?" he said.

Chanel was over-the-moon. She wanted to holler over the phone, but she managed to keep her cool. Of course she wanted to go out with Mateo. It was like a dream come true.

"Yes."

"I'll come pick you up tomorrow night."

Chanel gave Mateo the address, and when she hung up, she screamed at the top of her lungs. It was so loud that her pitch almost shattered windows. But Mecca was happy for her.

"So, he asked you out, huh?"

"Yes! Ohmygod, Mecca, I'm so nervous right now. I don't know what to do. I have nothing to wear and my hair looks a mess. I need to look perfect for him," Chanel chattered nervously.

"Girl, you know I got you. Just relax."

Chanel was overcome with emotions. This was going to be her very first date. When it came to men and love, she was a rookie. She didn't want to rush things; she wanted to take her time and fall in love with the right man, and Mateo seemed perfect.

It was Saturday night, and the temperature outside was a high 95 degrees. The heat wave was becoming ridiculous—almost unbearable. Every air conditioner in the city was on blast, and folks dressed in tank tops, shorts, and slippers loitered outside on the blocks of Harlem downing ice cold water and fanning themselves.

Despite the heat, Chanel was determined to look her best tonight. She wanted to impress Mateo with her beauty and her grace. Butterflies continued to swim around inside her stomach. She had never been so nervous about anything in her life.

"Mecca, you almost done? It's getting late. He's gonna be here soon."

"Just a few more minutes," Mecca replied.

Chanel's hair was the last touchup. She couldn't sport her go-to long ponytail or braids tonight. Mecca was giving her a blowout, and it felt like it was taking forever. Mecca was skilled at doing hair, and she promised Chanel that she was going to make her look dazzling tonight—that Mateo was going to be in complete awe at her transformation.

"What time is it?" Chanel asked.

"It's eight thirty-five."

"Shit! He's gonna be here soon, Mecca."

"You wanna look perfect for him, right?"

"Yes!"

"So, let me work."

Chanel sighed. She didn't want to be the late bitch on her very first date with a boy. But she also didn't want to look like Plain Jane or a sloppy bitch either. She had no choice but to trust Mecca.

"There. I'm finished."

Chanel stood up and stared at the final touch to her look. Her long hair was flowing past her shoulders in a black mane of beauty around her angelic face. She wore Mecca's black mini-dress with her same white sneakers. Mecca also had blessed her with a pair of earrings, cubic zirconia of course, and a thin necklace to match. Chanel smiled at her appearance. She was cute before, but now she looked stunning.

"I love it, Mecca."

"I knew you would."

"Thank you."

"You're welcome."

Just then, Chanel's cell phone rang. Knowing it was Mateo calling her, she hurried to answer it. "Hello?"

"Hey, it's me. I'm downstairs," he said.

"I'll be down in one minute."

She ended the call and then spun around with a nervous look about her and exclaimed, "Oh shit, he's here. I'm so damn nervous, Mecca."

"Chanel, just chill and take a deep breath. You go this. Just be yourself and have fun. Besides, he's the one that should be nervous—look at you. Damn, girl, I would fuck you."

Chanel laughed. "Thanks."

Chanel took one final look at the outfit Mecca let her wear. The dress showed enough of her long legs to captivate attention, and it was comfortable and cool enough for the July heat wave. The final touch was a small purse for her to carry.

"Now, go out there and have some fun. And, bitch, don't come back here pregnant," Mecca joked.

"Oh, shut up, Mecca." Chanel laughed.

"I'm serious. Shit, the way you've been carrying on about this nigga you've only met twice, you worry me, girl."

"I'm just getting to know him, and we're only going out to see a movie and get something to eat."

"Yeah, enough time to make a baby."

"I'll behave. I promise."

"It's not you I'm worried about."

"I trust him, Mecca. He's cool," Chanel said.

"Yeah. We'll see. But look, if you have any problems, call me right away. Okay?"

"Okay, Mom!"

Mecca and Chanel laughed. Their friendship was genuine, and Mecca was the sister Chanel wished she had.

Chanel walked out of the door still nervous, but she strutted with some confidence. Inside the elevator, she took a deep breath and said to herself, *Just be yourself, smile and have fun.* She exited the lobby to see Mateo standing outside the same pearl white Range Rover that she met him in. She smiled widely. He looked fine in his black cargo shorts, black sneakers, and a V-neck—dressed so simple and still looking too fine.

Mateo was taken aback by Chanel's transformation. "Damn, you look astonishing. You are so beautiful."

Chanel beamed brightly from the compliment. "And you look great too, Mateo."

"Thanks."

From there, their date started. Mateo escorted Chanel to the passenger side and opened the door for her. She couldn't stop grinning. She was giddy.

Mateo climbed into the driver's seat. "You want to see a movie first, or do you want to get something to eat?"

She shrugged. "It don't matter."

"You look hungry. Let's go eat first."

"That sounds great."

Mateo was completely smitten by her innocence. He had just had a huge fight with his girl, Nikki, and he needed relief. He needed something new and refreshing in his life, and Chanel was perfect.

The two of them dined at a Manhattan restaurant and talked for hours. Their conversation flowed so easily, they decided to skip the movie and just enjoy each other's company. They took a walk-and-talk around Riverside Park, where they had a view of the illuminated George Washington Bridge.

Chanel was glowing with happiness. She didn't want the night to end. This was her fairytale—her happily-ever-after ending away from home.

Chapter Eleven

D amn, you're going out with him again tonight?" Mecca asked Chanel.

"Yes. He's wonderful, Mecca. We have such a great time together. We talk about everything and he treats me so special."

"I see that. I'm glad that he's making you happy."

"He is." Chanel smiled, and her love for Mateo radiated from her.

She lit up every time she was around him or when she spoke about him. Throughout the summer, Chanel had spent more time in Harlem with Mateo than with Mecca. He was the perfect gentleman.

"Y'all had sex yet?" Mecca asked.

"What? No. He respects me."

"Yeah, they always do at first. But you do know that he's a drug dealer, right?" said Mecca. "Where you think he gets the money to treat you to nice things and take you to expensive places?"

"Yeah, I know. I thought about it."

"I'm telling you this because you seem ready to get serious with him, and that lifestyle can be treacherous."

"I love him, Mecca."

"I know you do . . . that's what worries me."

Chanel's cell phone chimed. "I gotta go. He's waiting for me downstairs," she said.

Chanel marched out of the apartment and met Mateo on the street, where he sat behind the wheel of his idling white Range Rover. Like routine, he got out to open the door for Chanel. He was spoiling her.

"You miss me?" she said.

"Always," he replied.

Chanel was treated to a special dinner at the River Café in Dumbo. It was a landmark restaurant nestled under the Brooklyn Bridge with a stunning view of the New York City skyline.

Mateo pulled Chanel's chair out for her at the table and sat across from her. He always took Chanel to places where it would be hard for him to get busted by his girlfriend. He wanted to keep Chanel far away from danger, and that danger came in the form of Nikki. She was a slick talking, rough-around-the-edges main chick. Dining in Brooklyn, far away from the Bronx, provided a safe distance.

"This is probably the nicest place I ever been to," Chanel said.

He raised an eyebrow. "Seriously?"

She nodded. "Yes. I don't go out much. I'm a Brooklyn girl with teenage problems."

"Well, I'm glad to be the first to treat you to a really nice restaurant."

She smiled. "And can I be honest with you?"

"Of course," he said.

"You're my first boyfriend."

"You serious?"

She nodded. "I am . . . and I already told you that I'm a virgin."

"Curious, a pretty girl like yourself and no boyfriend—not ever? And you're seventeen . . ."

"I know, I'm the oddball, but I have the right to be. Originally, I wanted to wait until I got married to have sex. And, yes, it does sound like a cliché, but if you know my family, you would understand why."

"Is your family that bad?"

Chanel sighed, rolled her eyes, and shook her head. "They're the worst."

"You care to elaborate?"

"My sisters have been using sex from the time they were young, and my oldest sister had two abortions before she turned eighteen. And it wasn't special. When I finally have sex, I want it to be special and I want it to be with someone I love and who loves me," she proclaimed. "And now that I've met you, I know you're gonna be my first."

Mateo was flattered—so flattered that he said, "I'm gonna marry you."

Chanel was surprised by the statement. Why did he say it? He didn't know why himself, but it made her happy. Yes, she would marry him when the day came.

"Would you really marry me?" she asked.

"Yes. I would."

It was becoming the best day of her life. She beamed so brightly that she could blind the entire room. Mateo moved closer to her and they kissed. It was a brief kiss, but it was passionate. Chanel was in love. She had never been in love, and the feeling was so overwhelming that sometimes it felt like she was going to explode from it.

"I love you," she blurted out.

He didn't hesitate to say it back. "I love you too."

Their dinner together was perfect. She could talk to and stare at Mateo forever. She was only seventeen, but Mateo made her feel like a woman—like she was a queen. The weeks they spent together were the best weeks of her life, and Chanel felt like she couldn't go one day without him.

After dinner at the Riverside Café, Mateo drove into Midtown Manhattan, and they stopped at Central Park. There, Mateo paid for them to take a horse and carriage ride through the park. It was the perfect summer night for it, warm and a full moon above. During the ride through the park, Chanel nestled against him and grinned as he held her in his arms. She'd never felt so secure and so safe. She was so happy.

The following day, Mateo took her shopping on 5th Avenue.

"My Chanel should have Chanel." Mateo beamed as he purchased his lady three very expensive handbags. And then he took her to the Dominicans in Harlem to get her hair done, where they washed, set, and blew out her beautiful long hair. They cut her bangs and evened out the back. Her hair looked like a long weave, but it wasn't.

"Should I dye it next time?" she asked Mateo.

"Dye it?"

"Yes. I was thinking maybe red?"

"Nah, baby. I love your hair as is."

"Really?"

"No doubts, okay?" Mateo leaned in and quickly kissed her.

Chanel looked in the mirror and drank in her new look. Mecca did a nice job, but the Dominicans did a fabulous job. She looked like a new woman—not a seventeen-year-old girl, but a gorgeous model. She was breathtaking, and Mateo couldn't take his eyes off of her.

Chanel had spent nearly three weeks in Harlem, and she knew it was time to go back home. Mateo was willing to take her back to Brooklyn in his Range Rover. He wanted to see where she lived, to see the nightmare of a place she told him about. Chanel didn't want to go back home, but she knew that she couldn't stay at Mecca's place forever. The only upside was that Chanel was going back to Brooklyn in style, with a new wardrobe and a new hairdo.

She stared out the window as the Range traveled across the Brooklyn Bridge. It was another beautiful night in the city. The balmy weather thickened the traffic into Brooklyn, and they were at a standstill.

Chanel turned her attention from the East River to her man, and asked him out the blue, "What is it that you do? I know I never asked you this before, but I'm just curious."

He said to her, "I promised that I would never lie to you."

"So don't."

He sighed and answered, "I'm a hustler. But I don't plan on staying in the game long."

"So you sell drugs."

"Yes, I sell drugs. Why, do you have an issue with that?"

"I don't judge anyone. I love you for who you are, not what you do."

"I have a plan, Chanel. I want to start my own company and go legit someday. I'm gonna invest in real estate and business. I'm even studying the stock market and some shit called cryptocurrency."

"It's good to have goals. I like that."

"I promise that I'll give you a better life, baby—a life that you deserve."

She smiled. "I know you will."

He took her hand in his across the console and held it in adoration. She exhaled and smiled. Her heart fluttered. God, she didn't want to leave him, but she had no choice. She still had her life in Brooklyn and he had his in the Bronx.

The Range Rover pulled up in front of Chanel's building. The locals were outside, and when they saw the pretty white truck come to a stop, their curiosity was piqued. Who could it be inside the SUV? Among those loitering outside the project building was Charlie hanging with a few of her girls from around the way. Claire was seated near the bedroom window and she too noticed the Range.

Chanel saw that the block was busy with people, including her sister. She sighed heavily.

Mateo noticed her apprehension. "You want me to walk you upstairs?"

"No, I'll be okay. This is home."

"You sure?" he said.

She nodded. "I want to keep you a mystery. They don't deserve to see you or know anything about you. Shit, they probably didn't know that I was gone for nearly three weeks. They don't care about me."

"Well, you know I do."

She smiled. "I know, baby."

Before her exit, they looked into each other's eyes for a few seconds. He moved closer to her, smiled, and pulled her in for a fiery and passionate kiss. The kiss sent shivers down her back. Mateo was intoxicating and addictive. It was going to be hard to leave him and go back to her family.

When their kiss ended, she exhaled and grinned. *Damn!* "That was nice," she whispered.

"It was. I could kiss you forever," he said.

The feeling was mutual. Finally, she made her departure from the vehicle and headed toward the building carrying numerous shopping bags. Mateo stayed parked and would watch her leave until she disappeared into her building. All eyes were on Chanel, wearing a designer crop top and pants, carrying a Chanel bag, and her long hair flowing naturally down her back. At first Charlie and Claire didn't have a clue that it was Chanel who got out of the Range, but once they recognized her, they had a million questions. Chanel ignored Charlie and marched into the apartment and ignored Claire, who was now in the living room staring at Chanel like she was an alien. The sisters became jealous of her newly noticed beauty and her straight hair. Claire accused her of having it permed, but Chanel explained it was a simple blow-dry.

Chanel went into her bedroom and went to the window. Mateo was already gone. She groaned. She was already missing him, but she knew she would see him again soon. Chanel lay across her bed and started to daydream about how her first time would be with Mateo.

Chapter Twelve

It was a beautiful day outside, but Chanel didn't feel so beautiful. She felt forgotten, unwanted, and lied to. It was early September, and she hadn't heard from Mateo since he dropped her off. She didn't want to be angry, but she had strong feelings for Mateo and she thought they were mutual. He had told her he loved her. So how could he not contact her for two weeks? Every time she tried to call him, his phone went straight to his voicemail, and Mecca said she hadn't seen him around Harlem lately. Chanel went from floating on cloud nine to misery and upset. She was back in school, but it was hard for her to focus when she couldn't stop thinking about Mateo.

Charlie didn't make things better. When she saw Chanel, Charlie would constantly tease, "Where's ya baller nigga at now, bitch?"

Chanel tried to ignore her, but Charlie was persistent in trying to make her life a living hell. And Claire didn't miss out on the verbal abuse. Although she was away at school, she would call and taunt Chanel about how dumb it was to get involved with a hustler. "I'm only going to date doctors and lawyers," she admonished. "You see a street nigga don't care nothing 'bout your dumb ass!"

Claire had become more egotistical since her acceptance into Harvard. It was still a hard pill for Chanel to swallow. She felt that Claire had to suck or fuck some nigga to get into such a prestigious school. Others believed it was possible, because Claire put up a front by always reading and looking like she was studying something. Though Claire wasn't an idiot, Chanel remained skeptical, believing that her sister wasn't Harvard-smart.

Chanel's heart was broken. She missed Mateo so much that she would cry herself to sleep at night. She wanted to disappear. But when it rains, it pours.

The school bell rang. It was Chanel's last period class and it was time to go home. The September weather still allowed her to look cute in her short skirt and white top. She rode the bus in silence, wishing she had some other place to go after school besides home.

The bus moved through the city street and Chanel stared out the window. With Claire now away in school, she had one less sister to deal with—to take abuse from. But Charlie's boyfriend God seemed to take Claire's place at home. Chanel hated the way God would look at her when she came into the room. His eyes lingered on her for too long and it made her uncomfortable. It almost felt like when he stared at her, he was undressing her young body with his eyes. She wanted to tell Charlie about the uneasiness she felt around God, but she knew telling Charlie about the issue would be like telling a rock. Charlie most likely wouldn't do anything about it.

For Chanel, it truly sucked that she didn't have a big sister to have her back. She hated to feel alone with her own family. With Mateo disappearing from her life, Chanel felt like she had no one but Mecca who gave a fuck about her.

The bus came to a stop on Ralph Avenue and Chanel got off. She minded her business as she walked two blocks to the Glenwood Housing Projects. Her area of Brooklyn was a busy place, especially on a warm September day. A few boys wanted to holler at her, catcalling to her from a short distance, but she ignored them. She wasn't interested and they weren't her type. They weren't Mateo.

It appeared that no one was home when she entered her apartment. For a moment, it seemed Chanel had the place to herself. She wanted to make herself a snack and lock herself in the bedroom and start on her homework.

But then things changed. Upon walking into the kitchen, her eyes widened with shock. There was Butch, sprawled out across the kitchen floor, and he looked dead. Near his reach was a bottle of Jack Daniels that had spilled out onto the floor.

Chanel hurried to him. "Daddy!" she cried out. "Daddy, wake up!"

She tried to wake him, but he wasn't coming to. She didn't know what to do. She tried to give him CPR, but to no avail. She ran to the phone and quickly dialed 911. She shouted breathlessly to the dispatcher, "My father—I think he had a heart attack or something. He's not moving! He's not breathing!"

"Ma'am, what is your location?" the 911 dispatcher asked.

Chanel quickly gave them the address and prayed that Butch wouldn't die. He was a drunk and treated her like shit, but he was still her father, and Chanel hoped the ambulance got there in time.

Butch lay unconscious on the gurney in the hospital room. Bacardi, Charlie, and God had finally made it to Brookdale Hospital to see about his condition. Chanel lingered in the hallway. She had saved her father's life, but her family would never give her the credit she deserved. Everyone was worried about Butch. He was an unemployed drunk who was mean and abusive when he was sober, but he was family.

The doctor came into the room and he had everyone's undivided attention. His diagnosis of Butch was simple. He had a seizure brought on by consuming too much alcohol. He would have to stay a few nights in the hospital for observation, and the family was told that if he continued to drink the way he did, then he would probably be dead within a year. But Butch not drinking was easier said than done.

Bacardi was a bit relieved, but it was bittersweet news. How could they stop Butch from drinking? Liquor and Butch went together like a horse and a carriage, and if Butch couldn't have his liquor then he would become an unbearable muthafucka to be around.

"Someone needs to call Claire and tell her what happened," Bacardi said.

"I'll do it," Charlie said.

She turned and walked out of the hospital room and moved right past Chanel without saying a word. She didn't even have the respect to tell Chanel what Butch's doctor had said. She marched down the hallway with her cell phone in hand to call her sister and to get everyone a snack.

Chanel stared into the room and observed Bacardi praying over her husband. She felt sickened by her mother's action. She thought, *How can a demon like her pray?* Although she saved her father's life, Chanel knew that nothing was going to change. They already ignored her and treated her like she was a plague—like her black skin was a virus inside the home. It wasn't her fault that she was born with dark skin and her two sisters were light with hazel eyes. She was still blood—still a Brown—but yet, she was a child without a home and without love. Chanel thought that she'd found love with Mateo, but was it only a façade?

She sighed and turned and left. She would take the bus home. She would lock herself inside her room and stay there all night. The benefit of Claire being away at college was that she no longer had to share the bedroom. The solitude she craved was granted—a minor blessing in such a hellish household.

Chapter Thirteen

Cigarette smoke hung thickly in the air of the strip club. It was a scene of debauchery. Every square foot of the club was thick with paying customers and scantily dressed women. Two naked dancers were wrapped around the poles while four other girls danced on stage. The rest of the girls paraded around the urban club while Big Sean's "Bounce Back" thumped through the speakers.

In their element like children at a playground were God and Fingers. Both men were being entertained with lap dances by two half-naked ladies. Fingers clutched a fistful of dollars and eagerly tipped the smiling, caramel complexioned girl with a big booty and matching big tits.

God downed a bottle of champagne and grinned at his lovely company. Her name was Miracle. She was pretty, dark, and curvy in all the right places. She straddled God in the folding chair and grinded her thick body against his—arousing her customer to the fullest. She thought he was cute. And he wasn't cheap. As she grinded her booty and pussy into his lap, he continued to make it rain on her. She smiled. He smiled. His hands roamed freely all over the dancer's body, and tonight he wasn't thinking about Charlie.

They looked like ballers in the club with their designer clothing and jewelry, purchasing bottles from the bar and tipping healthily. It was their way to unwind and enjoy life.

"I like you," said Miracle to God.

"I like you too, shorty," said God.

"What's your name?" she asked.

"It's God."

"God . . ." She thought it was an odd name for him. "Why do they call you God?"

"Because I make things happen and I see everything," he said.

He was amusing, and Miracle found him intriguing. She continued to work her sexiness on him and even kissed the side of his neck as she gave him a sensual lap dance.

"Well, God, do you want a private dance with me?"

He smiled. "How much?"

"Two hundred."

Just as things were about to get hot and heavy, his cell phone rang. He definitely needed to take the call.

He slightly nudged Miracle off of his lap, indicating that she was somewhat irrelevant at the moment, and he answered the call. "Hey, baby. What's good?"

"I miss you, God. Where are you?"

"I'm chilling with Fingers. What's good?"

"You. I wanna see you tonight. But can you come pick me up?" she said.

"A'ight, no doubt. Where are you?"

"I'm at Mack's bar," she said.

"I'll be there in a few."

The call ended. Right away, God turned to Fingers and said, "C'mon, nigga. Let's go."

"What? Nigga, I'm ready to fuck tonight."

"I gotta pick up shorty, and we need to talk," said God. "Get that bitch's number and catch her on the rebound."

Fingers frowned and the voluptuous, half-naked girl straddling his lap frowned too. God was being a party-pooper. To compensate the girls for their time, God gave them each a hundred dollars and they were appeased.

Fingers picked himself up and said, "You lucky ya my nigga."

God smiled. "Ride or die, nigga."

The two men left the strip club and climbed into God's Jeep. They drove to Canarsie, Brooklyn, and during the ride, God told Fingers that he'd gotten wind detectives were asking around about them. The streets were talking, and they weren't saying anything good.

"They still on that dead cop shit?" Fingers asked.

God shook his head. "I don't know. I just heard shit through the grapevine. But you know they ain't gonna give up on that case. A cop got killed and they wanna crucify some nigga, or niggas."

"Shit happened like eight months ago. Fuck that bitch-ass cop."

"Anyway, I think you should leave town again fo' a minute," God suggested.

"And go where, back upstate?"

"We just gotta continue to keep a low profile."

Fingers grimaced. He ran once. He hated to run from anything.

God pulled up to a quaint bar on Rockaway Parkway. He sat behind the wheel staring at the entrance, waiting for his girl to exit the place. He called to let her know he was outside.

Fingers lit a cigarette and tried not to worry about what God had told him. But as they sat idling outside the bar, his eyes darted around and he kept his gun close to him.

The entrance to the bar opened and a beautiful young girl emerged. God fixed his eyes on Kym and smiled. He admired the outfit she had on— dark jeans that hugged her luscious curves, a white shirt that highlighted her balloon tits, and a pair of white heels. Kym was dark-skinned with bantu knots styled in her hair. God loved her afro-centric look.

He climbed out of the vehicle and greeted Kym with a passionate hug followed by a lingering French kiss. Fingers simply watched them make out from the passenger seat.

Kym had been God's side bitch for nearly six months. She was the complete opposite of Charlie—dark skin, legit, and she had a blossoming career. He had to admit to himself that Kym was a bit freakier than Charlie, but Charlie was his ride-or-die bitch. Kym was unaware about Charlie, and vice-versa. Both women brought something different to the table for God.

Kym greeted Fingers by his government name. "Hey, Frederick."

"Hey," Fingers replied halfheartedly.

She continued to smile. She was happy to see her man. She intimately hugged God again, fondling his masculine frame. "You spending the night with me again?"

"Yeah. I just need to drop Fingers off and we can chill," he said.

She smiled brightly. Kym loved everything about God. He was handsome, manly, and intriguing. They'd met at Mack's bar. God found her attractive and offered to buy her a drink. She accepted the drink and a conversation was sparked. Right after that, she became his number-two.

Kym got into the backseat and God drove off.

The night was still young, and the two lovebirds wanted to make the best of it. That meant going back to her place for a few drinks, followed by some Netflix and chill. Kym was God's escape from Charlie and her dysfunctional family. When he needed to get away, Kym was always there with her open arms and spread legs.

God drove the Jeep several blocks until he finally came to a stop at a red light. The traffic had been sparse and the night was going good, until it wasn't. While idling at the red light, God glanced in his rearview mirror and noticed a black Dodge Charger approaching from behind. It stopped awkwardly close behind the Jeep, and he could see several silhouettes inside the car. Not wanting to overreact, he kept his cool. Under his seat was a loaded Ruger SR9c. It was a clean gun with no bodies on it.

Before the light turned green, another black vehicle sped toward them and came to a screeching stop at the bumper of his vehicle. Police lights were flashing, quickly indicating to them that it was the NYPD. God again glimpsed into the rearview mirror and he could see men flying out of the Dodge Charger with guns drawn and badges showing.

"Shit!" God shouted.

"Police! Put your fuckin' hands up! Put your hands up!" they all screamed simultaneously.

God and Fingers had no time to react. They were boxed in with high caliber weapons pointed at them. If one of them moved wrong, it was lights out, bullets spraying, and bodies slumped in blood-soaked seats.

Kym was wide-eyed and panicking. She shrieked at the heavy police presence but did what she was told, throwing her hands up so they could see that she wasn't a threat.

The cops swung open all three doors and dragged everyone out of the car and threw them down to the ground. They were immediately handcuffed and detained. Fingers seethed. God frowned. They didn't see it coming. The police had come out of thin air. But what were the charges? Why were they being arrested?

God growled, "What the fuck is this about? We ain't do shit!"

He had a cop's knee on his back and the handcuffs felt extra tight around his wrists. He felt it was done purposely, for he and Fingers were suspected cop killers.

Kym was bewildered by it all. She was only a passenger, but they arrested her too. While searching the vehicle, the officers removed God's black Ruger and found Fingers' 9mm Beretta. They were pleased with the results. It was a gun charge easily slapped against them.

The streets were snitching a great deal, and God and Fingers kept coming up in interrogation rooms.

Charlie was worried about her man. She had tried to call his phone numerous times, but he wasn't answering. She felt something was wrong.

So when her phone rang around two in the morning, she answered the call believing that it was God finally calling back. She was furious and ready to curse him out, but it wasn't God on the other end of the phone. It was an acquaintance of the two men telling Charlie that God and Fingers had been locked up earlier.

Hearing the tragic news, Charlie was struck with fear and concern. "What? What the fuck happened? For what?"

"I don't know. But they got locked up in Canarsie wit' some bitch in the car," the man said.

The caller hung up and she was left with a million and one questions. Did they get locked up for the home invasion? If so, were the cops coming for her too? Or was it because of that cop that got killed in January? Or was it another crime she didn't know about?

No matter the crime, Charlie was devastated. Her man and her money were gone, and she had no idea for how long—maybe life.

Chapter Fourteen

Harvard University was an entirely different world to Claire. Everything felt so surreal. She wanted to be better than everyone, and she had something to prove to those who doubted her.

The jealousy she felt before she left home to attend school on a partial scholarship was palpable. Claire Brown was leaving the ghetto to better herself in life—to get a higher education from a prestigious school. She'd graduated high school with a 4.1 GPA, and she scored a nearly perfect score on her SAT.

The entire school was wonderful. It was 210 acres of historical and contemporary buildings, students, staff, and knowledge—210 acres a world away from the Glenwood Housing Projects. Her dorm room was a bit larger than the bedroom she shared with Chanel in the projects, and she had two roommates—a white girl named Becky, such a cliché, and an African-American girl from Chicago named Tiffany. Though Tiffany was from Chicago, she didn't have an ounce of ghetto in her. She talked proper and dressed white. Claire thought, *Brady Bunch*.

In fact, Tiffany and Becky quickly bonded. Tiffany had a lot more in common with Becky than she had with Claire. Tiffany was sheltered and privileged and grew up in the suburbs, yet, she still represented Chicago. *Fuckin' fraud*, Claire felt.

Two weeks at the school and Claire found out she had a lot to learn. The classes could be grueling. The professors weren't going to hold your hand. Either you got it or you didn't. And if you were an undergraduate, they expected you to fully understand their lessons. The school wasn't going to coddle you.

In Claire's first two weeks, she found out that Harvard was a very extreme place. Everyone was extremely smart, extremely driven, and they were extremely focused on attaining their goals. She observed several students suffer from panic attacks in public. The school could become so extreme that it could be scary from time to time. Claire found herself surrounded by highly intelligent classmates with very competitive spirits—and a lot of students were full of themselves.

Claire figured that because she was from the gritty streets of Brooklyn, she could handle anything that came her way—and that no school or pompous, educated fool was going to scare her. Although her first two weeks started out shaky, she believed that she was built to last and there to stay. If she could survive Brooklyn, then she could survive this.

It was her third week into the semester and October was right around the corner. The Massachusetts weather was chillier than New York in late September. Claire had a lot of assignments to complete and projects to work on. She was in her dorm room alone, trying to study. She had heard about her father's seizure and she wished she could be there for the family, but she had a lot on her plate and she didn't have transportation back to New York.

She called her family to check on her father's condition. He was stable.

The knock on her dorm room door interrupted her time with her books. She sighed, stood up, and marched toward the door to see who was knocking. She opened it to find one of the school's administrators standing in front of her.

She gazed at Claire and asked, "Is your name Claire Brown?"

Claire nodded. "Yes."

"You need to come to the Dean of Admissions' office," she said.

Claire was taken aback. What did the Dean of Admissions want with her? She was a freshman who kept to herself, and she didn't know anyone at the school. Not having a choice, Claire followed the woman to the dean's office. It was a place she didn't expect to see so early in the school year, but there she was, meeting face to face with Dean Convoy, an aging white man in his late fifties with a serious look on his face.

"Have a seat, Miss Brown," he said.

Claire felt extremely nervous. She took a seat in the leather armchair and waited to hear the reason for the sudden meeting with him.

Dean Convoy sat behind his neat looking desk and didn't beat around the bush, saying to Claire, "It's come to this administration's attention that your SAT scores and your GPA are fraudulent."

Claire was shocked by the news. "I don't understand," she said. "Are you calling me a cheater?"

"How you were accepted into this university is beyond my understanding, Ms. Brown. Our vetting process is meticulous, yet, you still made it into the system—and with a partial scholarship. We are conducting a full investigation into this matter."

"A full investigation? I didn't do anything wrong," she exclaimed.

"As I explained, some things have come to our attention, and until we investigate, your enrollment is suspended until further notice."

Claire couldn't believe what she was hearing. She tried to deny the accusation of cheating and being a liar, but she knew the truth.

"Who told you this lie?"

"I can't divulge that information to you," he said.

"Someone out there is calling me a cheater and a liar, and you can't fuckin' tell me who it is!" Her Brooklyn side was coming out for sure.

"I would appreciate if you didn't curse at me," he said politely.

Claire wanted to do more than curse at him.

"As I stated earlier, until this matter is resolved, your enrollment at this school has been suspended."

A group of youngsters had openly admitted that they'd been part of a sophisticated cheating ring since the eighth grade, and Claire was part of it. The ringleader of the group was a boy named Trevor. He was extremely smart and manipulative. The group had access to exams a week before they were taken, including the SAT. How it was possible, no one knew. These kids were smart cheaters.

They'd dropped a dime on Claire, explaining that she had cheated her way all through high school and managed to get herself into Harvard. She was the only one to get accepted to a prestigious school, which had been their goal.

The kids were of different races and backgrounds, but Claire was the only African-American among the nine. Seeing this, the other eight were consumed with envy. None of them could sit back and watch Claire have a good life with Harvard on her resume. They'd provided a thick folder with incriminating evidence not only to the folks at Harvard, but to the media too. Claire pleaded her innocence.

The university wanted to avoid a scandal or a lawsuit for wrongful expulsion, so they decided to give Claire a test. She failed miserably.

After their investigation was complete, Claire was expelled from Harvard, and it became the talk of the town. Claire's fall from grace had made for a story to read in the newspapers, and somewhat became national news—an intricate group of cheaters who'd all lied their way through high school.

Claire was a smart girl. She'd started off as an A student in elementary and middle school, but in high school, she fell in with the wrong crowd of cheaters, and she'd gotten lazy and stopped studying because she already had the answers to tests and exams. She felt it was a win-win situation for her.

Claire had become a disgrace. She was ashamed to go home, but she had nowhere else to go. How could she look her family in the eye after being kicked out of a prestigious school like Harvard? How could she walk around Brooklyn without being laughed at and talked about?

Her family didn't understand how an intelligent student like Claire could be part of such a cheating scandal. They believed that she was always studying, always learning. It certainly had to be a lie. Claire continued to deny the accusations against her, and Bacardi was ready to fight for her daughter. She even threatened Harvard with a lawsuit and slandered the school by calling them racists. She wasn't going to take this lying down or stay quiet about it. She saw it as a payday for Claire and herself. The school had tarnished her daughter's reputation, and she wanted some money for her pain and suffering, claiming that Claire was completely distraught by the incident.

Day after day, Bacardi called different lawyers to file a lawsuit against the school, but none of them would take it on. They all felt Claire had no case against the school. The evidence of her deceitfulness was stacked against her. Bacardi became furious, and she felt that they were all in cahoots against her family.

Claire wanted it all to go away, but the story of cheaters from high school and the one who'd swindled her way into Harvard continued to play on repeat until the next big story or scandal broke. Now she was back home, living with her family. All three sisters were once again under the same roof, and things were more strained than before.

It didn't take long for the other project girls to talk that slick shit and taunt Claire about the cheating scandal. They called her a stuck-up bitch who thought she was better than everyone. She was a big-word-speaking fraud. Those were fighting words and, of course, Charlie went to battle for her sister and warned the bitches to keep her sister's name out of their mouths.

Shockingly, Claire and Charlie's biggest battle was with Chanel. Chanel had always had her doubts about Claire, and she suggested that the evidence against Claire pointed to it being true. The entire household erupted in anger and felt Chanel had betrayed their code.

"What code is that?" Chanel asked.

Bacardi replied, "We family! We stick together no matter what!"

"Since when?" That earned her a five-finger slap across her face from Bacardi.

Chapter Fifteen

Remember, no drinking," the doctor reminded Butch before discharging him from the hospital.

Butch frowned. The doctor might as well have told him not to breathe. "Not even a damn beer?"

"This is a serious issue, Mr. Brown. I would assume that your life is more important than alcohol."

"How can a man live?"

"Just take it one day at a time, and try to find yourself a constructive hobby," the doctor said.

It was grim news for Butch. His hobby was drinking and having a good time. If he continued to drink, parts of his brain could shut down due to alcohol poisoning—and his long-term abuse of alcohol was manifesting as cirrhosis of the liver.

Bacardi and Charlie were there to take Butch home. His doctor had a brief conversation with the family, and he gave them the same warning. Butch ranted and cursed from the hospital room to the car, a friend's Accord that Charlie had borrowed.

"I don't fuckin' need no fuckin' doctor telling me what to do wit' my fuckin' life," Butch cursed inside the car. "I'm a damn man, y'all hear me?"

"You need to listen to him, Butch. Do you wanna die?" Bacardi said.

"I'm not goin' any-fuckin'-where!"

Bacardi and Charlie sighed. Butch was being stubborn.

"I need me a fuckin' drink. You fuckin' hear me?" he shouted.

"No!" Bacardi shouted back.

"Bitch, you don't fuckin' control me," he retorted.

"Call me a bitch again, and I swear it won't be the alcohol that'll fuckin' kill you," she shouted.

Normally, Butch would have laid hands on his wife, but a beatdown wasn't on the menu today. Butch wanted a drink. He frowned heavily and muttered incoherently. He was a like a drug addict with the monkey on his back, craving the taste of liquor to appease his pain—to quench his thirst.

The whole family knew they needed to keep him sober or else he was going to die, but it wasn't going to be an easy task. Things were tense inside the apartment. Every day with a sober Butch was more unbearable than the last.

While Butch became everyone's concern, no one picked up on Claire's sudden depression. Her abrupt dismissal from Harvard had more of an effect on her than everyone thought. Chanel would walk into the bedroom to find her sister lying in her bed in silence in the dark. Claire refused to interact with the family. She sulked alone. She even refused to abuse and bully Chanel.

When Chanel asked, "You okay?" Claire wouldn't respond.

The first week back had been bumpy with Claire and Chanel, and although they weren't close, Chanel couldn't help but to worry about her sister. She knew something was wrong, but her family didn't pay any attention to the signs. While the rest of the family was trying to keep Butch from killing himself by drinking, Claire had sunken into a deep depression. She had fallen into Chanel's world of being an outcast, and somewhat being ignored. She would spend hours and hours inside the bedroom.

It was a depressing sight for Chanel. She had her own problems and the last thing she wanted to see was her depressed sister. *Why should I care?* Claire brought the trouble upon herself by cheating and lying her way through high school. She got caught, and now she wanted people to feel sorry for her. No, it wasn't happening.

Chanel was still heartbroken. She couldn't stop thinking about Mateo and his sweet kisses every day. She felt like a drug fiend that needed her fix. It was hard for her to grasp the thought that maybe Mateo would never come back—that maybe she was just a fling and he'd lied to her about love and wanting to get married.

With the scenery transitioning from warm and green to chilly days and falling leaves, for the Brown family, the worst was yet to come. They had their own changes coming.

Chanel got off the city bus and started her walk home. It was a breezy afternoon and she was on the phone with Mecca. Almost everything out of her mouth was questions about Mateo.

"You haven't seen him around lately, Mecca? He still hasn't called me," Chanel said.

"Girl, he got you that sprung? I'm saying, maybe it's time for you to move on from him, Chanel. You haven't talked to him in almost two months, and he doesn't call you. That's a hint. He forgot about you, so you need to forget about him," said Mecca. "And I told you, he's a player and he has more than one bitch in his life."

Chanel didn't want to believe it. Why couldn't she move on from Mateo? What was so special about him? Mecca was right. He had forgotten about her and he wasn't calling for a reason.

Chanel had to admit, life at home hadn't been so bad lately. Butch was making things miserable for Bacardi and Charlie, and Claire was in her own world of depression. That kept Chanel out of everyone's crosshairs for the moment.

Chanel walked into the building lobby and got inside the elevator.

"Chanel, you're a pretty girl and I know you can find some other nigga to treat you special. Shit, girl, you better be glad that you didn't fuck that nigga and give him your virginity. You know how mad you would be?" Mecca said.

Chanel sighed. "Yeah . . . I know."

"So, you cool at home? What's been going on?"

"My father is still trying to fight sobriety, but that's Bacardi and Charlie's problem. He curses and yells at them more than they ever do me. So, I stay out the way. And Claire, she's like not there most times. She just lays there looking fuckin' pathetic and sad."

"You know what that is, right?" said Mecca.

"What?"

"Girl, that's karma coming after their trifling asses."

"You think?"

"How they be treating you? Yes."

"I guess."

"All you need to do is just focus on you, get yours, and find you another man," Mecca said.

"I'm trying, girl. I'm trying. I spend most of my time either at the library or just in the bedroom reading."

Chanel stepped off the elevator and moved down the hallway. Conversing with Mecca was always uplifting. She smiled as she entered the apartment. It was quiet. She didn't see Butch or Bacardi. God was locked up, and she was thankful for that. She figured Charlie was somewhere out in the streets trying to help her man make bail. Chanel hoped he would rot in jail. She knew God was bad news. She felt it in her entire body. Jail was the perfect place for him, she believed.

"What are you doing this weekend, Mecca? I wanna come by."

"I'm free. Maybe we can go and see a movie."

"I'm definitely down for that. Shit, I need to get away."

"Bet then. It's a date," Mecca joked.

Chanel giggled. "It's a date then."

Chanel walked into her bedroom to find the usual—Claire sprawled across her bed. But she was lying face-down. She took one look at her sister's position and immediately suspected something was wrong. The room felt too still. Chanel soon noticed the empty pill bottle on the floor.

Quickly, she said to her friend, "Mecca, let me call you back."

Chanel hurried toward Claire with worry. *This isn't happening again*, she screamed to herself, thinking about when she found her father unconscious on the kitchen floor a few weeks earlier.

"You stupid bitch!" Chanel shouted. "Why?"

She shook Claire, desperately trying to wake her up, but to no avail. Chanel screamed with heavy frustration. She had no choice but to call 911—again.

It felt like a nightmare to Chanel. It was happening in a blur. The paramedics arrived and hurriedly went to work on trying to save Claire's life. The only thing Chanel could do was watch. She wasn't a big fan of her sister—some days she hated that bitch—but she didn't want her to die.

She rode in the ambulance with Claire to the hospital and called Bacardi and Charlie to tell them the grim news. The paramedics frantically tried to pump Claire's stomach. She was unconscious with low vital signs. Claire was still alive, but barely.

Once again, Chanel found herself at Brookdale hospital with another family member.

Why me?

When Bacardi got to the hospital, she was devastated. She wanted answers. Why was Claire in the hospital?

Chanel was in the waiting area alone, and the moment Bacardi set eyes on her youngest, she went off on Chanel. "What the fuck did you do to her? What the fuck happened?!"

"She tried to kill herself, that's what happened!" Chanel shouted.

Bacardi didn't want to believe it. She argued with Chanel, but Chanel stood her ground. They weren't about to blame her for this. No way!

First Butch, now Claire. Bacardi felt like her family was cursed. "This fuckin' family!" she hollered.

When Bacardi was finally able to see Claire, her condition was stabilized. The medical staff at the hospital had to insert plastic tubing into Clair's mouth, down her throat, and into her stomach to quickly empty the contents.

Claire was asleep on the gurney. Bacardi went toward her daughter with a disheartened expression. She blamed Harvard. She blamed the media. She blamed the people in her neighborhood for mocking her daughter—for calling Claire a cheat and a liar. They all drove her precious daughter insane.

She released a deep sigh and had to fight the tears from falling. Her family and her livelihood were under attack.

"She needs help, ma," Chanel uttered from behind her.

Bacardi turned and glared at her youngest. She didn't say a word. She was defeated by grief, along with the trials and tribulations of life.

Bacardi committed her daughter to a 72-hour hold for psychiatric observation. She couldn't help but to wish that it was Chanel.

Bacardi sat by her bedroom window and smoked cigarette after cigarette. If it wasn't one thing, then it was another. Everything was falling apart. Since her arrest and the cop killing on New Year's Day, it had been a troublesome and hectic year.

With God in jail and her unemployed, there wasn't any income coming into the household. She had to swallow her pride and march her ass down to the welfare office and apply for government assistance and food stamps. She had a sick husband, a disgraced daughter, another daughter that she felt was trouble, and Charlie, who was of no use without God.

Bacardi sighed heavily and frowned. She gazed out the window. It was a rainy day—a downpour outside had been going on for the past hour. The heavy rain cascaded against the window. The day was lousy like her life. It was October and the holidays were looming. Bacardi needed Charlie to do something. She needed her to find a way to get God out of jail so they could live again, so they could get back on top.

Bacardi felt she was too old to look for new employment. And she wasn't slim and curvy enough to go back out there to find herself a baller to spoil her, young or old. She felt washed up.

She took a drag from the Newport and continued to gaze at the gloomy and wet weather outside. She was dressed in an old nightgown that covered all of her flab. Butch was asleep on the bed. He was no use to her—no good dick, no damn income, and no quality conversation came from him. He was a wet, dumb log trying not to die from his drinking—a limp dick inside her bedroom. *What a waste of a man.*

Bacardi was broke, tired, and she was sexually frustrated. She always wanted a better life than this. She always wanted nice things, to take nice trips, and to have a rich man spoil her. Now in her early forties, she lived that life vicariously through Charlie, and now the dream had come to an end with God locked up.

What now? she asked herself.

Chapter Sixteen

Charlie stepped off the bus that took her to Rikers Island and followed behind the other ladies that were also there to see a loved one. It was a breezy October day with a gray, overcast sky. The gloomy weather matched her mood. This would be her second trip to the sprawling jail, and once again it was met with both anticipation to see God and a feeling of hopelessness that he was locked up. The good news was, he and Fingers were arrested on a gun charge—no murders, no robberies. The bad news was that his bail was set at fifty thousand dollars by the judge. Going through a bondsman for 10%, Charlie would have to cough up five thousand dollars she didn't have.

Immediately, the corrections officers started shouting instructions at the visitors. Charlie followed behind the other long line of folks into the reception building, where she had to give her information and go through a metal detector.

It was a tedious and tiresome process and almost degrading—the questions, going through various metal detectors, the bus ride, and the waiting. But she arrived at the visiting room, sat at the small table, and tried to look her best for God in such a deplorable looking environment.

Rikers Island had a strict dress code—nothing too skimpy or short, no jewelry, no gang emblems or colors. Charlie sat looking cute in a pair of jeans, white sneakers, and a green tee. Her reddish-brown skin with freckles and hazel eyes caught the attention of the male guards and a few inmates. She was a pretty girl.

She sat and waited, and ten minutes later, a guard escorted God into the visiting area with a few other inmates. They all wore gray jumpsuits.

Seeing God, Charlie smiled. Even incarcerated, his presence was commanding, and he still looked like he was the man in charge of things. He coolly walked Charlie's way and wrapped his arms around her and planted a loving kiss against her lips. He didn't want to let her go, but the guards and signs made it clear that lingering displays of affection were not allowed during visits.

They took a seat opposite each other and held hands across the table. It was good to see him again, although he only had been locked up for a short period.

"How are you holding up?" he asked.

"I'm fine. I miss you."

"I miss you too."

Not one to beat around the bush, God then asked, "So, what's goin' on wit' my bail?"

"I told you, God, I don't have the money."

"You can get the money, Charlie. I told you to sell those mink coats and your Rolex and get me up outta here."

Charlie felt slighted by his words. "Why I gotta sell my shit?"

She kept on refusing God's request. She liked her material things. They were all she had. And it was his mistake for being careless, not hers.

"Bitch, don't ask me no stupid shit like that," he replied. "Didn't I bail you, ya fat-ass moms, and ya fuckin' insane sister out?! How you gonna do me like this?"

"You have your own shit to sell, God. But you won't tell me where it is. So, I'm supposed to sacrifice my shit? And now is not the time to be takin' Claire's coat. She's fragile, but she's not insane!"

"You love me, right?"

"You know I do."

"So, do what's right and get your man out of here."

Charlie sighed and replied, "I'll see what I can do. Your bail is high, though."

"You're my ride-or-die, Charlie. You always will be. You got this."

Another deep sigh escaped Charlie's mouth. She worried why her man couldn't tell her where his stuff was. What was he hiding?

When God got arrested with Fingers and Kym, Kym left the police precinct with their belongings. She was keeping them in a safe place until God told her what to do with them. Kym also placed money on God's books, and therefore, he was able to call Charlie. When Charlie asked him who the girl in the car was, God lied and told her she was Fingers' bitch. She believed him.

Kym still didn't know about Charlie, and Charlie still didn't know about Kym. God was using them both. He liked the street, gangster side in Charlie—his ride-or-die—and he liked the educated and responsible legal assistant Kym. For God, it was the best of both worlds.

Charlie hugged and kissed him goodbye. Their visit was over. Charlie left with a profound void inside her. God was like the air she breathed. She needed him home.

Butch had the kitchen smelling like a backdoor restaurant with his fish frying in the pan, his baked beans simmering in the pot, and French fries sizzling in the skillet. The porgies he fried were his specialty, and he seemed to know his way around the kitchen.

He was barefoot in a wife-beater and shorts, and his limber frame danced around the kitchen seasoning his meal. Though he was mean and cranky, some people started to see a slight change in Butch. He still cursed like a sailor and could be meaner than a junkyard dog, but seeing Butch cooking in the kitchen was an anomaly.

Claire's suicide attempt was somewhat of a wakeup call for him. He had almost lost his daughter, and he wanted to comfort her and be there for her the best he knew how. He decided to help cheer her up by cooking.

Chanel walked into the kitchen after arriving home from school, and she was completely astounded by what she saw. Her father? In the kitchen? Cooking?

Butch looked at her and smiled, "You hungry?"

Chanel was speechless. Did hell freeze over? Did pigs start to fly? And did her father ask if she was hungry?

Befuddled, Chanel stammered, "Um . . . um, I guess."

"Sit down and I'll make you a plate," he said.

Whoa! Where is this coming from? she said to herself.

She sat down at the table and suspected that it was all a dream. Shit, she even pinched herself to see if it was, and it hurt like hell. This was real.

"How was school today?" he asked.

"School was fine, Daddy."

"And how are these fuckin' boys treatin' you?"

"Boys will be boys, right?"

"Well, them boys better be treatin' my little girl with respect," said Butch. "You got a fuckin' boyfriend?"

"No," she answered.

"Good. You stay in school n' learn somethin'—get ya education. Don't be like me, a stupid drunk. Ya hear me, girl? Ya smarter than this."

Chanel nodded.

"Fuckin' doctor gon' tell me I can't drink no more. Shit, a nigga been drinkin' all his life. It's what I do best—drink and have a good time. I never knew how to be right when I'm not drunk. But drunk, I'm in a different place . . . I'm happy. I'm fun," he proclaimed.

He took a deep breath and went on, "But you don't need to be like me, ya hear? You smart, Chanel, and you let the world know it. You get ya respect from everyone, even these niggas, and you behave and dress like a lady, cuz no nigga gonna want to marry a whore. Ya hear me?"

Chanel sat there and listened to him ramble. She wondered where all of it was coming from. The speech about respect from men was ironic coming from him, because for so many years he never gave his youngest daughter any respect. He always treated her like a whore and a problem child, constantly laying hands on her like he was fighting an enemy on the streets.

"Ya respect yourself? If ya fuckin don't, then these muthafuckin' young niggas won't," he continued to ramble on.

He fixed Chanel a plate and served it to her at the table. It was the first time in a long while that someone had cooked and brought her a plate of food at home. Chanel couldn't help but to beam and relish the moment. She didn't want it to end.

Butch continued his talk about life and respect and how she needed to be careful in the streets. He also took a plate to Claire in her bedroom, but she refused, claiming she wasn't hungry.

For two weeks, a sober Butch surprisingly tried to be a father to his girls and fight the urges to drink. He was cooking and talking, or lecturing, and he also was becoming overbearing and overprotective. He would call his daughters' cell phones to ask when they were coming home, and he would sometimes meet them at the elevator like he was a concerned and doting father.

Charlie didn't care for his fatherly attitude and somewhat resented him, and Claire felt the same way. They both felt that it was too late for his fatherly love and words of wisdom. All their lives, Butch had been a selfish drunk, and a mean, cranky, and abusive father when sober. For them, it was too late for a change.

Chanel wanted it to be true—to be real and lasting. She liked who he was trying to become—someone different. She hoped and prayed that her father wouldn't touch a drop of alcohol and that he'd continue to treat her like his little girl. For her, it wasn't too late to be loved by her father. For her, it was a new beginning with the year coming to an end and a new one about to start. For her, there was no better way to bring in the new year than with her father's love.

Chapter Seventeen

This Christmas Day was a direct contrast to the one they'd had last year. There were no extravagant gifts from Charlie. In fact, the Browns hadn't heard or seen Charlie for several weeks, but she was home today. Butch wasn't a drunk and dancing fool, and there was no Christmas tree. Christmas Day was dry like a desert. It came and it went. That same dryness and cheerless mood continued into New Year's Eve. There was no party, no crowd of people crammed into the Browns' apartment having a good time, and no Bacardi making a small fortune from selling food and liquor.

It was January, and Butch was still sober and unemployed, and Bacardi was just unemployed. Claire was a disgrace who even failed to kill herself, and she was the laughingstock of the projects. Without God around, Charlie had fallen into the slumps of poverty with her family. She still had a few nice things to boast for the New Year, but that way of life was becoming only a memory. Her cash was really low. She wasn't much of a stick-up kid without God and Fingers in her corner, so she was reduced to petty crimes like shoplifting and minor scams to get by.

Chanel simply minded her business. She went to school, the library, and home, and she occupied her time by studying and hanging out with Mecca in Harlem on the weekends. Her hopes of seeing or hearing from

Mateo had faded. It was a new year, and she figured she should let the past stay in the past.

It was a cold Friday evening with the city feeling like Antarctica. The wind chill felt like it had dropped to -70 degrees. Chanel took warmth and comfort inside her bedroom. She occupied one end of the room, and Claire had the other. They said nothing to each other. Chanel was reading a book and Claire had her headphones on listening to music.

Her sister had gotten better. The psychiatric observation that Bacardi put her in helped somewhat, but Claire still had her issues to deal with.

It was too cold to go outside, so everyone was inside doing something. Butch was in his bedroom watching TV, and Charlie and Bacardi were hanging out in the living room smoking a blunt together and talking shit.

It was a regular day for everyone, or so it appeared. Chanel was grateful that the house was quiet. The January weather was making it impossible for her to escape to anywhere else—especially to Harlem. She was stuck indoors until it got a bit warmer and the ice melted.

So, the sudden knock at the door surprised her and everyone else. They were rapid knocks that echoed through the apartment. No one had any idea who it was. Who could be visiting them on such a frigid evening?

Bacardi jumped up from the couch with the blunt in her hand. She cursed, "Who the fuck knocking at my door? You expecting company, Charlie?"

"In this cold? Nah."

Bacardi walked to the door looking like she belonged in an old hoochie mama movie, wearing curlers in her hair and a colorful robe that could blind the blind. She swung the door open and saw two niggas standing in front of her. She had never seen them before, but by the way they were dressed, she could tell that they were some money niggas. One was wearing a mink jacket, and he was really fuckin' handsome. Bacardi sized him up quickly, seeing the Rolex around his wrist, the clean Timberland boots, fresh haircut, and she even peeped the .45 tucked in his waist. The second nigga wore an expensive leather jacket, jewelry that glimmered, and stylish jeans and boots that looked costly. Both men were Hispanic.

Who these Spanish niggas here to see? she wondered. She figured they were there to see Charlie. She figured that Charlie had come through for the family and probably met the next money nigga to leach off of while God was in jail.

"Hello, ma'am," said the nigga with the mink coat.

Ma'am? Bacardi thought. She wasn't that old.

"My name is Mateo, and this is my boy Pyro. Is Chanel home?"

Bacardi's mouth dropped open. *Chanel?* Bacardi couldn't believe what she was hearing.

"You mean Charlie?" she wanted to correct him.

"Nah, Chanel. She a dark skin beauty with long hair and a beautiful smile," Mateo said.

Bacardi was blown away. She quickly ushered the men into the living room and told them to make themselves at home.

Charlie was shocked too. She sat there staring into the faces of the two well dressed Hispanic men who were now crowding her living room.

"Shit!" Charlie muttered in admiration of them. *Chanel? How? Why?*

Bacardi sweetly called out Chanel's name. Her youngest daughter had some explaining to do. She wasn't mad, just shocked that Chanel was able to attract two fine niggas like Mateo and Pyro.

Hearing Bacardi call her name, Chanel meekly walked out her bedroom expecting her evening to go from calm to chaotic. Bacardi never called her name unless it was some trouble coming her way. Chanel expected her mother to riff and rant about something to her—some wrong she had done.

Chanel slowly traveled down the hallway and could see her mother standing at the edge of the hallway with her eyes zeroed in on her like she was the warden and Chanel was an inmate taking her final walk to the death penalty. Bacardi always had this uncomfortable look toward her youngest.

But when Chanel walked into the living room and saw Mateo and Pyro standing in her home, she had no idea what to think or what to say. She was stunned. Was she dreaming? But then she saw his pearly white smile and heard him say, "Hey, beautiful."

Mateo didn't get the greeting he thought he would get.

"What the fuck you doing here?" Chanel chided. "It's been how fuckin' long since I saw you?"

She stood there standoffish. She hadn't heard from or seen Mateo since that day he'd dropped her off in August. It was January.

"What's that, five months?" she added.

"I can explain."

"I don't wanna hear your excuse."

"Chanel, what the fuck is wrong wit' you?" Bacardi exclaimed.

"This isn't your business, Ma," Chanel snapped at her.

Bacardi twitched and the corners of mouth turned downwards into a frown. Did her daughter just talk back at her?

"I know you're upset, and you have the right to be. It's been a while since I saw you," said Mateo coolly.

"Every day, I waited for you and waited for you . . . but not a single phone call, no visit, no text, nothing!" Chanel exclaimed.

"Well, if you don't want him, shit, I'll take him," Charlie uttered.

Charlie moved closer to Mateo and placed her hand against his chest, wanting to feel his muscles. But Mateo quickly shut her down and slapped her hand away. He made it clear that he wasn't interested in her. Her next move was to Pyro, but Charlie got the same reaction—the cold shoulder.

When Claire entered the room, she too was taken aback by Chanel's handsome company. Mateo and Pyro were definitely eye-candy.

"Can we talk?" Mateo asked Chanel.

"No, not right now."

Bacardi couldn't believe what she was hearing. Was Chanel crazy? A nigga like Mateo wanted her daughter's attention and she was treating him like he was some kind of STD.

"Chanel, why don't you talk to the man? He came out in the damn cold to see you," Bacardi said.

"No. I'm not just something for you to play with, and then get bored, and then come back to it when you want," said Chanel. "I got feelings, Mateo."

"It's not even like that," he said. "Let me make it up to you and take you out to dinner."

"It's too cold outside."

He chuckled. Chanel was being stubborn, but he liked that about her. Shit, most females would have given in and surrendered themselves to him once they saw him standing in their home—like her sisters. Chanel was different. He liked different.

"Damn, Chanel, that's why you don't get dick now," Charlie rudely said.

Mateo cut his eyes at the sister. He wasn't too pleased by her comment. Both her sisters were red, pretty, and took after their father, and Chanel took after her mother. Now he understood why she wanted to dye her hair. She was a black beauty and Mateo loved a dark skinned woman.

"This ain't about sex," Mateo announced. "Chanel's too special to be treated like a hoodrat. She's a queen and the most beautiful woman I've ever laid eyes on and I fucked up. So I'm here to show her that I won't make that mistake twice."

The sisters didn't like to hear that. They started to envy Chanel.

Mateo smiled at Chanel and he wanted her to forgive him, but Chanel was still being stubborn. She was still angry.

"Mateo, let's just go. Give her some time," Pyro said.

Mateo looked hesitant to leave, but he knew his friend was right. Chanel needed some time, and he didn't like how her family was all in their business.

"I'll be back, Chanel. Just think about us," he said.

She turned from him and marched back to her room. Mateo wasn't upset. He loved how feisty she was. She did love him and that was why she was so upset.

Mateo pivoted and walked out the front door. Bacardi looked at him like he was a million dollars walking out the door. She wanted to try and pimp her other two daughters onto him and his friend, but they both made it clear that they weren't interested.

Pyro smiled and uttered, "It was nice meeting y'all," and he made his exit behind Mateo.

When the door closed behind them, Bacardi turned and shouted, "Chanel, what the fuck is wrong wit' your foolish ass!"

"I told you she's a stupid bitch," Charlie chimed.

Chapter Eighteen

The next day, Mateo parked his Range Rover on the Brooklyn Street and climbed out into cold air that matched yesterday's brutal weather. This time he was alone. He wanted to give talking to Chanel another shot. Yesterday was a shock to her, and she was upset. He had been gone without an explanation for quite some time, and he understood that. Today, he came with some flowers for her along with his stubbornness. He wasn't going to give up on Chanel. He wanted her back in his life.

He stood under Chanel's apartment window and called her cell phone. She answered, and before she could hang up on him, he uttered, "You gonna have me freeze to death. Cuz I'm gonna wait out here all day until I get to see you alone."

Chanel hung up on him. She went to the living room window and there he was, standing outside her apartment window dressed in the same mink jacket and clutching a bouquet of expensive flowers that looked like they were ready to freeze and turn to ice. The winter day was no place for flowers, but Mateo didn't care. He wanted to impress her.

Bacardi gazed out the window too, and seeing Mateo standing in the winter cold holding flowers for her youngest daughter was the best thing she could see at that moment—along with the pearl white Range that was parked behind him.

Damn-it, her youngest daughter done hit the jackpot. In her eyes, Mateo was a keeper. But seeing Chanel's reaction, how she appeared stubborn and standoffish to the man's advances, Bacardi had seen enough. That bitch was about to ruin a good thing coming.

Bacardi spun around to face her daughter. "Are you a stupid bitch or what? This nigga out there in the cold waitin' fo' you to see him, and you in here looking like we don't need his help. Ya a stubborn little bitch wit' hurt feelings."

Chanel stood there in silence.

Bacardi angrily continued with, "You either go out there with him or you can get the fuck out my house! We all up in here struggling and starvin', and maybe that nigga can help out. You need to fuckin' pull ya weight around here, Chanel. Now get dressed and go handle ya man."

Chanel sighed. She wasn't about to go against Bacardi, not because she was scared, but she felt her mother was right. She was being stubborn, and she didn't want to lose Mateo. Yesterday, she didn't give him a chance to explain. She gave him the cold shoulder because he'd hurt her deeply. But if he were to leave and disappear for good this time, Chanel knew his absence was going to hurt more the second time around.

She went to the window and hollered at him, "Just give me five minutes."

He smiled.

She marched into her bedroom and threw on something that was appropriate for the cold outside. In her thick winter coat and snow boots, she went out the door and took the stairs down to the lobby. Even in the lobby, she could feel the cold air from outside. She went through the doors and it felt like she got hit in the face by a brick. She bundled up inside her coat and trekked toward Mateo. He kept his eyes on her with a bright smile.

"I'm glad I could change your mind," he said.

She sighed. "So, are we just gonna stand out here and freeze to death?"

Mateo handed her the dying flowers and escorted her to his ride and opened the passenger door for her. She climbed inside. Being inside his vehicle again felt soothing to her and brought about some nostalgia.

Mateo got behind the wheel and sat there for a moment. His eyes lingered on Chanel, manifesting his feelings.

"Are we just gonna sit here with you looking at me, or did you have someplace in mind?" she said.

"You hungry?"

"I can get something to eat."

Mateo put the car in gear and drove off. Moving farther away from the projects, he glanced at Chanel and said, "I know I owe you an explanation for my sudden disappearing act for a few months."

"You do."

"I'm sorry."

Chanel sat in silence and simply looked at him. She was ready to hear what he had to say to her.

He sighed and uttered, "I had a girlfriend—"

"Girlfriend?" she uttered in disbelief.

"Yes. Her name is Nikki. Right after I dropped you off that day, I went to see her and she told me she was pregnant."

Chanel could feel the sickness of jealousy and betrayal swimming around in her stomach. Mecca had warned her that he had other women, but she didn't want to believe her. She wanted to be Mateo's one true love. Truth was, she was still young and vulnerable to his charm. But hearing "girlfriend" and "pregnant" was thrusting her into pain and envy.

"Anyway, she lied to me about the pregnancy. She had found out about you and threatened to abort my child if I continued to see you. And I believed her. I wanted to be a father, so I sacrificed our relationship for fatherhood," he proclaimed.

Chanel took a deep breath. She didn't know what to think. She wanted to believe him.

Mateo added, "I wanted to have a baby, and since you were new in my life, I felt that it was best to let you go. But, Chanel, believe me when I say that I thought about you every day. And it hurt me to cut you off so suddenly over a lie that I wanted to believe. Nikki was never pregnant. She said that to keep me in her life and to get rid of you. I realized the mistake I made in December and her lie nearly tore me apart. It took me weeks to get myself together . . . to move out and move on."

She looked at him and asked, "So she's no longer in your life?"

His expression was reassuring, and he said, "She's gone from my life, I promise you that—and everyone else. I only want to be with you, Chanel. I want to give this thing we have a chance."

Chanel wanted to pout and frown. She wanted to stay upset with him, but she couldn't. Hearing the explanation about his long absence, and then hearing his pledge to be with her and only her to give their relationship a try, she smiled.

"So, what do you say? You want this? Because I do," he said.

"Yes. I want this, Mateo. I always wanted this."

At the next red light, the two leaned closer to each other and kissed passionately. It was a kiss that could melt the ice outside and turn the cold into summer.

"Damn, I missed you," he said.

"I missed you too."

They kissed again. Chanel didn't want to let him go. She wanted to kiss him forever, hoping that the red light never turned green again. She was happy again.

"You still hungry?" he asked.

She chuckled. "I am. You have a lot of making up to do, and that starts with feeding me."

He laughed too. "A'ight. Your wish is my command."

With Mateo back in her life, and the two forming a relationship that seemed like a fairytale, Chanel started to blossom a lot sooner than the flowers and leaves did in the spring. It seemed like nothing could separate her and Mateo. Mateo treated Chanel like his queen and made sure she didn't want for anything. They constantly went out on dates, talked, held hands, and went for long, romantic walks around the city. Mateo paraded his young beauty around town like she was a new car, washed and shined and looking spectacular.

On Valentine's Day, Mateo ordered two dozen roses, several teddy bears, and chocolate to be delivered to her home. Chanel was blown away by the surprises delivered to her front door, and so were Bacardi and her sisters. It was clear to everyone that Mateo was there to stay.

In March, Mateo took her to see *The Lion King* on Broadway in Times Square. *The Lion King* was one of her favorite Disney movies growing up, and Chanel was excited to see it in live action on stage. Mateo had gotten them the perfect seats up front, and she could feel herself on the stage because they were so close. She got to experience the African savannah come to life on stage with Simba, Rafiki, and an unforgettable cast of characters as they journeyed from Pride Rock to the jungle and back again.

In April, they took trips to Coney Island, frequented museums in the city, toured the Empire State Building, and enjoyed horse and carriage rides through Central Park, something that was becoming a favorite for Chanel. Though she was a native of the city, Mateo had her feeling like a tourist. A day with him was always breathtaking and busy.

Bacardi and Butch started to treat their youngest like she was their world. Suddenly, Chanel could do no wrong. Chanel would wake up to Bacardi cooking breakfast for her—her favorite, French toast, omelets, and bacon. Her parents were starting to spoil her with kindness. If Chanel had a dispute with her sisters about anything, Bacardi right away took Chanel's side and fussed at Charlie or Claire.

It felt like she was living in a parallel universe.

Because of her relationship with Mateo, Chanel was now able to buy groceries, pay the rent, and hit Bacardi off with money and gifts, turning the other cheek and proving that she was the bigger woman by forgiving them for how they treated her before Mateo came into her life.

Now, to Bacardi, Claire was the cheater in the family, the fraud and exposed loser, who was dumb and was going in and out of depression for months now. Then there was Charlie, her oldest daughter who had fallen from grace and couldn't bail her man out of jail because she didn't have the money.

When Mateo would come to the apartment, Bacardi would roll out the red carpet for him and pull out the good china. Mateo became her favorite person in the world. She started to call him her son and treated him like he was.

"Look at how handsome my son is," she would say.

Mateo took her flattery and compliments in stride. He wasn't too fond of Chanel's parents. He remembered the stories Chanel would tell him about how they would constantly mistreat her and abuse her. The only reason he was nice to them was because of Chanel.

Even with all the gifts and the kindness Mateo showed her, Chanel remained as sweet as ever. She didn't allow his money to go to her head. He tried to push a lot of really nice things on her, but Chanel would only take what her family needed and nothing more.

Chapter Nineteen

Mateo's alarm clock rang at seven in the morning. Lying next to him was a naked young woman who had given him the time of his life last night. But it was only sex. He looked at her and frowned. She was just pussy, nobody special.

He yawned and stretched and got out of the bed butt-naked. He went to the window to take a look outside. The morning sunshine percolated through the bedroom window, indicating that it was a beautiful spring day in April.

A deep sigh, a long stretch, and then it was a few calisthenics on the bedroom floor—nearly a hundred push-ups and almost as many sit-ups. Mateo liked to work up a sweat before he got his day started. He was in great shape and in the prime of his life. He was an early riser and didn't believe in sleeping in and waking up late mornings or early afternoons. He believed that the early bird always gets the worm.

After completing his calisthenics, finally, his sexual plaything from last night decided to wake up. She rose up, propped herself against the headboard, and spotted Mateo naked on the floor after he'd just completed sixty sit-ups.

She smiled and said, "Now that is something nice to wake up to in the morning."

He stood up, looked at her, and said, "You need to go."

"Go? Why? It's still early, baby," she said.

"Don't call me that."

She removed herself from the bed, her voluptuous figure eye-candy from head to toe, and tried to wrap her arms around Mateo to give him a sweet good-morning kiss. But he pushed her away.

"You need to get dressed. I got things to do today."

"Damn, it's like that? I fuck you good wit' this wet pussy and suck your dick and swallow your seeds and you gonna dismiss me like that?"

He stared at her coldly and replied, "Yes."

"Fuck you then, Mateo. Fo' real, fuck you!" the girl shouted.

She stormed around his bedroom collecting her clothes from off the floor and sloppily got dressed. Mateo donned his shorts and a shirt. Playtime was over, and she needed to leave. Besides, he started to feel guilty about cheating on Chanel so soon.

As the girl stormed out of his apartment ranting and carrying on, Mateo thought, *Good riddance.*

He cooked himself some breakfast and then got dressed. Soon after, his cell phone rang. It was Pyro.

"Yo, what's up?"

"You. Did you kick that bitch out yet?" Pyro asked.

"How you know I had a bitch in here?"

"Because, nigga, old habits die hard. And I know you love Chanel, but, nigga, you got needs too."

"Nigga, stay out my business," said Mateo.

"Anyway, Lorraine called and said she gonna need us there at the closing to sign some papers."

"What time?"

"Around six," Pyro said.

"A'ight, I'll be there."

"And we still got that class tonight," Pyro reminded him, like he was his personal assistant.

"I didn't forget. But P, I'll see you at the barbershop in a few. I got some runs to make," said Mateo.

"A'ight. One love. I'm out."

Mateo ended the call. It seemed like his schedule today was on overload. He mixed himself a healthy drink in the kitchen and downed it.

Mateo's Bronx apartment was a luxury in the borough. For $3,100 a month, he had a 1,400-square-foot apartment with two bedrooms and two bathrooms, along with gorgeous hardwood flooring, granite countertops, and full sized stainless steel appliances. It was the ultimate bachelor's pad with a 60" flat screen and a high-end stereo system with surround-sound.

Mateo liked nice things, and he and Pyro did their best to stay under the radar. They sold mostly weed and didn't dabble in cocaine or other hardcore drugs like most dealers. Both men wanted to make enough money to start their own legit businesses, from real estate investments to cryptocurrency. Mateo was a man who did his homework, and it seemed like cryptocurrency was the future. There was no central bank to manipulate the value.

Mateo sat down at the kitchen table and opened his laptop. First, he went into his portfolio to look at a few of his investments and saw that Bitcoin was up 5.2%, and things were moving well. He smiled.

After going through several of his portfolios, he started to write in his small journal that he started a few months ago. Mateo was a meticulous individual. He was organized, smart, and believed that the pieces will always fall into the puzzle if you visualize the entire design.

After his early morning routine, he exited his apartment and took the stairs down to the lower level. He carried a .380, for that *just in case,* and he carried a few thousand dollars on him.

The first stop on Mateo's list was to Washington Heights to meet with his weed connect, a cool player named Marty. Marty was a white man small in stature, but very business savvy and influential around town. He wore thick bifocals, always dressed in bohemian clothing, and was a down-to-earth guy.

Mateo parked in front of the brick building near Amsterdam Avenue and entered the five-story structure. He walked up three flights and knocked on apartment door 3F. Marty answered the door with a smile on his face, happy to see a friend and lucrative client at his door.

"Mateo, my friend, c'mon inside," said Marty with a hug and dap.

Mateo took a seat on the sofa. The décor of the place was neat and comfortable. Marty had a bit of OCD, and he liked things in place and rarely touched. Mateo knew how to move and where to sit.

"What you need from me, my friend?" asked Marty.

Marty considered everyone a friend, but he hardly trusted anyone. Mateo was one of a few allowed at his location in Washington Heights. Seated in the kitchen was Marty's goon, Large D, who stood six-four with muscles and who was very protective of Marty. It was even rumored that they were lovers. But it wasn't Mateo's business. Gay or not, Marty was his connect and they'd been working together for nearly two years.

Mateo reached into his pockets and pulled out a wad of cash and dropped it onto the glass coffee table in front of him.

"I need a ki."

"Big baller, you are, Mateo. This is your second ki in two weeks," said Marty gleefully.

"I'm a busy man, Marty."

"I see, I see."

Marty picked up the wad of cash and Large D came into the living room to collect and count it. But they both knew Mateo was always correct with the cash. While Mateo waited for his product, Marty happily lit up a joint and asked him, "So, have you looked into those business investments I told you about?"

Mateo nodded. "Yeah. You always on point, Marty, I gotta hand it to you. I put down a few thousand dollars on some cryptocurrencies, and the returns are looking nice."

"What did I tell you? Digital currency is the wave of the future, and right now I'm sitting on a few hundred grand—money, money, money. I came out the pussy with a dollar bill in my hand," he joked.

Mateo laughed.

Large D came back into the living room with Mateo's ki of marijuana. It was potent shit—Kosher Kush. Mateo's clientele couldn't get enough of it. Mateo grinned and placed the shrink-wrapped and vacuumed sealed ki in his bag and stood up. Their transaction was complete. What he paid $4,500 for could net him ten grand or more in profit with his customers—supply and demand, it was great business. Mateo and Pyro were moving one to five kilos a month. But it wasn't much compared to the heavyweights in the game that were moving triple that.

Mateo left the apartment and went back down the stairs and out the lobby doors with his high quality purchase concealed in his bag. He got back into his Range Rover and drove off.

It was back to the Bronx, where he made most of his money. He loved living in the Bronx. Mateo loved the culture, the food, and the music. When he would bring Chanel to the Bronx, it was a different world for her with all the Puerto Ricans around and the numerous Spanish restaurants in the neighborhoods.

At times Chanel felt like she wasn't in America anymore. Mateo loved bringing her around and introducing her to his peoples, and everyone fell in love with the dark skinned beauty. There were the female haters, though, the ones who wanted Mateo for themselves and felt that he needed to stick with his own kind and not some young black bitch from Brooklyn.

Mateo parked in front of the barbershop on the Grand Concourse. He could see that the inside was already busy with customers and it wasn't even noon yet. But Spanish Fly Barbershop was a popular place in the neighborhood.

Inside the shop, there were three barbers—two Hispanics and one black male. Each of them had a client in the chair, and seated on the opposite side of the barbers were a half-dozen men waiting to get a haircut. There was a decent sized flat screen mounted nearby to entertain waiting customers, and it played everything from the latest music videos to movies and sports.

The chitchat inside was vibrant and sociable, with laughter and shit talking. The moment Mateo entered the shop, all eyes were on him and he was greeted with love and respect. Mateo gave a few guys dap and said hello to them, and then he went toward the owner of the barbershop. Bolo was a hefty man with some pretty features, including diamond earrings in both ears and dark waves on top of his head that stayed spinning. He had swag and was about his business and his customers.

"What's good, Mateo?" Bolo greeted with dap and a brotherly embrace. "We good?"

Mateo smiled and nodded. "Yeah. We good."

"Fellows, excuse us for a minute," Bolo said to his peoples in the shop.

Bolo and Mateo disappeared into the back of the barbershop, a medium sized break room that could also be transformed into another business for a beautician. It was windowless room and cluttered with a few crates and boxes and black garbage bags.

Mateo set his bag on the table and asked, "What you need, Bolo?"

"Let me get four ounces. I got customers ready for it right now."

Mateo nodded and grinned. "A'ight!"

Bolo was one of Mateo's distributors on the Bronx streets. He was a frequent buyer with a string of clients looking forward to the Kosher Kush that Mateo provided him.

Four ounces of high quality weed at $300 an ounce was a very profitable gain for Mateo. Bolo pulled out a wad of cash and handed it over to Mateo.

"Yo, I heard that you been chillin' wit' some fly black shorty lately, and more than once. What's that about, huh?"

"Just my personal life, Bolo."

"I hear you're in love."

"Yeah, well, is that a bad thing?"

Bolo chuckled. "A man like you, I never thought it would happen. This chocolate mami, she must be something special for you to sport her around town the way you been doing lately," said Bolo.

"You good, puta?"

Bolo chuckled. He could see that Mateo was somewhat offended by having his personal life brought up, so he left the subject alone.

"Yeah, we're good, Mateo."

Mateo packed up his shit, gave Bolo dap, and was on his way. He expected Pyro to meet him at the barbershop, but he was nowhere around.

Chapter Twenty

"Chanel, you okay?" Mecca asked.

Chanel turned around from staring out the window. "Yeah, I'm okay. I'm just thinking about something, that's all."

"Is it about Mateo?"

She sighed. "Yes. I think he's cheating on me."

It wasn't surprising news to Mecca, and she wanted to say *I told you so,* but she didn't. She was Chanel's best friend and her comfort. Whatever Chanel needed to talk about, she was there to listen and give her friend the best advice she could give without being judgmental.

"Why do you think he's cheating on you?" she asked.

"I don't know. It's just that feeling you get. We've been together for a while now and he's never touched me other than kissing."

"So, are you trying to fuck him?"

Another sigh escaped Chanel's lips. She knew he was the one to take her virginity, but the strangest thing was, he wanted to take things slow.

"I want us to make love, Mecca. I'm ready. I've never felt so ready in my life."

"I bet you are."

"Do you think something's wrong with me?"

"No, girl. Shit, everything is right with you, and if I was gay, then we probably would be having sex right now," said Mecca.

Chanel laughed. Mecca always made her laugh.

Chanel believed that Mateo was having an affair with a few Puerto Rican girls. When she would bring up the issue, he would explain that he was into black women, and that he always had an attraction for dark skinned women.

"I love your complexion, baby. It's Nubian—it's beautiful. Sometimes I wish I was darker. Chanel, you know you got my heart," Mateo would say to her.

His reassurance made her feel good and it made her feel wanted. Still, she couldn't shake the feeling that he was hiding something from her.

"I just find it weird that a man like him would wanna take it slow."

"Maybe's he overloaded on pussy," Mecca joked.

Chanel didn't find the comment funny.

"I'm sorry. Bad joke, huh?"

Chanel raised her eyebrow. "Mmpf. Anyway, he has this new place and he claims he never brought any bitches there before and I'm the only one he's brought there. I get to come over and chill, but he never allows me to stay the night. He always takes me home."

"I gotta be real with you. I do find that shit weird, Chanel."

"It is, right?"

"You ask him why?"

"He says if I stay the night, he won't be able to control himself."

"So Mateo is actually trying to be a gentleman, huh?"

"I guess so. But girl, I'm not trying to be a lady."

Mecca laughed. "So let me get this straight. Mateo treats you like the queen you are, and for some strange reason, he wants to wait to have sex with you, but you don't want to wait any longer, and he brings you to his new crib, but he don't want you staying the night because he sees you as temptation. Wow!"

"My life is weird."

"Well, y'all need to talk. And you need to let him know that you don't like the way he's moving, and no matter what he tells you, you're seeing different."

Chanel agreed.

The next day, Chanel was nestled in Mateo's arms on the couch at his condo. Watching a movie on Netflix, the two engaged themselves into passionate kissing and some touchy-feely. Chanel could feel a twitch between her legs. Mateo's touch was riveting and his deep kisses were always mesmerizing. He held her lovingly. The aroma from his breath was winter fresh, and her scent was intoxicating to him. Being with her man always meant security and desire.

"I love you," she said.

"I love you too, baby," he said.

It was approaching midnight, but things started to really heat up with them on the couch. Mateo cupped her breast and caressed her butt, and their tongues wrestled, fighting for dominance. The movie was now watching them. Chanel wanted to take things to the bedroom. She wanted to know what sex felt like—to feel him inside of her.

They had been together for months and their conversation was still strong like they'd met yesterday. They were getting to know each other really well. Chanel felt like tonight she could take things to the next step. She could finally exhale and breathe.

He unbuttoned her shirt and she thought, *This is it*.

But then, Mateo pulled away from her, and their passionate moment came to a halt.

"Baby, what's wrong?" she said.

"I need to take you home," he said.

"Take me home! Why?" Chanel lamented.

"It's getting late."

"I don't want to go home. I want to stay the night with you. I want to be with you, Mateo, not home!" she exclaimed.

"Chanel, just chill—"

"No, fuck that! What is really going on, Mateo? We sitting here on the couch making out, you groping me, and I'm finally ready to have sex with you, and you want to take me home!" she shouted.

"Baby, calm down."

"Don't tell me to calm down! Are you fuckin' some other bitch?"

"What? No," he lied. He was still seeing a couple of jump-offs.

"You told me that you would never fuckin' lie to me! So don't!"

"Baby, listen." He tried to reach out to grab her, but Chanel angrily pushed him away. She didn't want him to touch her right now.

"You got my heart, Chanel, and you will always have my heart."

"Then why don't you want to have sex with me? Why do you always want to take me home, huh? Explain that shit to me, Mateo!"

Mateo took a deep breath. "It's . . . it's complicated," he stammered.

"Then don't make it fuckin' complicated," she cursed. Chanel found herself sounding like Bacardi with so much cursing.

"I love you, Chanel. I love you too much," he admitted wholeheartedly.

By now, Chanel had some tears trickling down her face. She was in love, and the last thing she wanted was to be hurt by the man she loved. Regardless, she simply wanted the truth from him.

"Look, I've been with a lot of women, baby. A lot," he said. "And you—you are special and so unique in my life that I don't want to ruin a good thing," he said.

She sighed. Chanel had become an emotional wreck so fast. She continued to throw a jealous tantrum, and no matter how Mateo tried to appease her, she strongly felt that he wasn't telling her the truth.

She hollered, "You don't want to have sex with me because you got an STD from some other bitch?"

Mateo was shocked by the accusation. "What? No! I'm clean, baby, and I told you that I wasn't having sex with anyone else."

"I just don't understand you, Mateo. First, I don't hear from you for months, and then you pop back into my life and give me this story about your ex-girlfriend and her fake pregnancy. And now you don't want to make love to me and you don't want me spending the night at your place. How do you think that makes me fuckin' feel?"

"I promise you, baby, I'll make it up to you."

"No! If you gonna hurt me, then do it now and tell me the truth."

"It is the truth."

She didn't believe him. That feeling of being betrayed was eating away inside of her. She didn't want to hear it.

"Fuck this and fuck you, Mateo. I'll take an Uber," she replied.

Chanel quickly gathered her stuff and stormed off.

Mateo gave chase behind her. "Chanel, why are you acting like this?"

Chanel spun around with anger contorting her pretty face and she yelled, "Because I love you too much, Mateo. And if you gonna do me dirty, I rather find out right now."

"Beautiful, I promise you that I'm not doing you dirty," he replied.

They looked into each other's faces. He seemed sincere. *Damn.* Chanel wanted to believe him.

He drove her home that night, and still being somewhat upset with him, she got out of his SUV without giving him a kiss or telling him goodnight. She needed to be alone for a moment and think.

Mateo sighed deeply and once again yelled, "I love you, Chanel."

She didn't respond. She marched toward her project building without turning back to look at him or saying that she loved him too. Mateo sadly drove off.

That night, Chanel could be heard crying from her bed. Claire, lying on the opposite side of the bedroom, slyly grinned at her sister's grief, assuming that Mateo had broken up with Chanel. Now things could go back to normal in the household, with Chanel once again being the outcast.

Chanel sat in silence and stared aimlessly out the window as the city bus navigated its way through the Brooklyn traffic. It was a sunny afternoon on a warm spring day, and she was on her way from school. She didn't want to think about Mateo, but she thought about him all the time. She missed him. It had been a week since their argument and he was calling her every day to apologize for his actions. Chanel wanted to be stubborn for a moment. She proclaimed to Mateo that she needed time to think.

The bus traveled down Ralph Avenue and approached the next stop, where she would get off. She was shocked to see Mateo's pearl white Range Rover parked near the bus stop.

She stepped off the bus and Mateo climbed out of the SUV and approached her with a wide, bright smile and clutching some colorful flowers in his hands. Chanel was surprised by his unexpected presence, but she looked at him deadpan. He always had a knack for finding her at the right place at the right time. She remembered not giving him her apartment number inside the building, and yet he and Pyro were knocking on her door on one of the coldest days of the year.

"Are you stalking me?" she joked.

"I missed you, and I had to see you," he said.

He handed her the flowers and she happily accepted them. "I missed you too."

"Can we go for a ride somewhere?" he asked her.

After a brief hesitation she said, "Sure."

Always the gentleman, Mateo escorted her to the SUV and opened the passenger door for her. Chanel slid inside with a lot of eyes watching her from afar, seeing her being courted by the young and handsome Hispanic male with the nice truck. Some of those eyes were envious.

Mateo started the vehicle and drove away from the area. Chanel always felt like a queen inside his white chariot. *Where is he taking me?* But she didn't really care. Being with him again felt good.

Mateo drove to the nearby park. He liked parks. He told her that they were always a relaxing place for him—the greenery, the playgrounds, and the kids. Parks were temporary escapes from the bustling cities.

They went for a walk around a trail that neighbored a small pond and talked. Mateo was very apologetic. He wanted her to forgive him about the other day, but she already had. Mateo took her hand in his. Every time they touched, there was a spark between them.

"There is no one else, Chanel, and there will never be—not now and not in the future," he said.

"Why don't you want to have sex with me?" she asked.

They stopped walking and he looked at her with deep love and concern. "Because you're the purest thing I have ever been with. And-and, I don't want to treat you like all the other women I've been with—like you're some whore, because you're not. You're ready to give me your virginity and I truly respect that, Chanel. You're giving me something special, and I want to give you something special in return."

Suddenly, Chanel found Mateo bending a knee in front of her, his hand still in hers. She looked at him with some alarm and astonishment. "Baby, what you are doing?"

She kept her eyes on him and his eyes were locked on her. *Is he doing what I think he's doing?* she asked herself.

"Chanel, you're the most beautiful woman I have ever laid eyes on, and I fell in love with you swiftly, and I know you love me for who I am, and . . ." he paused for a moment and reached into his inner jacket pocket and removed a black velvet case. Chanel couldn't take her eyes off of him.

He opened the case to reveal a rose gold, 5-carat diamond engagement ring.

He continued with, "Will you marry me, Chanel? I want you to become my wife."

Chanel stood there with her mouth open. "Mateo," she uttered in amazement.

"Say yes, beautiful, and I promise to always take care of you. You're willing to give me your virginity and I'm willing to give you my last name and make your very first experience count. It's my special thing for you."

No other nigga would have done this. They would have probably fucked her and used her. But Mateo wasn't an ordinary dude.

"Of course I'll marry you," Chanel excitedly accepted.

Mateo smiled so big that he got his ears wet. He slid the engagement ring on her finger and it was a perfect fit. How did he get that right? But her man was always full of surprises. Mateo finally stood up from his knee and Chanel threw herself into his arms and they kissed so passionately that things almost became X-rated in the park.

It was hard for them to pull away from each other. Their love was strong and Mateo wanted to show the world how much he loved Chanel. He wanted the young girl to become his wife. He didn't want to lose her.

"Listen, baby, I want us to get married on your eighteenth birthday, on June twenty-fourth," he said.

"Seriously?"

"It'll be my birthday gift to you. Marriage."

Chanel was completely overwhelmed. Her birthday was in two months. There was a lot to do, many arrangements to make, and of course Mecca was going to be her maid of honor.

"I have another surprise for you," said Mateo.

Chanel wasn't sure if she could take any more surprises from him. She was becoming inundated with happiness. It was already the perfect day, so how could Mateo make it any more perfect? But knowing him, he could.

They walked hand-in-hand out of the park and back to his Range Rover. Chanel was floating on cloud nine the entire time. From her view, she could see everything and it was so beautiful—sprawling blue skies and bright sunshine. There was no way she was going to come down from the cloud. Being so high above everything else with Mateo, she felt so safe and secure and far away from all the bullshit and drama.

He drove her to a dealership in Queens. She had no idea why she was in Queens. That borough was definitely foreign territory for her. All Chanel knew was Brooklyn and Harlem, and some of the Bronx, thanks to Mateo.

And why were they at a dealership?

Mateo was close with the owner of the dealership. He was an affable white male in his early forties named Michael. He approached Mateo's Range with a smile and introduced himself to Chanel.

"So, this is the lucky lady, huh?" He shook Chanel's hand and added, "Mateo tells me a lot about you. Now I see why he's willing to go all out for you. Congratulations."

Chanel smiled.

"Beautiful, come out the car. I want to show you something," Mateo said.

Chanel coolly climbed out of the car and she was still soaring high. Mateo and Michael guided her through the car lot where there were a lot of nice cars for sale, Beamers, Benzes, Jags, and SUVs. Mateo led her toward a pearl colored Range Rover Sport that sat in the rear of the lot. It had a bright red bow on the hood of the trunk. Mateo pointed to it and said, "It's yours, baby."

Chanel didn't know what to think.

"What? What you mean, Mateo?"

"That's your new car."

"But Mateo, I don't even have my license."

"You got your permit, right?"

"Yes."

"So we'll work on getting your license. And I trust you in driving because you drove my truck plenty of times. And you having your own ride saves me from not having to drive to the projects all the time," he said.

"Ohmygod, Mateo, you're gonna spoil me. I don't deserve all—"

Before she completed her sentence, he approached her and softly placed his index finger against her lips. "Shhhh . . . you deserve it all, beautiful, especially after everything your family put you through."

Chanel could feel her eyes welling up with happy tears.

"I got you, beautiful, and I always will. I promise you that. Just enjoy it, Chanel."

She took a deep breath and smiled as one of the tears escaped. In one day, she was engaged with a giant rock on her finger and she had a brand new car.

Although Mateo would occasionally hit her family off with some money, once he was married to Chanel, he planned on excluding them from their lives completely. The generosity was a ploy to keep the peace between Chanel and her family after all the horror stories she'd told him. Bacardi was a greedy bitch, and he wanted that bitch to enjoy it while it lasted, because in two months, they were going to get married on her birthday and then he planned on flying them off to Hawaii for their honeymoon.

Mateo wanted to fulfill her wish and marry her as a virgin.

The diamond engagement ring and the new Range Rover Sport that Chanel had were all too much for Claire and Charlie to take. Overnight, it appeared that Chanel had hit the jackpot—a man with money who loved her, and she was getting married on her birthday.

Bacardi was over-the-moon. Chanel marrying Mateo meant a step up for the family too, she assumed. She was already treating him like he was her own son, and now it was about to become cemented.

Charlie felt the opposite. It bothered her that her little sister was getting all the attention from the family, and that Chanel had a baller to take care of her while her man was still locked up. It bothered Charlie that Chanel now had better things than her. That bitch had a Range Rover Sport to drive around in, and she didn't even have her license. The envy ate away at Charlie.

Now Charlie had to go to the extreme to help get God out of Rikers Island. She decided to pawn everything she had to make that happen—because now, her ugly duckling of a little sister was becoming that bitch.

God and Fingers were going back and forth to court, and their lawyer was able to get their bail reduced to a lower amount, which meant that Charlie could get the both of them out. But she had to go to some extreme measures to raise the money, because pawning her shit wasn't quite enough. So, unbeknownst to God, she started to dance in some shady clubs and perform sexual favors to raise the rest of the bail money. It was a degrading act, and Charlie had hit an all time low, especially now that her little sister was soaring high with material things and respect.

Chapter Twenty-One

*C*hanel, this dress is almost fifteen thousand dollars! Are you serious? You really wanna pay fifteen grand for a wedding dress?" Mecca asked.

"Mateo said whatever I want, I can get, and it's gonna be my special day," Chanel said.

"But damn, fifteen stacks for something you're only gonna wear once?"

Chanel smiled. "It's beautiful, isn't it?"

Mecca's furrowed brow softened a touch. "I mean, it is . . ."

"I can't wait, Mecca. I'm getting married!"

Mecca smiled. "And I'm happy for you, girl. You deserve to be happy."

Chanel did a graceful twirl in the wedding dress she was trying on and stared at her image in the long mirror. It was beautiful. It was a Monique Lhuillier wedding gown, in all white to signify her purity.

The two were inside Kleinfeld Bridal located on 20th Street in Manhattan. It was an upscale bridal boutique, and the woman helping them eyed them suspiciously and wondered how such a young girl could afford such an expensive wedding dress.

Mecca was happy for her friend and the fact that she was doing it the right way, although she wasn't too pleased about her friend spending a small fortune on a dress. She eyed Chanel in her white, flowing gown. Her friend was so breathtaking—so beautiful.

Chanel turned and beamed toward the saleslady, a middle-aged Caucasian woman who seemed snobbish at first, but lightened her mood when she knew the girls were serious about purchasing the dress.

"I'll take it," Chanel said wholeheartedly.

"Perfect!" said the saleswoman. "And how will you be paying?"

Chanel handed the woman a credit card with a fifty-thousand-dollar limit. It belonged to Mateo.

"It's my fiancé. He's spoiling me rotten," she said.

The woman smiled and replied, "Whatever makes the misses happy. Happy wife, happy life."

"Yes. We're going to have a very happy life. We're getting married on my birthday next month."

"Well, congratulations. I'm sure it will be a beautiful wedding."

The purchase went through and Chanel and Mecca walked out of the upscale boutique with a very expensive dress.

"Where are you gonna keep the dress, Chanel? I know you're not about to take it back to your mama's place."

"No. I was hoping that maybe you could hold it for me at your place until the wedding," Chanel said.

"Of course, girl. I got you. I'll put it in the closet and it will be safe there."

Chanel was grateful.

Originally, Mateo and Chanel were going to get married at the Justice of Peace, but things changed. Mateo wanted to give his queen a small and intimate ceremony. Chanel left Landy numerous unanswered telephone calls because she wanted her there. Mecca was going to be her maid of honor, and Pyro was going to be the best man. The whole thing would take place in Hawaii, where they would have their honeymoon too.

Chanel was excited. It was a life changing event for her, and she felt that nothing could ruin her moment—her high.

Mecca secretly had her eyes on Pyro. She was hoping that Mateo's right-hand man would sweep her off her feet like Mateo had done Chanel.

Chapter Twenty-Two

*C*harlie waited anxiously in the parking lot of Rikers Island jail complex and watched the traffic come and go across the bridge that stretched toward the correctional facility. It was a gray day with light drizzle, but no matter how colorless the day was, Charlie was grateful and excited. God and Fingers had finally made bail and were being released. She missed her man deeply, and the first thing she wanted to do was lock herself in her bedroom with him and have sex for hours.

Dressed in a blue parka and her beige Timberland boots, Charlie smoked a cigarette and kept her eyes fixed on every bus that came to a stop near the parking lot. She watched every passenger getting on or off the bus. Still, no God or Fingers.

She needed her man back in her life, especially with her sister Chanel getting married in three weeks. Charlie needed the money and she needed the excitement again. It had been nearly nine months since God had been locked up, and longer since they had hit a lick.

Another bus coming from Rikers Island crossed over the bridge and came to a squealing stop at the bus stop parallel to the parking lot. The doors opened and Charlie fixed her eyes on the bus as she had with every bus before it. Finally, she spotted God and Fingers exiting the bus. Charlie couldn't control herself. She immediately ran their way, ready to attack her man with an aggressive and loving hug and plenty of kisses.

"It's good to see you outside them walls again, baby," God said.

Charlie wanted to fuck him right there in public, but she had to put her sexual feelings on hold and simply hug and kiss her man. She hugged Fingers too. The team was back together again.

That night, God received a lukewarm welcome home from Butch and Bacardi. They used to fall all over him with gratitude and hospitality, and now they acted like he was a virus they didn't want to catch. God wanted to know what that was about, and Charlie explained that her mother and father were now sweating Chanel's man, Mateo. He'd been giving the family money and gifts and winning her parents over with his street wealth. God didn't like it. Being down and out inside Rikers for nearly nine months was too long, and everything done changed.

"Don't worry, baby. My heart still beats only for you and that will never change," Charlie said.

She locked the bedroom door to make sure they wouldn't be disturbed. She wanted to give her man a proper welcome home gift—a night that he would always remember. God nearly did a bullet inside of Rikers Island with no pussy and no oral sex, and his manhood was ready to pick up where they'd left off.

Charlie unzipped his jeans, kneeled in front of him, and took his hard dick in her mouth and gave him a blowjob that nearly knocked him dead. God felt himself being thrust into paradise from her deep throat swallowing him whole. The way she cupped his balls and jerked his big dick was divine.

From oral sex, God undressed completely and took her from behind—doggy-style. He rammed inside her like a jackhammer trying to crack concrete. Charlie liked it rough with her man. She wasn't fragile. She wanted her man to smack her ass, pull her hair, and beat her pussy up like it had stolen from him. Her pants and moans echoed from the bedroom throughout the apartment.

They switched from doggy-style, to missionary, to Charlie riding his dick like she was trying to win a race. The sex was phenomenal. The months he'd spent inside had her man going animalistic on her, and she loved every moment of it.

"Fuck me, nigga!" she hollered.

They came like two planets colliding with Charlie's legs quivering from the aftermath of her intense orgasm. She collapsed against God's bare chest with him nestling her into his arms.

"Baby, I missed you so much," she said.

God didn't respond. He stared up aimlessly at the ceiling and appeared to be thinking about something.

"What you thinkin' about, baby?" she asked.

With his eyes still on the ceiling, he said, "Who this nigga your sister started fuckin' with?"

Charlie didn't want to talk about Chanel. She wanted to relish this moment and go a few more rounds with her man in the bed.

"I don't know, some clown-ass Spanish nigga from the Bronx."

"So your little sister done came up, huh?"

"Fuck that little bitch. I don't wanna talk about her, God. Tonight, it's only about you and me, remember?"

She removed herself from his arms and slowly straddled him again, feeling his big dick penetrate her. They moaned and started to fuck again.

An hour later, God was sound asleep. It had been a long day for him and lying on a soft mattress in a quiet room was like paradise.

Charlie sat by the window and smoked a cigarette. The light rain from earlier had subsided and it was now a warm, spring night. The activity outside her window was bustling with local folks enjoying the night with gossip and chitchat, some card playing, and laughter. The spring weather brought about movement from everyone. Foot traffic, fiends, dealers, police, and even stray dogs were seen wandering on the block.

Charlie soon fixed her eyes on the Range Rover Sport that was parking across the street. It was a spectacular looking vehicle that stood out on the block. Charlie knew who the vehicle belonged to. Seeing it move and park, she envied the driver inside.

The driver's door opened and Chanel climbed out of the stylish SUV. She looked like a million bucks in her new designer black dress with lace and feathers, and her hair was long and sensuous. The worst part about it for Charlie was the giant engagement ring on her sister's finger. Chanel looked like a brand new bitch, and Charlie hated it. She hated *her*.

Frowning and drowning in jealousy, Charlie angrily flicked her cigarette out the window and turned away. She couldn't take it anymore. Her little sister had found happiness and some wealth, while she was putting her life back together, trying to fit the pieces in a puzzle that she felt no longer mattered.

It wasn't fair. Charlie felt she should be the one driving a Range Sport and looking like she had just come from a shopping spree. The one good thing about her life at the moment was that God was back in it.

Charlie hadn't seen God in days. The other day he abruptly left the apartment without informing Charlie of his whereabouts. Four days later, God came back to the apartment with his Rolex watch and mink coat, though it was spring and he had no use for it.

Charlie was stunned to see God with a few of his goodies again. *Where were they? Who had them? And where the fuck did he go for four days?* Charlie was irritated that he still had his stuff, while she had to pawn everything nice she had, dance in clubs, and perform sexual acts just to pay his bail.

The tension between Charlie and God was palpable inside the apartment, but Butch and Bacardi minded their business. Bacardi no longer cared about the condition of their relationship. When Charlie argued with him about being gone for days, God griped that he was sick and tired of how everyone was dick-riding and obsessed with Chanel's new man. He'd never met Mateo, but immediately God didn't like him.

God also couldn't keep his eyes off of young Chanel. She was growing into a beautiful and mature young woman. He would slyly watch her around the apartment, admiring how she had her hair blown out—no more long braids or kiddy pigtails. He peeped the diamond earrings she sported and the diamond engagement ring that sparkled brightly. God had to admit to himself that Charlie's little sister was looking right. There were even a handful of times when he would come out of the shower and be tempted to drop his towel in front of Chanel to show her what he was working with.

Chapter Twenty-Three

I want you out of that place, baby. I don't want you staying there anymore," Mateo griped.

"So you want me to move in with you?" Chanel asked.

"Yes. As long as that nigga your sister is with is living there, I don't want you in that apartment."

Chanel was flattered—happy. Mateo was protective of her. The moment he found out that God was back in the apartment, he wanted his fiancée out of there—even if he had to come and move her out himself. He didn't trust God or her family.

The next day, Mateo showed up with Chanel at the apartment to help her pack her things and leave that hellish place she used to call home for good, while Pyro waited for them in the SUV. Mateo wanted Chanel to bounce up out of there and never look back.

In a few weeks, they were going to fly to Hawaii and Chanel was going to be his bride. Her family wasn't invited. They didn't even know about the wedding. Mateo wasn't about to pay for their trip or their expenses so they could ruin what was going to be the best day of their lives, especially Chanel's. So they both felt that it was best to keep everything a secret. They saw the ring and knew about the engagement, but Chanel refused to tell any of her family members that Mateo was going to fly her to Hawaii to marry her on her birthday.

They entered the apartment to find that it was a full house. Butch was sleeping on the couch, Bacardi and Claire were in the kitchen, and Charlie was in her bedroom with God.

Seeing Mateo walk through the front door, Bacardi instantly became excited. It was always good to see her new son. Her home was his home. But Mateo wasn't there to give out cash or gifts, and he clearly made it known to them.

"She has something to tell you," said Mateo.

"Oh? What's going on, Chanel?" Bacardi asked. "Is everything okay?"

Chanel glanced back at her man. He was her confidant and her protector. Chanel felt safe with Mateo standing behind her. She knew he was going to back her up.

She took a deep breath. All eyes were on her in anticipation.

Charlie came out of the bedroom and saw Chanel looking fly in her stylish pants and back-zipper crop top that showed off her slim waist. Then she eyed Chanel's red bottoms and the glimmering accessories, including a tennis bracelet, necklace, and her diamond engagement ring. Mateo had his woman looking like a diva, and Charlie swelled with envy.

"I'm moving out," Chanel said to everyone.

Bacardi's mouth dropped open. "Moving out?"

"Yes."

"Chanel, this is your home, and we love you," said Bacardi.

Chanel had nothing to say to her mother. They never loved her. The only thing Bacardi and everyone else loved was what she or her man could do for them. As long as there was money and nice things, Bacardi became a caring, loving parent.

"You moving in wit' that nigga?" Charlie chimed.

"Yes."

"More room in here for us. Have a great fuckin' life," Charlie added sarcastically.

"I just came to pack up my things and leave," Chanel said.

Claire was silent. She didn't care if her sister stayed or left. She had her own issues to deal with. It was Bacardi and Charlie that were making the most noise about the situation.

"So, what about us, Chanel? You wanna leave and forget about family?" Bacardi asked with some disdain in her voice.

"What about you, Ma?"

"I just want you to be well taken care of."

Mateo finally intervened. "My woman is always going to be well taken care of. I'm gonna make sure she has everything she needs until the end of time. And that, I promise."

Chanel smiled.

Bacardi looked at Mateo and had the audacity to ask, "And what about her parents? Are you gonna take care of us too? Don't forget about us." She didn't want her cash cow to cash out.

Mateo had to chuckle at that bitch's ridiculous comment. Was she serious? He wasn't there to take care of her family, only his woman. He was tired of everyone taking advantage of Chanel and him, particularly after knowing about the abuse and mistreatment Chanel had endured.

"You need to get a job, Ma," Chanel said.

Bacardi didn't want to hear that, especially from her youngest. She had a job, but they fired her, and over time, she'd become lazy. She believed that her kids should be now taking care of her since she had taken care of them.

God emerged from the bedroom and came into the living room wearing a pair of boxer shorts—indecent attire with women in the home. But he didn't care.

"Hey Chanel," he greeted her with a smirk.

Chanel didn't acknowledge him. She kept silent. He always made her uneasy and uncomfortable.

God and Mateo locked eyes, and it was clear that these two men didn't like each other. Mateo held his hard stare against God, knowing his type—a grimy nigga, a user.

God continued to smirk and finally acknowledged Mateo, saying, "So, you the new nigga in her life, huh?"

"I'm the *only* nigga," Mateo corrected.

Chanel went to the bedroom to pack her things. She couldn't wait to finally be free of the place. Mateo stayed in the living room to hold things down and to size God up. God did the same thing. He coolly eyed the jewelry on Mateo, the clothing, the style. God knew the nigga was a definite payday for him if he ever got the chance to go after him. The sight of Mateo's money and shine was making his dick hard.

"So, where you from?" God asked him.

"Around," Mateo uttered with a frosty response.

God chuckled. "I was just tryin' to make conversation, that's all. No need to get all emotional."

Mateo wasn't about to let this nigga bring him out of character, unless he didn't have a choice. He was simply there to help his fiancée move her stuff out of the house.

"Anyway, y'all be safe out there, ya feel me? It's a treacherous world out there . . . too many grimy niggas tryin' to come get what you got wherever you turn," said God.

"We good."

The unlocked front door opened with authority and Pyro was standing on the other side. He needed to check on his man and make sure that things were moving along without incident. Pyro's eyes scanned his surroundings before settling on a dusty looking nigga. God gave him a chilly glare before Mateo spoke up. "We'll be down in a minute, Pyro."

Pyro nodded. As he backpedaled out the front door, he smirked at God.

God was unfazed as he pivoted and went back into the bedroom, and Charlie followed behind him and shut the door.

It didn't take long for Chanel to pack her things. She soon emerged from the bedroom with a rolling suitcase, which Mateo helped her with. Bacardi was sad to see her go. Chanel moving out definitely meant that Mateo would stop coming around.

"Bye!" Chanel uttered coldly.

Bacardi sighed.

Mateo decided to leave them with a final parting gift. He reached into his pocket and removed a large wad of cash. It looked like if he threw it at the wall, it probably would leave a gaping hole.

Bacardi's eyes lit up. She watched Mateo peel away a few bills and hand them to her. She didn't hesitate to take it. In fact, she snatched it away so quickly, that she nearly took off his hand. It was five hundred dollars.

"Thank you, Mateo," she said.

He didn't say anything else. He and Chanel left the apartment expecting to never return. Chanel was ready to get married and live her life with Mateo, hopefully in absolute bliss.

Chapter Twenty-Four

*M*ateo and Pyro sat in the early morning real estate and investment class in the financial district, and they were taking notes. They sat at the front of the room and were focused on the lecture coming from one of the top investors in the city. Mateo and Pyro looked more like eager young men ready to plant their feet into real estate and investment deals than drug dealers. They were trying to make legitimate moves with their lives, including caring about their credit scores so they could get loans, investing in properties, and using most of their illegal gains as down payments on prime real estate and legit cash making businesses.

After the two-hour class, the men left the room to continue their day of conducting business.

First, they went to a shooting range in Long Island to put in some target practice. Mateo and Pyro were always in friendly competition of each other, and they were both good shooters.

Mateo aimed at center mass with the Glock 17 in his hands and squeezed off several shots at the target, which was about 10 meters away. Pyro was in the booth nearby, and the two let off some steam by putting holes into the hanging silhouettes. When they were both done, they retracted the silhouettes to see their results.

"Look at that shit—center mass and four headshots. You ain't fuckin' with me, Mateo," Pyro teased.

Mateo compared his target to Pyro's, and Pyro was definitely the sharpshooter of the two.

"You got lucky," Mateo joked.

"Nigga, luck ain't got anything to do with skills."

Mateo laughed. "Let's go again."

"You know you can't win in this," said Pyro.

"We'll see."

Both men replaced the target silhouettes and went for 20 meters down the line of sight. Once again, Pyro was the better shot. Mateo ultimately had to give him his props.

After target practice, they went to one of their favorite diners in Valley Stream for a hearty meal and conversation. Seated in a window booth with a view of the park across the street, they were like two old men talking about business over their afternoon coffee and lunch.

"I talked to my lawyer the other day," Mateo said.

"Oh word? And what he talking about?"

"I just ran some paperwork by him . . . told him that we opened an escrow account to get this sale completed. Going through this neutral third party is taking longer than I expected."

Pyro laughed. "You know how it is. Legit money is slow money."

"Tell me about it. But he ran the title search and obtained title insurance," said Mateo.

"And how did that go?"

"Everything came back legit."

"How much do we already got invested into these properties? Remind me," said Pyro.

Mateo sighed. "Too much."

"Well, we needed this."

"I know," Mateo replied. "But Alex assured me that there will be no red tape with this deal."

"For what we're paying that fool, shit better go smoother than a Jamba Juice."

Mateo agreed.

Alex Mont was their experienced real estate attorney who had fifteen years in the business. He was expensive, but for Mateo and Pyro, he was well worth it. They needed a professional legal opinion on their closing documents. It was a lot of paperwork and a lot of red tape that many well-educated folks couldn't comprehend. Alex Mont knew where to look for potential problems in their paperwork. Doing a title search and obtaining title insurance was something that gave them a peace of mind and a legal safeguard, so when they bought their property, no one else could try to claim it as their own.

"So what happened the other day with Chanel?" Pyro asked him out of the blue. "Y'all ain't say shit once you were back in the car."

"I had to get my woman out of the madhouse. You saw that nigga her sister got living up in there."

"I saw dude, and he looks like a grimy nigga."

"And he got the nerve to call himself *God*," Mateo said.

"God?" Pyro chuckled.

"Yeah, cornball nigga staying with his girlfriend's parents in the projects," Mateo said.

"Now that's some pathetic shit."

"Tell me about it. But Chanel good, though . . . moved her in and she loves the place, even though it's temporary."

"So you're ready to go through with buying that condo?"

"Yeah, it's gonna be my wedding gift to her."

"She's a lucky woman."

"Nah, I'm the lucky one," Mateo corrected.

"I'm glad to see that you're happy with her."

"I am."

The two men finished their meal, left the waitress a nice tip, and left the diner with full bellies.

From Long Island, they traveled to the Bronx to Spanish Fly Barbershop, where they got haircuts from Bolo and talked shit. Although Bolo was a heavy buyer from them, he was also a good friend who they grew up with.

While cutting Mateo's hair, Bolo joked, "So, when are the wolves of Wall Street gonna make their first million? If y'all haven't already."

Mateo and Pyro laughed.

"So tell us, what we need to invest in to make money like y'all?" one of the barbers asked.

"Municipal bonds, stocks, cryptocurrency, real estate, et cetera, et cetera, et cetera . . ." Pyro joked.

Mateo and Pyro were like the investment gurus of the Bronx, but everyone also knew that their primary income came from weed sales.

"Nah, but on the real, Bolo, we ain't doing shit you can't do. We've been sittin' in here for years schooling you, yet you ain't get in. What you waiting on?" Mateo asked.

Bolo shrugged. "Investing is a rich man's hobby."

"See that's where you're wrong. Do you see a rich nigga in your chair?"

Bolo looked at Mateo with a side eye. "Yes! You got a helluva lot more cash than most of us."

"We built up to that. You don't gotta go big. Buy what's called odd lots. It's where you buy less than a hundred shares. Take this challenge. For one year save all your tip money and once a month buy three or four shares of a stock, whatever you can afford. Nike, Twitter, Amazon, mix in some Municipal bonds and cryptocurrency. One year from now we'll discuss your portfolio and how it's grown."

"My tip money, huh?" Bolo gave him a look of skepticism.

"Only your tip money. Don't go investing your rent and car note cash."

Bolo smiled. "It's on. I'm in."

Pyro patted Bolo on the back and then added, "Mateo's bill for investment advice will be in the mail."

All three men laughed and gave each other dap. Today was a good day.

Chapter Twenty-Five

Charlie felt like she'd traded places with her baby sister. It felt like she was now the one living in squalor with no respect and nothing to her name. Seeing Chanel in those red bottoms and witnessing Mateo drive her off into the sunset in a pearl white Range Rover sent Charlie past her breaking point.

Mateo had money to burn, while God was shacking up with her in her mama's place, and she had seen better days. It wasn't fair.

Chanel's birthday was two weeks away, and Charlie cringed at the thought of what Mateo would get her for her birthday. He'd already spoiled her with jewelry, a car, a diamond engagement ring, clothes, and money. What else could he give Chanel? *A baby?*

Charlie lounged on her bed smoking a cigarette. She sighed deeply. She needed some action again before she died from boredom or broke-assness. As she lay there, it occurred to her. It was like a light bulb came on over her head—like a crystal clear dream.

When God came into the bedroom, Charlie stared at him like she was ready to tell him the truth about life.

"You got another cigarette, babe?" he asked.

She tossed him her dwindling pack and said, "God, we need to talk. I got another lick for us."

God removed a few cigarettes from the pack for later and placed one between his lips and lit up. He took a few drags and said, "What you mean?"

"We need to start gettin' this money again, nigga. You know I don't like being fuckin' broke."

"Like I do! Whatever happened to that other mofo you had lined up?"

Charlie had forgotten her lie. "Who?"

"Forget it. I'm already on it, Charlie. I'm scouting niggas out now."

"Not fast enough. But no worries, because I always come through. I already got someone we can hit up."

"I'm listening."

"My little sister and her man. They can get got," she said.

He took another drag and raised his eyebrow. "You serious?"

"Yes! Like fuckin' cancer, nigga."

God chuckled. "You my bitch fo' real, Charlie. Damn, I fuckin' love you."

She grinned. "So, I guess you down wit' it?"

"Charlie, you and I think so alike it's fuckin' scary. Fingers and I was already plotting on that bitch-ass nigga. He holdin' too much money and weight to keep it all for himself."

"Fo' real?"

"Fo' real, shorty. I'm hungry to go after those fools, especially after he come up in here all smug and shit. Yo, you know that nigga dog food for us, and we gonna eat that nigga for everything he got," God exclaimed.

Hearing her man talk like that turned Charlie on. She couldn't stop beaming. She felt a surge of power flood her body like a dam breaking open. She wanted to be back on top, and if Chanel was the next sacrificial lamb then so fucking be it.

"Yo, let's get this fuckin' money," God said.

Chanel couldn't believe that this was her home. It was neat, quiet, spacious, and it was comfortable. Most importantly, she didn't have to share it with her evil sisters and her wicked mother. The two-bedroom, two-bathroom apartment in the Bronx with pre-war details and a 9-to-5 elevator attendant was a far cry from her family's project apartment in Brooklyn.

For an hour, Chanel danced around the entire apartment in her panties and bra. She laughed and smiled like a kid in a toy store, wide-eyed with excitement. She didn't know what to do with herself.

Mateo kept a very tidy place, one of the many things she loved about him. Still, it definitely needed a woman's touch, and she couldn't wait to add a piece of her personality to the apartment.

Chanel was able to stretch out on the couch and watch a full movie in peace. She added her culinary touch to the kitchen, making the apartment come alive with her delicious cooking. She took lingering, warm bubble baths and listened to her favorite songs through the pimped out system.

It was paradise. It was what she always wanted; something she could call her own. But most of her excitement came from knowing she was flying to Hawaii in two weeks and getting married to the man she loved.

For the moment, Mateo was out of town on business, so she had to hold down the fort. She wanted to invite Mecca over for a girls night of junk food eating, movie watching, and girl talk. Mateo was explicit that no one could know where they lived, but she trusted Mecca to come over to keep her company. Unfortunately, Mecca had to cancel on her because she had a date. Chanel wasn't upset; she wanted her friend to find love too. She wanted her friend to be happy.

Enjoying her Saturday afternoon, Chanel snacked on cookies and peanut butter and took pleasure in lounging in the bedroom and watching a few Netflix movies. When her cell phone rang, she was surprised to see it was Charlie. *Why is she calling me?*

She answered the call with some reluctance, asking fretfully, "Is everything okay at home?"

"Yeah, things are fine," said Charlie. "We miss you, Chanel."

"Y'all miss me?" Chanel replied with skepticism. *Or do y'all miss picking on me?*

"I'm not gonna lie, Chanel. It's not the same without you around."

I bet.

"How's Bacardi?"

"Miserable," Charlie said. "She's still broke and drinking; don't know what to do wit' herself. But I'm really happy for you, Chanel. You definitely makin' sumthin' out ya life, fo' real."

"Thank you."

Although Chanel was cautious about Charlie's unexpected hospitality, being the little sister of the three, she yearned to be wanted and accepted by her sisters. There was a part of her that wanted their approval—and she wanted to show off somewhat.

"So, is Mateo treatin' you okay?"

"Things are great."

"Love is a wonderful thing, ain't it?"

"It is, Charlie. I'm happy."

"You sound happy. But, baby sis, I called because I want to truly apologize to you for everything I put you through. I'm sorry. You didn't deserve that. I guess . . . I guess I was jealous of you."

"You were jealous of me?" Chanel asked with doubt. "Why?"

"You're a beautiful black woman with the perfect skin tone, and you're smart and humble. You're so many things that I'm not."

Chanel didn't know what to say. Was it true? Was Charlie really jealous of her all these years?

"Listen, can we just talk?"

"We're talking now, Charlie."

"I mean, can we come over—Claire and I—to sit down and have a sisterly talk? I really want that, Chanel—to end the beef between us," Charlie said with conviction.

"I never had any beef with you or Claire," said Chanel sincerely.

"I know. It was us being the assholes all the time. But let's start over, okay? You and I."

Chanel remained silent for a moment, contemplating the offer. It sounded genuine. She wanted to build a bond with her sisters, and she was naïve to believe that it could actually happen.

She sighed through the phone and finally said, "Okay. I don't have a problem with that."

"Cool. Just give me your address and we'll come have some sister time," Charlie said with some giddiness in her voice.

"Okay, but only you and Claire. No one else."

"I promise, Chanel. It will only be us two."

Chanel smiled. She gave Charlie the address, and Charlie promised again that it would only be her and Claire. Although Mateo was clear that he didn't want anyone to know where they lived, Chanel felt this was an exception. These were her sisters. They weren't close, but she finally felt like one of them. She finally felt that they were going to have a sisterly relationship.

The following afternoon, Charlie and Claire walked through the front door of Chanel's new home. Right away, they were wide-eyed and impressed.

"Damn, Chanel, ya man got you living nice. Shit! I ain't mad at y'all," Claire said.

"Y'all like it?"

"Shit, I love it. I wish I was living here," Claire said.

Chanel smiled.

Like she'd promised, Charlie only brought Claire to the apartment. Things looked like they were going to work out. Chanel didn't feel threatened by them. They came in peace—so she wanted to believe.

"Y'all hungry?" she asked them.

"Yes."

"You cooking?" Charlie asked.

"Of course. I got y'all."

Charlie and Claire shrugged. They were ready to eat.

The girls followed Chanel into the kitchen, and it was a lot bigger than their ghetto kitchen in Brooklyn. The place had the latest amenities. Charlie rubbed the granite countertops and opened and closed the new microwave.

They continued their oohs and ahhs.

"Damn, girl, I know you be cooking like some five course meals in this kitchen," Charlie said.

"I try," Chanel replied, being modest.

But Chanel finally had something that was worth their praise.

While Chanel got started cooking up a meal in the kitchen, her sisters reclined in the living room and took advantage of the high-end home theater system. It was a beauty, from the 60" flat screen TV, to the Sony stereo system, and the latest Xbox below the TV. Mateo was like a big kid with his toys.

Charlie took it all in. Everything from wall to wall, it was all valuable stuff. While Chanel was busy in the kitchen, Charlie took it upon herself to sneak inside the master bedroom to briefly snoop around. She glanced inside Chanel's closet and saw the expensive outfits and shoes and jackets and coats. She opened a few drawers and saw gleaming jewelry, trinkets, more clothes, and even some cash.

She wondered if Mateo had a safe somewhere on the premises. A nigga like him, he had to.

Charlie nodded. She was pleased with everything she saw, and she was ready to get back to God with the information.

She was leaving out the bedroom and coming down the hallway when she bumped into Chanel.

"What you doing, Charlie?"

"Oh, I was just looking for the bathroom, that's all. You know for a Bronx place, this shit is huge," Charlie said.

"It is, right? You do get your money's worth in the Bronx. But the bathroom is the door to your left."

Charlie smiled. "Thank you."

The sisters' evening continued smoothly. Chanel cooked a healthy and delicious meal of baked chicken, green beans, and brown rice. Charlie and Claire devoured her cooking like they hadn't eaten in months. They weren't getting home cooked meals at their place. Bacardi wasn't the devoted cook in the kitchen, and Butch was mostly gone for days at a time. They suspected that he'd started drinking again, or worse.

The two sisters praised Chanel's cooking. They were full and content. Chanel made her home their home, and she treated them with kindness and forgiveness. They'd spent the entire day together talking, laughing, watching movies, and gossiping. Chanel felt like she had formed some kind of bond with her two sisters. As the day progressed, she grew more comfortable around them, and it felt like Charlie's reaching out was genuine.

Night came, and it was time for Claire and Charlie to leave. Chanel offered them to stay the night, but Charlie refused.

"We intruded on your life too much already," said Charlie.

"It's cool. I can use the company."

"Nah, we gotta go, but it's been fun," Charlie said.

"I enjoyed it," said Claire.

"Me too."

Chanel hugged her sisters goodbye. Ironically, she didn't want to see them leave. As they were about to exit the front door, Charlie turned to Chanel with an afterthought, saying to her, "Hey, don't mention to your man that we came by."

Chanel became somewhat baffled by the request. "Why not?"

"Because he seems real protective of you. Let's just keep this day between us—our little secret. I don't want to create any problems between y'all," Charlie explained.

To Chanel, it sounded like a genuine explanation. Mateo already told her that he didn't want anyone to know where they lived.

Chanel nodded. "Okay."

Charlie smiled. She hugged her little sister one last time and left.

It was a day that Chanel was never going to forget. Besides meeting Mateo, this special day with her sisters was one of the best days of her life.

The following day, Mateo gave her a call to check up on her. They talked briefly, and she told him about her sisters coming by for a visit. She was going to be his wife, and she didn't want to keep anything from him.

"What, Chanel? Why? I told you, don't let anyone know where we stay at," he fussed.

"But they're my sisters, Mateo, and I got lonely."

He sighed profoundly, knowing Chanel was still naïve about a few things.

"It's okay, I understand," he said. "I just want you to be careful."

"I will."

But he knew it wasn't okay. There was something about Charlie and God that really rubbed him the wrong way. He didn't trust those two at all, and knowing that Charlie had been to their home, a feeling of anxiety and trouble crept upon him.

When Mateo ended the call with her, he turned to Pyro and said, "I need to move ASAP. I got a bad feeling about her sister and her man."

"It's like that?"

"Yeah. I can't shake that shit, Pyro. Them two are bad news."

Chapter Twenty-Six

God placed two Glock 17's on the bed, along with a .380, a Walther PPQ, and a sawed-off shotgun. It looked like he was ready for war.

"You think you got enough guns?" Charlie said with sarcasm.

God was a gun fanatic. "You can't ever have too many guns."

God was ready to move on Mateo and Chanel. Charlie came through with the information they needed, and now it was up to them to go in like a beast and take what they wanted. And they wanted everything.

God and Charlie didn't know that Chanel and Mateo were about to fly out to Hawaii soon to get married. God was ready to move in now, but Fingers wanted to plot first. The Bronx was a tricky location. It wasn't the suburbs, and Mateo lived in an apartment, not a private home. An apartment meant close neighbors, nosey folks, and more of a risk. But they weren't amateurs. They'd raided couples in apartments before and gotten away with it.

"We need to do this soon, God," Charlie said.

God cocked back the .380 to check inside the chamber, inspecting his tools of death. When he heard Charlie say "we," he turned to look at her with bad news.

"You not comin' wit' us," he said.

"What the fuck you mean? Yes I am. She's my fuckin' sister and I was the one that set this shit up," she barked.

"No, Charlie. Fingers and me got this shit."

"I'm coming! I wanna make sure shit don't get out of hand."

"What the fuck I say, Charlie? No! You stayin' here. Even ski-masked up, your sister can recognize you, and we can't take that chance," he said.

Charlie frowned. She knew he was right. Chanel knew her too well. Even behind a mask or disguise, she would be recognized.

"Fine. But only Mateo gets got, not Chanel," she said.

God looked at her deadpan.

"I'm serious, God!" she exclaimed. "Do not touch her. I don't want her hurt or injured at all. Kill Mateo, take what you need to take, and leave her alive," she commanded.

"I won't hurt her, Charlie," he replied halfheartedly.

Charlie didn't like his reply. She stepped closer to God while snatching one of the guns from off the bed. She placed the barrel of the Glock to God's head and looked squarely in his eyes and sternly repeated, "Don't pistol whip her, don't stab her, slice, or fuckin' shoot her anywhere. I'm serious, God!"

God smirked. He looked undaunted by the gun in his face. Nonchalantly, he replied, "You done?"

Charlie removed the pistol from his face and was immediately met with a backhanded smack that sent her crashing to the floor.

"Don't you ever put a fuckin' gun in my face like that again, bitch," he threatened.

She glared up at him. She had a trickle of blood coming from her mouth.

"You got my word, Charlie. I ain't gonna touch your fuckin' sister," he growled. "I'ma kill that fool and take it all, but Chanel won't be harmed." God continued to ready his weapons.

Charlie picked herself from off the floor. She had to believe him. She knew that they were all killers, and she wanted to be specific with him.

The plane tickets had been purchased and the venue in Hawaii had been secured. Mateo and Chanel were to be married at a lovely resort on the beach. It was going to be an intimate ceremony. Chanel's family still had no idea that she was getting married in a few days.

The couple had sent the wedding dress and the tuxedo ahead of time to be delivered to the lavish hotel on the beach. Chanel and Mecca planned on arriving 72 hours early to have Chanel's "last days as a free woman" shenanigans. This meant that Mateo would also have his free time as a single man in New York. Chanel didn't want to spend one day without Mateo. She was jealous and she also feared that he would fuck someone during his final moments as a single man. And then there was the bachelor party Pyro had planned for him.

But Mecca, like always, was there to comfort her friend and give her some friendly advice, telling Chanel not to worry about anyone because he was putting a ring on her finger. To help bolster her point, Mecca used Jay-Z cheating on one of the hottest chicks in the game and how Beyoncé made lemonade out of it.

"Fuck those dumb bitches, Chanel. He only wants you. Your nigga is about to fly you to Hawaii to marry you on your birthday. Mateo is giving you the world—a car, money, a ring, and he's marrying a virgin, girl."

"What if I'm whack in bed, Mecca?"

Mecca locked eyes with Chanel for a moment before they both burst out in laughter.

It was four days before the wedding, and Mateo wasn't supposed to spend the night with his fiancée. Chanel and Mecca would be leaving on a 6 a.m. flight to Hawaii, and the next time he would see her again would be on the afternoon of their wedding.

However, Mateo didn't want to be away from her for so long. He wanted to hold her and kiss her lips, touch and caress her face, hold her hand, and just stare at her.

Chanel had looked incredibly beautiful when he'd left the apartment that morning, and he was rushing home to see her off. Originally, they'd wanted to miss each other—some cloak and dagger type of setup.

He'd called and told Chanel that he was coming to her tonight instead of staying at the hotel. He wanted one more moment with her. They talked dirty to each other for a moment. It was an exciting time. They couldn't believe they would be husband and wife in a few short days. For Chanel, it felt surreal.

"I love you," he proclaimed.

"I love you too," she happily replied.

Charlie paced around the bedroom looking impatient. A few days had gone by, and she wanted to know when they were going to rob Chanel and her man. Charlie wanted to get back on top. She wanted the finer things in life by any means necessary, even if it meant taking from her little sister and putting her in harm's way.

She kept listing off her demands to God.

"Make sure you take her engagement ring and her earrings. Oh, and I saw that bitch's closet, and it's stuffed with furs and a bunch of nice shit that she won't wear. Make sure you get all her shit. Don't leave her with a fuckin' crumb. Take her shoes, clothes, everything!" she demanded.

"Yo, we ain't about to walk out that bitch wit' just trash bags of clothes for you. Any trash bags we got, that shit gonna be filled with cash and jewelry," God exclaimed. "Shit, this ain't a fuckin' shopping spree for you. You can't wear her shit anyway. We ain't tryin' to get caught."

Charlie knew that she couldn't wear any of her sister's clothing. She didn't want Chanel to have it, though, after they took from Mateo and killed him. She would rather toss all of Chanel's belongings in the trash than to have her own little sister out-dress her.

"Then destroy that shit, God. You fuckin' hear me? Fuckin' throw bleach on all her shit—burn that shit or sumthin'," Charlie uttered with absolute scorn pouring from her voice.

God looked at Charlie like she was this parasite all of a sudden. The contempt she had for Chanel was unreal. What did she ever do to her? She didn't want him to harm one hair on her head, but she wanted him to take everything from her and destroy it. God had done a lot of grimy shit over the years and he would continue to do so, but this was Charlie's little sister. She was a good girl who was naïve and nice and wanted to please everyone. God somewhat liked Chanel, even though she always gave him the cold shoulder and an odd look.

Why be extra cruel? he thought.

He didn't care that his behavior was abhorrent because she wasn't blood. If he had a brother, he would never do such a thing to his blood.

However, Charlie felt that she was doing Chanel a big favor by setting them up a few days before her birthday. She felt that getting robbed and losing her man violently on her birthday would be extra cruel. Wouldn't it?

She did have some kind of heart. She thought so, anyway.

Chapter Twenty-Seven

*I*t was a balmy night with a full moon shimmering in the sky. Four more days and Mateo was going to be a hitched man. He was excited about the date. He was excited about becoming a one-woman man—an honest and married man. He was excited about having their honeymoon in Hawaii, and he was excited about their wedding night, when he would finally have Chanel sexually. He was willing to wait until they got married to experience something special, and Chanel was special. He didn't want to treat her like some regular whore or bitch. Chanel deserved a ring on her finger.

Mateo remained upbeat as he drove home to spend one more night with Chanel before she and Mecca headed to Hawaii. It was a beautiful night, and he was living a beautiful life.

Mateo made it a habit to always check his side and rearview mirrors to make sure he wasn't being followed. He was a cautious man, knowing he lived in a dangerous world with wicked people, and he always took extra precaution with his safety and his woman's, along with the safeguard of his finances. He was satisfied that he wasn't being followed. But God and Fingers didn't need to follow him home because they already had his location.

Mateo had already made arrangements and bought a larger condo apartment in a more affluent area of the Bronx. He and Chanel would move in as soon as they came back as husband and wife. The building had tight-knit security with CCTV cameras and a doorman, and it was near a police station. He wanted his new bride to be safe at home. While they were off in Hawaii relaxing, sunbathing, swimming, and having sex, he would have a moving crew and an interior designer come to the new condo to put everything in order. He had it all planned down to the letter.

Mateo parked on the block and climbed out of the vehicle. He observed his surroundings and there appeared to be no abnormalities in the area. Everything looked copasetic. With a concealed .38, he made his way toward the building. He punched in his code to get into the main door and made his way toward the elevator. Alone and composed, he stepped inside the elevator and rode it silently to his designated floor.

"Four more days," he said to himself.

He already had his luggage packed and the arrangements made. The only thing everyone had to do was get to Hawaii via plane.

Before Mateo could step off the elevator, he felt the presence of two shadowy figures charging his way, and before he could react and remove his .38, they accosted him inside the elevator. God brought the butt of the gun across Mateo's face, spewing blood and right away dazing him. Fingers quickly threw duct tape over his mouth to keep him silent.

"You wanna die tonight, muthafucka?" Fingers said into his ear.

It was a bold move, attacking him in a public building. He had neighbors, but it was late, and the two goons knew what they were doing and when and where to confront him. Most of the scuffle took place inside the elevator, away from any neighbors' eyes and attention.

"Chill the fuck out, muthafucka, or I'll kill you right here!" God scolded him at gunpoint.

They disarmed him and told him to take them to the apartment and open the door. Mateo became defiant—*no way*. He refused to put Chanel in harm's way.

If he could speak, he would have shouted, "Kill me right here, muthafuckas!" But with the duct tape over his mouth, his insults and voice were incoherent. He wanted to curse and rant, but he could only mumble angrily. His heart was pumping a mile a minute. So many thoughts darted around inside his head. How did they get inside his building? How did they know the code? And how did they know where he lived? He was going to die. He knew it.

God struck Mateo in the head with the butt of the gun again, leaving a gash across his forehead. "Don't fuck wit' us, nigga! We can make this go easy on you and your bitch," God growled.

Mateo's mind was on his innocent and beautiful Chanel. He refused to tell them the apartment. He feared what they would do to her. Mateo huffed and puffed and cringed for the worst. He said a prayer to himself and hoped they killed him quickly.

"You wanna be a tough guy, nigga?" Fingers said. "We already fuckin' know the apartment. So let's do this shit the hard way."

Fingers snatched Mateo's keys from him, and they hurriedly forced him down the hallway toward his apartment. Mateo wanted to struggle, but his mind and vision were still blurry from the attack. He could barely stand now.

Fingers used the key to open the door. They pushed Mateo inside the apartment with an unsuspecting Chanel. She was in the living room, lying on the couch watching TV, until the sudden disturbance. When she saw the masked gunmen and Mateo being violently pushed onto the floor, her eyes swelled wide with fear and she couldn't move. She was frozen.

At once, both of them were subdued with duct tape around their mouths, wrists, and ankles, and thrown to the floor in the corner, their fate unknown. They looked at each other in fear. Mateo felt that they'd caught him slipping; now they both were going to pay the price. He didn't care what they did to him, as long as they left Chanel alone and let her go.

God and Fingers started to rummage through the entire apartment looking for valuables. They took their time. They went room to room, finding money, jewelry, coats, and a kilo of high grade marijuana.

"Shit! This nigga is definitely a fuckin' payday!" Fingers hollered.

They stripped Mateo of his Rolex, diamond earrings, and the cash out of his pockets—at least $1,500.

For nearly an hour, God and Fingers went through the apartment like they were in a shopping mall, stuffing everything that wasn't nailed down into black garbage bags.

The couple could only speak through their eyes as they sat there helpless and vulnerable. Chanel's tears were streaming from her eyes. She didn't want to die. She was supposed to be happy and be getting married on her birthday.

The couple watched as one gunman whispered to another. Something else was brewing between them. Mateo knew it wasn't anything good. He feared the worst. The two men towered over them with two garbage bags full of their things, and one of them had this perverted gleam in his eyes toward Chanel that made them both uncomfortable.

All of a sudden, one of the men grabbed Chanel and roughly pulled her off the floor and started to drag her away from Mateo. Mateo knew what time it was, and his worst nightmare was coming true. Chanel panicked and screamed under the duct tape, but her pleas for help were muffled. Mateo frantically squirmed against the floor with a look of anguish and horror written on his face as he desperately wanted to try and stop what was about to take place. He started to cry.

God forced Chanel into the master bedroom and pushed her against the bed, having her fall on her side. She was in full-blown fear. She wanted to fight and resist him, but her hands and feet were tied. The only thing she could see was his eyes behind the ski mask, and they were devious and malicious with a strong hunger for her.

Chanel, knowing what was coming, pleaded with her eyes for him not to do this—not to take away something that she was saving to give Mateo on their wedding day. But God didn't care. He saw what he liked and he wanted to take it.

He turned her over and positioned her face-down on the bed. Chanel tried to resist, but he was strong and willing to take it from her by force. God cut away the duct tape from around her ankles and tore away her pajama bottoms, leaving her exposed. She tried to kick him fiercely, but a swift punch to the back of her head made her become docile and dazed.

He undid his jeans and slid the condom back onto his growing erection. He was hard, and he knew this was going to be fun. For a while now, he had desired Chanel, knowing that she was a virgin. He'd never fucked a virgin before.

He pinned Chanel against the bed and forced her legs open from behind. He wanted to penetrate her from the back. She continued to fight to keep her virginity, but she could feel God heavily against her. His hand was firmly wrapped around the back of her neck, keeping her in place against the bed, and his sour breath was in her ear. He was going to rape her, no matter what. Chanel was helpless to stop it. Her hands were tied, the duct tape muted her cries, and her body was his to take.

Abruptly, God thrust himself inside of her—a strong jerk that pierced inside Chanel like a knife through her heart. She felt his big, hard dick fully inside of her, and it was a feeling she'd never felt before. It was excruciating to feel him moving in and out of her brusquely. She cried and cried, and the tears flooded her eyes to the point where they clouded her vision. She felt herself being ripped apart below and the blood oozing from the rough penetration. She felt everything like her body was super sensitive. If it wasn't for the duct tape around her mouth, her cries and her anguish would have been banshee like—echoing through the room and probably shattering glass.

God could feel that he was taking her virginity. He took his sweet time in the pussy. When it got really good, he pulled out and quickly flipped her over onto her back and untied her wrists. He wanted to feel her perky tits against his chest. He wanted to see her face as he was fucking her. He wanted this rape to be more romantic in his sick and twisted mind. Falling between her legs, God thrust himself into her again, and pounded and pounded inside of her as he stared directly at Chanel's anguish. He panted and huffed and fell closer to her petite frame and felt waves of exhilaration from taking her virginity with brute force. He could feel Chanel's fingernails digging deep into his back from the pain he executed. It turned him on, and he fucked her deeper and deeper.

What lasted about ten minutes felt like a lifetime for Chanel. God huffed and puffed, and then came inside the condom, and inside of her, and quivered on top of her. He was finally done. He removed himself from her flesh and looked completely relieved. But Chanel was sobbing. She was torn apart and in pain. She couldn't move from the bed. Between her legs felt like a bloody mess and she was sore. He didn't care. God stood there looking absolutely aloof from the violent incident.

He tucked his dick back into his pants and zipped up, but not before removing his condom and stuffing it in his pocket. His DNA was leaving with him. When he left the bedroom, Fingers was eager to go inside and get a taste too. But God pushed him back.

"Nah," God said.

"Fuck outta here, nigga. I wanna fuck her too," Fingers exclaimed.

"I said no."

Fingers became furious and shouted, "So you get to fuck that virgin and not me?"

"What I said, nigga!"

Fingers wanted to go to blows with God, but he decided against it. Never had they raped anyone, and the last person God should have raped was Chanel, his girlfriend's virgin sister. So why couldn't he get a turn? Everyone noticed how beautiful, sweet, and pure Chanel was. And Fingers never fucked a good girl virgin before. And why hadn't Mateo fucked her yet? There were so many questions, but he didn't care for the answers. It was time to get down to business.

Meanwhile, Mateo was tucked in the corner nearby, still bound with duct tape and powerless to aid the woman he loved. He was completely destroyed and devastated, especially after overhearing the two goons' conversation. He knew what they had done to his fiancée—the horrors Chanel had endured. He cried and cried, suffering greatly.

God walked over to the grief-stricken man and placed a pillow over his head to muffle the sound of the gunshot. He didn't hesitate to squeeze the trigger and put a bullet into Mateo's head.

Poot!

Mateo's body fell over, and from the bedroom, a terrified Chanel heard the muffled gunshot and she knew her fiancé's fate. She figured they were coming to kill her next.

However, God and Fingers picked up their blood money and the loot they'd picked from the place and made their exit, leaving behind a nightmare of a scene.

Chanel heard the door slam. She assumed the masked men had left. Still shaken-up and terrified from being assaulted and raped, and not knowing what she was going to find in the next room, she mustered the strength to remove the duct tape from her mouth and hurried to call the police and help for Mateo. She raced from the bedroom and into the living room and her worst nightmare became reality. She saw Mateo sprawled across the hardwood floor motionless. He had been shot in the head and his blood was pooling thickly on the floor.

She rushed to apply pressure to his critical head wound and tried to comfort him with loving words. She clutched his limp body in her arms and begged Mateo to fight for his life. She cried as she tried to be strong for him.

"C'mon, baby, don't do this to me. Please don't leave me. Please, Mateo, please. I love you too much to lose you now. I can't live without you," she cried out.

Chanel couldn't believe it. She was supposed to get married in four days, but now it looked like she would be planning a funeral instead.

Chapter Twenty-Eight

I t was two in the morning when Bacardi's cell phone rang and rang. Lying next to Butch in the dark bedroom, Bacardi didn't want to move at all to answer her phone. She was a bit tipsy from drinking earlier. The only thing she wanted to do was close her eyes and sleep—become catatonic to the world. But her ringing cell phone wouldn't allow that. It became infuriating.

Finally, she removed herself from the bed and angrily snatched the phone from the night stand beside her. Whoever was calling her this late was about to get a tongue lashing and a curse-out so strong that it would leave marks through the phone.

"Who the fuck is this calling me so got-damn late?"

She heard Chanel's voice roar with tragedy from the other end. Her daughter screamed frantically into the phone, "I think he's dead! Ohmygod, I think they killed him!"

Chanel's unexpected devastation now had Bacardi fully awake and worried. "Chanel, what the fuck is goin' on?"

"They shot Mateo!"

"What? Who shot Mateo? What the fuck happened?"

Chanel was mostly incoherent and upset. Bacardi could barely make out what Chanel was saying to her. She heard her repeat that Mateo had been shot.

"Chanel, calm down . . .just calm down and talk to me," Bacardi said.

But it was hard for Chanel to calm down. She had just gone through a terrifying ordeal. She was scared, angry, and filled with so many emotions that she couldn't think straight. She didn't know what to do.

"Chanel, what's goin' on? Fuckin' talk to me. What happened to Mateo? Who fuckin' shot him?" Bacardi wanted to know.

"They . . . they . . ."

"Chanel, where are you right now?"

"I'm . . . I'm at the hospital . . . in the Bronx."

"What hospital?"

"Umm, I think . . . I think Jacobi," she stammered.

"We'll be right there," Bacardi uttered with rush in her tone.

Bacardi woke up Butch and then she informed Claire that something was going on with Chanel. It was a new day for them, and although they had their differences with Chanel, she was still one of their own, and Mateo had been nice to them. Chanel had now become their golden child.

In the middle of the night, all three of them climbed into a taxi and headed toward the Bronx to meet Chanel at the hospital.

Mecca was already there to greet everyone. She was in bad shape too after hearing the news about her friends. Mecca's eyes were red from crying. She told the family what she knew. Chanel had been brutally raped and Mateo had been shot in the head by two masked intruders. At the moment, the medical staff was collecting a rape kit, clipping and swabbing her fingernails for DNA, and performing an exam on Chanel. Mateo was still in surgery. He was touch-and-go. Bacardi and everyone else was floored by the news.

"I need to call Charlie again," Bacardi said.

She had been trying to reach Charlie since they'd left the apartment in Brooklyn, but she'd had no luck. Charlie's phone was going straight to voicemail.

"Fuckin' bitch, answer your fuckin' phone! This is an emergency!"

Everyone was breaking down while sitting or standing around in the emergency room. How could this happen to such a sweet girl like Chanel?

They'd hit payday. God and Fingers had dumped the loot onto a motel bed somewhere in Brooklyn, and it was a goldmine. There were large amounts of cash, lots of jewelry, some clothing, and a few minks. But the mother lode was the kilo of weed they'd taken from the place.

Charlie was pleased with the lick. She noticed that there was some tension between God and Fingers, but she didn't mention it. The only thing she said to God was, "Is my sister still alive?"

"What the fuck you think, bitch? Yeah, she's fuckin' still alive. She's good—no fuckin' harm to her," he replied matter-of-factly. "Don't ask me no shit like that!"

Fingers frowned at him.

Charlie couldn't put her finger on what the sudden tension between them was about. What had happened?

"And what about Mateo?"

"What you think? I personally put a fuckin' bullet in that nigga's head," said God.

She was pleased to hear the news. She believed God when he said that Chanel was still alive and that no harm came to her.

The trio started to go through their score, separating the cash, the goods, and the weed. They had the motel room all to themselves and weren't worried about anyone intruding on them.

Charlie's phone was constantly ringing on the dresser, but she chose to ignore it for the moment. She assumed that it was either her mother calling, or one of her sisters to inform her about the tragic news about Mateo and Chanel. She wasn't in the mood to talk to them. What was important to her at the moment was counting money and getting what was hers—what was owed to her.

The guys needed to sell the weed and the jewelry to give Charlie her cut. In total, they felt that they came off with at least fifty or sixty thousand in stuff, and split three ways, that would probably leave her with fifteen to twenty thousand dollars. It was a good day, Charlie felt.

Charlie's cell phone rang for the umpteenth time that night, and once again, she continued to ignore it.

God looked at her and said, "You need to act surprised when you hear the news, Charlie. Ya feel me? Fuckin' act concerned about ya sister an' shit. Can you fuckin' pull that shit off?"

"I got this, God. Don't worry about me," she assured him.

He sighed heavily. He didn't want to worry about her, but he wondered how she would react when she heard the news about Chanel being brutally raped.

Charlie arrived at Jacobi hospital in the Bronx the following morning where she was met by everyone, even Mecca. Bacardi shot her a foul look and right away tore into her oldest daughter with, "I fuckin' tried to call you and you don't know how to fuckin' answer your fuckin' phone."

"Chill, Ma. I was busy."

"Busy..."

"What the fuck happened? What happened to Chanel?" Charlie asked with concern pouring from her tone, though it was fraudulent.

Butch, Claire, and Mecca simply looked at her with sadness. Did God lie to her? Did he kill her sister too? Now Charlie started to worry.

"Is Chanel okay?"

"No! There was a home invasion, and Mateo was shot and Chanel was raped."

"Raped?" Charlie repeated the word with ample bewilderment. "What the fuck you mean she was raped? By who?"

"We don't know."

"And is Mateo dead?"

"No, he's in critical condition," said Bacardi.

"Ohmygod!"

"He made it through surgery, but it's still touch-and-go wit' him."

Charlie was shocked for two reasons. Mateo was still alive and Chanel had been raped. That wasn't part of the deal.

"They don't know who did it?" Charlie asked.

Bacardi suddenly lost her cool. "If they fuckin' knew who did it, they would be fuckin' locked up by now or fuckin' dead already, don't you fuckin' think!"

"Where's Chanel?" Charlie asked.

"She's still with the doctors," Mecca answered.

Charlie all of a sudden looked visibly sick. The family thought she was finally showing some concern for her little sister.

"I need some fuckin' air," Charlie announced.

She immediately departed from the room and dashed out of the hospital. She needed to call God. She needed to confront him. Everything was fucked up. They done fucked up. She walked up the block and called God from her cell phone.

When he finally answered, she screamed from the top of her lungs, "You grimy fuckin' nigga! You fuckin' raped my sister! You nasty-ass bastard! Fuck you, God! I swear, nigga, you ain't shit!"

God indifferently replied, "Yo, I don't know what the fuck you talkin' 'bout, Charlie. I ain't rape nobody. And don't be coming at me wit' this shit over the fuckin' phone. I'm on my way."

He curtailed their call.

Charlie was left standing outside looking dumbfounded. She sobbed.

Unbeknownst to Charlie, Claire had followed her outside because she was concerned about her. She overheard Charlie cursing God out on the phone and was shocked by what she heard.

Could it be true? Did God have something to do with this tragedy?

Claire didn't know for sure, but she knew what she'd heard Charlie scream out. Her sister was truly upset. Claire walked back inside the hospital without Charlie seeing her.

Butch excused himself from the waiting area and went and stood in an empty corridor. Ten minutes later Bacardi went to check on him. She bent the corner and found a pitiful sight. Her husband was coiled over, hands clenched in a tight fist, his face drenched with tears. His veins were bulging in his neck and his eyes were puffy, almost swollen shut from crying. He looked almost unrecognizable.

"They hurt my baby," he sobbed. "I'll fuckin' kill 'em. I'll kill 'em all!"

Bacardi embraced Butch. He squeezed her waist tightly and buried his face in her shoulder. He was torn up inside, grieving, and blaming himself for not being able to protect his youngest child from the wolves.

"Why, Bernice? Why her? Why Chanel?"

Briefly, Bacardi wondered if Butch had ever had a clue that Chanel wasn't his blood. And then she pushed that thought to the back of her mind. What did that matter now?

A few hours later, God arrived at the hospital in the Bronx. He came alone and brought flowers for Chanel. By now the adrenaline had worn off and he suddenly felt the pain from the scratches Chanel had dug in his back. He didn't want to panic, but he knew that his DNA would be under her fingernails and hoped that the hospital staff would somehow overlook this evidence.

Charlie had mixed emotions about God being there.

To Charlie, he emphatically denied the rape—whether it was between him and Chanel, or Fingers and Chanel.

"Then why the sudden tension between you and Fingers?" she asked him.

"That's some other shit, Charlie, not this. I promise you, we ain't touch that girl," he replied vehemently.

He continued to lie and said that Chanel was lying to get attention. Charlie didn't know what to believe. God went on to say that he bet the rape test would come back inclusive, no DNA.

She narrowed her eyes at him. What did he mean DNA?

"Maybe they wrapped up," she said. "My sister was fuckin' raped!"

God became easily offended, and shouted, "I ain't no fuckin' rapist! I would never touch ya fuckin' sister, especially some black, ugly bitch like her. Shit is like fuckin' incest. She's like a sister to me too."

"But she's not your fuckin' sister!"

"You never gave a fuck about her anyway!"

"That don't mean shit!"

"I didn't fuckin' do it, Charlie, so get that shit out ya fuckin' mind," he shouted.

They argued right there, and God remained adamant about his innocence in the rape. Eventually, Charlie backed down, but she couldn't shake the uneasiness she felt around God. The thought of her man putting his dick inside her little sister disgusted her. Inexplicably she still loved him, even with the allegations of rape lingering over his head.

He was right, though. She never cared about Chanel, so why did she start to now? Was it jealousy that Chanel fucked him too, though it was by rape? She already had everything, and now God had to give himself to her too—taking her virginity.

Chapter Twenty-Nine

Bacardi stayed by her daughter's side in a room chair, while the rest of the family went home. Chanel's doctor had come out and confirmed that she'd been raped. There was trauma and tears to her vagina, and her hymen was viciously torn. They'd swabbed her for DNA, but they wouldn't know if they had a profile for some time now.

Bacardi was shocked that Chanel was still a virgin. She didn't think that it was still possible at her age. Bacardi had been having sex since she was twelve years old.

Grief and guilt overwhelmed Bacardi, and she realized that she had been a terrible mother to her youngest daughter. The fact that a long time ago she'd had an affair and had gotten pregnant with a man she loved had haunted her until this day.

Bacardi wanted revenge.

A few detectives came to the room to ask Chanel some questions about the home invasion and the attack. Did she recognize the two men? She didn't. They wore masks. Did she notice any distinguishing marks on either man? She couldn't tell. It happened too quickly, and she was terrified. They were dressed in black and wore gloves, therefore, left behind no fingerprints. The men came and went, vanished suddenly, leaving behind her fiancé to fight for his life—and her definitely scarred for life.

With nothing to go on, the detectives were disappointed. They really wanted to catch these culprits. There had been a wave of deadly home invasions in the Tri-State area in the past few years, and the culprits still hadn't been caught. The detectives were hoping that Chanel could give them their first lead to catch these murderous thugs, but they left empty handed.

"We were getting married," Chanel uttered faintly.

"Married?" Bacardi was shocked to hear.

Damn it, the man was going to officially become her son-in-law, and now they didn't know if he would live or die. Just like that, Chanel's world—and she felt like her world—had been turned upside down.

Bacardi sat with Chanel for a few more hours, and then she decided to go check on Mateo. He was in ICU—comatose from the shooting and the intense surgery, with machines and tubes monitoring his vitals and trying to keep him alive.

"I'll give you fifteen minutes with him," said his nurse.

Bacardi nodded. She moved closer to Mateo's bed, a bit nervous to see him in such a fragile condition. Then there was this anger that started to develop inside of her. Why was this happening to her daughter? Mateo was supposed to be her golden goose out of the hood. He had money and he was kind to her—a cool dude. Maybe he had enemies, or stick-up kids came to violently take from him like they always do. There were so many questions as to why this happened, but Bacardi knew that she probably would never know the answers.

She gently took Mateo's hand into hers and said to him, "Chanel is gonna be okay, Mateo. And she needs you to fight. She told me that y'all were getting married. That's wonderful news. So you fight, so you can be with my daughter and take care of her—take care of us. But I need you to fight because someone hurt my daughter and we need you to get better so you can get your revenge."

Pyro sat parked outside the hospital in heartache over his friend. He sat behind the wheel of his car in total disbelief. It all had to be a bad dream. What the fuck happened? Who did this to his friend and his fiancée? He seethed like never before. And he cried. He was all over the place with emotions. In a few days, they all were supposed to be in Hawaii to witness a beautiful union on the beach. He, his best friend, his fiancée, and Mecca, they were supposed to see glory. And Pyro was looking forward to the wedding and the escape to paradise.

He sat inside the car, deep in thought. He was not able to move. He was not able to go inside the hospital to see his friend. He couldn't see Mateo in his condition, comatose from a bullet to his head. He strongly felt he should have been there to watch Mateo's back.

"Fuck!" he cursed. "Fuck! Fuck! Fuck! Fuck! Fuck! Fuuccck!" he screamed madly while repeatedly banging his fist against the dashboard.

What he really wanted to do was take the 9mm Berretta that was by his side and blow someone's brains out. He wanted to avenge his friend.

Pyro already had his suspicions on who was behind the violent attack. He knew it wasn't random. It was carefully planned. Mateo and his fiancée had been targeted and stalked.

Mateo had told him that Chanel had invited her sisters, Charlie and Claire, to the apartment a few days before the home invasion. Mateo had always been extra careful who he brought to his home. He deduced that Charlie gave her man the intel he needed to execute the attack. He knew it had to be them.

Pyro sat there inside his Benz until he noticed Charlie's dirty looking man, God, leaving the hospital lobby. The sight of that nigga enraged him—especially seeing him at the hospital where Mateo and Chanel were. He glared at God with the urge to pick up his gun and march over there and murder that nigga in cold blood. Mateo was a nigga who'd bust his gun if he had to, but Pyro was a nigga who'd bust his gun when he wanted to.

Pyro climbed out of his Benz, wanting to start some shit with God. He continued his hard stare at God. He wanted to make it obvious that he was looking directly at him. And God soon noticed. God looked back at Pyro like, *What the fuck you looking at, nigga?* Both men exchanged menacing stares, and neither was intimidated by the other.

Pyro kept his eyes fixed on God until he climbed into Fingers' car and it drove away.

"I'm gonna see you around, nigga. Believe that shit," Pyro said.

He changed his mind and decided to go into the hospital to visit his friend. He owed Mateo that, to still be by his side no matter what. But he had the seed of revenge planted in his mind and heart. They weren't going to get away with what they did to Chanel and Mateo.

Chapter Thirty

God slammed the bedroom door behind him and immediately started in on Charlie, shouting, "What the fuck you been telling people?"

"What the fuck are you talkin' about, God?"

"Did you open ya big fuckin' mouth?"

"No!" she shouted, still baffled as to what was going on.

"You sure, bitch?"

"I'm sure!" she shouted.

"Then why this nigga's friend was looking at me sideways and shit at the hospital? Like he knew some shit—sneering at me all funny style and whatnot. I don't like that nigga, and I swear, he gonna get got too. He wanna fuckin' size me up, I'll kill that nigga Pyro! I swear, I'll fuckin' murder that nigga. I don't give a fuck, you hear me? I don't give a fuck!" God ranted in front of Charlie.

"God, just relax and chill. You're paranoid," she told him.

God cut his eyes at Charlie with a hard glare and unexpectedly slapped the shit out of her. Charlie spun around and stumbled backwards. The slap caught her off guard. He was becoming more and more violent toward her—utterly disrespectful.

"I ain't fuckin' paranoid, bitch," he barked.

Charlie stood there holding the side of her face in bewilderment. The look in God's eyes was demonic.

God seethed and stormed out of the bedroom. He refused to sleep there that night.

Charlie soaked up the wound. It wasn't the slap that hurt her physically, but mentally, she felt everything was falling apart. Going after her sister and her man, was it a bad sign? Was this an omen? Controlled by greed and jealousy, she couldn't tolerate Chanel having a bigger and a better life than her. So, she did what she knew best—steal and have people killed.

But she didn't want this to be their downfall. No way. Charlie wasn't about to be beaten by her little sister. She needed to do something before the situation grew out of control and came barreling down on her like a runaway locomotive and destroyed everything in its way.

Bacardi wiped away the few tears that trickled down her face. She didn't know exactly what it was, but seeing Chanel's condition and knowing she had been brutally raped and her virginity had been violently taken from her, it did something to Bacardi. Her youngest daughter was truly innocent and pure. The only thing she wanted from everyone was to be loved.

Bacardi knew that she was eighteen years too late to become a mother to Chanel now, but she wanted to try. The grudge she held against her daughter because of a broken heart wasn't fair.

Chanel suffered some trauma and the tragedy affected her heavily. Being raped and seeing your fiancé shot was too much of a nightmare for anyone to endure. Bacardi could only imagine what that girl was going through right now. The doctors informed Bacardi that her daughter would most likely need some counseling.

At night, Bacardi slept in an uncomfortable chair next to Chanel's bedside, and during the day, she would hurry home to shower and bring back some food. Chanel would cry on her mother's shoulder, and Bacardi would walk with her each day to visit with Mateo in ICU. He was still alive, and he was still holding on through a miracle. Being shot in the head was a death sentence, but Mateo was strong and fighting to come back to her. Chanel believed he was fighting for their love. He'd promised her that he would never leave her, and it looked like he was desperately trying to keep his promise.

"I need to go back to the apartment to change clothes, Chanel. But I'll be right back," Bacardi told her.

"I'll be fine, Ma," Chanel replied faintly. She smiled.

Chanel always understood. Even though it was hard for her to be left alone because she had been severely traumatized, she still understood about her mother's departure for a few hours to travel back to Brooklyn.

Bacardi hugged Chanel and left the room.

Chanel sat back on the bed and closed her eyes, but sometimes the darkness became too overwhelming for her and she would suddenly see her masked attacker standing over her, assaulting her and raping her over and over again. She would abruptly wake up from her sleep screaming and clearly horrified. It felt like she couldn't escape from them. They were following her wherever she went.

Bacardi traveled back to Brooklyn via train and several buses. It was early afternoon when she arrived home. It was a clear, sunny day, but there was nothing sunny about her life.

The apartment was quiet, and it seemed like nobody was home. Lately, Butch had been doing his disappearing acts, and Claire had been in her own world doing God knows what. Bacardi couldn't worry about them. She had one tragedy to deal with already, and she was making good on her promise to Chanel.

She went to her bedroom to get a change of clothes, but she was soon intercepted in the hallway by Charlie and Claire coming out of their bedrooms. Charlie and Bacardi looked at each other, while Claire stood there quietly. A jealous Charlie, who knew that her mother was only there to come and go right back to Chanel's bedside, said, "I think she's lying about being raped."

Bacardi stopped dead in her tracks. She couldn't believe what had just come out of her daughter's mouth. "Excuse me?"

"I said, Chanel's lying about being raped."

"Are you serious, Charlie? So Chanel raped herself, huh? I saw the hospital report, and unless she fucked herself and caused the tears to her pussy, then you need to shut the fuck up!"

Charlie crossed her arms and poked out her lips. "So, that's it? Chanel cries rape and we're all supposed to kiss her ass?"

Bacardi's face tightened into an intense scowl and she stepped closer to her oldest daughter. She growled, "You need to stop being a selfish fuckin' bitch, you fuckin' hear me?"

"Looks who's talking," countered Charlie matter-of-factly.

"I'm sick of ya shit, Charlie. You need to be by your sister's side and not here fuckin' hating!"

"And you need to wake the fuck up! Now you wanna start caring about her?" Charlie retorted.

"Better late than never!" Bacardi countered.

The two argued in the hallway. Claire continued to stand there in silence. She was torn. Should she tell Bacardi what she'd overheard the other day at the hospital—what Charlie had fussed about with God, or should she mind her business? After she had been exposed as a liar and a cheater, Claire decided to mind her business. All Charlie would have to say was that she was lying and no one would believe her anyway.

So while Bacardi and Charlie argued in the hallway, Claire went back into her bedroom and closed the door.

The following day, Chanel was released from the hospital, and Bacardi was there to help her home. They rode back to the Brooklyn projects via cab. There was no way Chanel was capable of taking public transportation.

Inside the apartment, the only thing Chanel wanted to do was go to her room and lay down. She was quiet mostly, and when she did speak, it was a prayer to God to help save Mateo. She was fortunate to come home, but Mateo was still in ICU fighting for his life. Chanel wished she could do more for him, but she couldn't. She hated feeling helpless. She still was having nightmares, and the fact that she no longer had her virginity to give Mateo on their wedding night was heartbreaking. With her birthday looming, what was supposed to be a special day, Chanel only wanted to forget and disappear somewhere. She didn't want to think about her birthday at all.

She sobbed in her bed. It wouldn't go away.

That night, Chanel lay in the bed in a dark and silent room. Everything felt completely still. She wasn't hungry or thirsty, hadn't eaten in a day. The only thing she wanted to do was lay there. Saddened and depressed, she felt like concrete on her bed, unable to move from the weight of everything that'd happened to her—and sometimes not able to think.

As she lay there, she heard the bedroom door open and close. Thinking it was Claire coming into the room, she didn't turn around and paid it no attention. But then she felt someone take a seat on her mattress. She turned over to shockingly see God staring at her. It felt like her heart had stopped. She remained frozen on her bed startled and fearful.

"I didn't mean to scare you, Chanel. I just came in here to check up on you . . . to see if you were okay," he said.

She couldn't say a word.

"You good? Yo, I heard what happened to you the other day, and I'm sorry that you went through that shit. But if you need anything, I'm here, a'ight? I got ya back."

God reached forward to touch her leg in some kind of comfort, but Chanel jerked frightfully from his touch and flinched away from him.

"I know that shit got you messed up," he continued. "But you just need to be strong, a'ight?"

He finally stood up. Chanel couldn't keep her eyes off of him. Her heart started to beat a mile a second.

"And believe me, I'm gonna help find whoever did this to you and I'm gonna murder these fools that raped you, okay? You got my word on that," said God.

He turned and eventually left the room, closing the door behind him and leaving Chanel alone in the dark. His sudden presence did something to Chanel. She erupted into tears. She couldn't stop shaking. There was something about his presence that made her skin crawl and plunged her into deep fear.

It took her nearly an hour to stop shaking.

The following day, God was in the living room with Bacardi, and the two shared a blunt. They were engaged in conversation. Things were still tense in the apartment, and they figured smoking weed would relax them.

God took a long pull from the haze and then said, "Bacardi, you know I always will have love for you and your family. That shit that happened to Chanel, I'm already on it. I got my peoples out there lookin' fo these niggas that did that shit, ya feel me?"

"Fuckin' animals out there and I want these fuckin' niggas dead," Bacardi said with contempt.

"Don't worry 'bout it. Whoever did that shit, they gonna get theirs, fo' real. You know Chanel always been like a little sister to me."

"I know, God."

"That shit really fuckin' hurt me," he continued.

They passed the blunt back and forth and prolonged their conversation about how would they kill the two men responsible for raping Chanel. Bacardi came up with some sadistic ways that even made God cringe.

"Damn, you a foul and dangerous, bitch, Bacardi. Damn."

"You fuck wit' mines, then I fuck wit' you, no fuckin' mercy. I would cut these niggas' dicks and balls clean the fuck off and make them fuckin' eat that shit. I would watch them die fuckin' slow."

"Yeah, I feel you on that," God agreed.

He was really selling it to her and to everyone else that he was the concerned surrogate older brother for Chanel and that he really wanted to go after the men responsible for her rape.

The next night, God entered Chanel's room again to check on her. He was reaching for information, trying to see if she remembered anything about that night. He never removed his mask, they wore gloves, but he did leave with a few marks across his back after raping Chanel missionary. He knew it was a dumb move to untie her wrists so he could feel on her chest.

Once again, Chanel was lying in bed, not actually sleeping, but in a slight stupor. When she saw God come into the room again, she immediately cringed from the sight of him. He looked at her with concern, but there was a profound lie behind his eyes.

"Chanel, I just came in here to see if you were okay," God said sympathetically.

"Just get out!" she exclaimed.

"I'm sorry. I just wanted to make sure you were good in here."

"Get the fuck out!" she cried out.

"A'ight shorty, you ain't gotta yell. I'll leave. I care about you, Chanel, and I was just showing you some concern."

Not wanting to upset her even more, he did what she asked and left the bedroom.

Chanel was visibly shaken-up and uncomfortable around him. Her tears started to run down her face like a river. He was purposely invading her personal space and stirring up fear inside of her. To her, God was her nightmare and his presence gave her the chills.

It had been weeks since God had spent the night with Charlie. After he slapped her, he would come and go, and he didn't really pay Charlie that much attention. He'd sold off everything they gotten from Mateo's place and it was a healthy profit. He gave Charlie her cut, and she felt like she was the breadwinner in the family again. She used her share to buy a used car to get around in. While Chanel was left devastated, frightened, and alone, Charlie felt no contrition for what she did to her little sister. But Bacardi hadn't shifted her attention from Chanel. Nothing had changed inside the apartment except for Charlie's wealth.

One evening, while God and Charlie were fucking in the bedroom, Charlie ran her hands down his back and she could feel scabs. When they were done, God stood up naked and when he turned his back to her, she could see the deep scratches that someone else left behind. They were now healing, but they looked appalling, like Wolverine had attacked him.

Charlie puffed out and suddenly had to choke back her tears. She watched God walk around the bedroom naked, looking for some pants to put on. She didn't know what to think. The evidence was there. He raped Chanel and she had left her mark behind on his skin.

"I'll be in the shower," he said.

He left the room. Charlie lingered on the bed with a lot to think about. True or not, how could she betray her man? She was eating again, she had nice things, and they started to have great sex again. So, would she bring all that to a halt for Chanel? She doubted it. But still, knowing that God was the monster that raped her little sister was a sickening feeling.

God hopped in the shower and took his sweet time in the bathroom. He felt that he'd gotten away with the assault and attempted murder. For a few weeks now, he'd been subtly keeping tabs on Chanel. Although the girl was frightened of him, he was confident that she was clueless.

After his shower, he dried off and wrapped the towel around his waist. He smiled at his handsome reflection in the mirror and was ready to start another day. Fingers had been asking to do another lick. God wanted to wait a bit longer before they went after another target. Things had been too hot on the streets and the cops were putting pressure out there. It was a risk to move too soon, especially anywhere in the Tri-State area. Their work of deadly home invasions had been on the news, and a task force had been set up to catch the culprits. God didn't want to push his luck. If anything, he felt that it was time to move out of town and start fresh somewhere else—maybe the South or the Midwest.

As he was coming out the bathroom dressed only in a towel, Chanel happened to step foot out of her bedroom. The two crossed paths in the hallway. God smiled at her and said, "Pardon me."

He hurried into the bedroom to be with Charlie, while Chanel stood there frozen like she was cemented to the floor. In passing, she noticed the scratches on God's back, and an uneasy and queasy feeling swiftly came over her, and the night of the rape and assault came flooding back.

Could it have been him? God?

She ran back into her bedroom and slammed the door behind her. She crawled back into her bed with a flood of tears coming from her eyes.

Bacardi heard the door slam and worried about Chanel. She entered the girls' bedroom to find her daughter cowering and crying in her bed. Bacardi carefully joined Chanel on her bed and gently wrapped her arms around her daughter to comfort her. Something had upset her. The poor girl was shaking like a leaf in the wind. She assumed it was another bad dream.

Chapter Thirty-One

A crowd of men in a concrete Brooklyn basement hollered and cursed at rolling dice. There were large amounts of cash on the ground, and the atmosphere was rowdy as the thugs gambled, smoked weed, and drank.

Among the group of men gambling in the basement was Fingers. He gulped a 40oz, took a few puffs from the blunt, and clutched a handful of money.

"Yo, run that back, nigga," Fingers hollered.

"What you want on that, nigga?" a thug shouted.

"I got a C-note on that muthafucka."

"Bet, nigga."

Fingers took another swig from his beer. He felt comfortable in the thuggish and sketchy environment, especially with his .45 tucked snugly in his waistband. He didn't go anywhere without it.

The men continued to gamble, the dice rolled against the gray concrete floor, and the numbers did not come up favorably for Fingers. He lost a hundred, but he was willing to run it back. "Five hundred, nigga," he said.

"Nigga, you like losing money, don't you?" said Tony, the shooter of the dice.

"Just fuckin' roll 'em dice, nigga," Fingers said with a bit of irritation.

Tony chuckled. The crowd of men continued to be loud and sometimes vulgar. A lot more money was thrown into the pot, and it nearly totaled a stack. These were some heavy hitters and they won big or lost big.

The dice rolled again, and once again, Fingers lost. He shouted and cursed. "Fuck me!"

Tony laughed and taunted Fingers with, "You ready to ante up again, nigga?"

Fingers pulled out another wad of bills from his pocket. It was a sizable knot of cash totaling fifteen hundred. Fingers looked like he had money to burn.

He wanted to quickly win back the six hundred he'd already lost, so he tossed a few hundred dollars into the growing pot of cash. Things were becoming a lot tenser. He hated to lose. He wanted to win and he wanted to get his mind off his troubles.

Fingers was still offended that God hadn't allowed him a turn with Chanel. It wasn't as much about fucking Chanel, but more so the way God blocked him and looked at him like he was a piece of shit for wanting a turn. The thought of raping her never would have occurred to Fingers, and yet, it had entered God's mind, and he went through with it. So, God thought that only *he* was good enough to fuck the black beauty?

Fingers couldn't understand why it bothered him so much. God had made him feel like a thirsty pervert that night, and it was eating at him.

He downed more of his beer and continued to gamble, and continued to lose. Eventually, he ended up losing more than two grand. Now he was broke and angry.

"Nah, fuck this. Y'all niggas is cheating!" he shouted.

"Yo, you lost, so bounce, nigga. This shit right here is a fuckin' rich man's game, muthafucka," someone exclaimed.

Fingers didn't like the comment and he removed his pistol from his waistband to start some shit and get his money back. But surprisingly, no one was intimidated by the gun in his hand. They stared at Fingers like he was crazy, and then they pulled out their guns and aimed at Fingers.

"What, nigga, you think you the only nigga wit' a fuckin' gun down here?" said someone. "You either leave broke and alive or in a fuckin' body bag, nigga. Ya choice, fool."

Fingers relented, knowing he was outnumbered and outgunned.

Outside the building, he fussed and cursed to himself. He was a bit drunk and agitated. While he staggered to his car, he got it into his head to call Charlie. Her phone rang several times before she finally answered.

"I got sumthin' to tell you, Charlie," he uttered.

"Fingers, what the fuck is wrong wit' you?"

"This is important, and I wanna tell you in person. Meet me in the morning," he added.

"I'm not interested, Fingers. You sound fuckin' drunk."

"I ain't fuckin' drunk and this got sumthin' to do wit' our last lick."

Charlie abruptly ended their call.

Fingers was left standing there dumbfounded. "Why . . . why she hang up on me?" he stammered.

He attempted to try and call her again, but her phone was going directly to voicemail. He angrily tossed his phone and marched toward his truck and unlocked his doors. He was fully aggravated and felt disrespected by Charlie too. Fingers wanted to release his anger, and he thought about heading uptown to Harlem to fuck some chick.

He walked and stumbled a bit, and the moment he placed his hand on the door handle, a dark assailant emerged from the shadows—like he came out of nowhere. The man outstretched his arm with a Glock 41 in his hand and he fired coldheartedly into the back of Fingers' head.

Bac! Bac! Bac!

Fingers' body dropped to the pavement, his crimson blood thick and coating the street. The assailant fired two more hot slugs into Fingers' chest, officially making it overkill. But Fingers was dead before his body hit the pavement.

Pyro glared down at the body and squeezed off another shot. "That's for Mateo, faggot!"

He pivoted and hurried back to his vehicle. He peeled away from the scene unobserved. One down and one to go.

Fingers was dead. It hit God like a ton of bricks. The grim news of his friend being gunned down on the street with three shots to his head and two in his chest was unnerving. God knew the killing was personal. It had to be with five shots. His friend had been caught slipping.

God needed to be alone. He left out the apartment and went into the stairwell to smoke a cigarette and think. He still couldn't believe that his friend was gone.

He took a long pull from the Newport and thought, *Who did this shit?* He felt that they didn't have enemies, or did they? When they did the home invasions, they always wore masks and gloves, and they always picked their victims carefully. They didn't want anything to come back on them. But something had come back on one of them.

Word around the way was that Fingers had lost a lot of money at a gambling spot and ruffled some feathers. God was worried. With his right-hand man gone, what was next? And would they try and come for him too?

"What the fuck! Damn it, Fingers. Damn!" God griped. He had lost his best friend, and he was a wreck.

But no one took the news harder than Charlie. She had spoken to Fingers the night he was killed. She'd hung up on him. Now she wished she hadn't. Charlie had burst into tears and screamed throughout the apartment after hearing the news. The three of them were thick as thieves, because that's what they were—thieves. Now one of them had been gunned down.

How?

Charlie's family took the news in stride. No one really cared about Fingers' death. Bacardi, Butch, and Claire all pretended as if they barely knew him, and they refused to go to his funeral.

Chapter Thirty-Two

July 4th

What was supposed to be a festive holiday turned out to be the day Frederick Avery, AKA Fingers was laid to rest. The 23-year-old thug was dressed in a fitted ball cap and a black and white Nike sweat suit chosen by his single mother, Tonya. The morticians did a good job reconstructing his features, and the young thug looked more like he was sleeping than dead.

The funeral was pathetic. Fingers wasn't a well-liked guy, and only a handful of people showed up to pay their respects. But Tonya was absolutely devastated over his death. Her son was her bread and butter. Tonya wailed over his casket. He was her only son, and she couldn't believe he was dead.

His funeral was hard to pay for. When Fingers was murdered, Tonya had to beg and scrape every dime together. She went around asking for help from whomever she could, including God and a few friends. God only offered to give Tonya $500, claiming that he was broke.

With Fingers gone, she had to look out for herself, and money didn't grow on trees. But Tonya was particularly disgusted with God. She knew about all the things they'd done together. Her son told her about everything, including the rape of Chanel and every murder they'd committed. For

Fingers, it was like confession and his mother was his priest. The violent and turbulent life he lived was sometimes a lot for him to hold in, and when he talked to his mother, it was like therapy. They were really close.

Tonya felt God had disrespected her son. Only $500 toward his best friend's funeral? She was also convinced that Fingers was murdered because of their last job. Tonya felt that it was no coincidence that no one was left alive in their other robberies. *Why rape the girl and leave her alive?* Tonya wondered. Now her son was conveniently murdered, and she didn't believe that it was over a dice game. Nah, it wasn't going to end like this. She wanted justice for her son.

Dressed in all black and in tears, Tonya looked around the funeral home. What hurt her was the attendance. It was a mostly empty room. God and Charlie stopped by to pay their respects and to give their condolences, but something about them rubbed her the wrong way. They were dressed like they were about to go to a barbecue, and God seemed hurt about his friend's death, but he didn't seem too upset to Tonya. He was supposed to be crushed and devastated, like she was—and he was supposed to stay longer to give her some comfort.

She wanted them to stay, and she wanted God to pay for her son's funeral. He didn't. Five hundred fuckin' dollars wasn't shit.

As the couple left, Tonya glared at them until they were out of her sight. She used to treat God like he was one of her own, but now she saw his true colors. He only cared about himself and that bitch.

Tonya seethed in her seat. Something had to be done.

As God and Charlie left the funeral home, they were unexpectedly met by two detectives who flashed their badges. They were there to pick up God.

"You need to come with us," said the detective.

"Y'all niggas serious? This is my friend's fuckin' funeral!" God chided.

"Do you really want to make a scene then?" said his partner.

God mean-mugged the detectives and Charlie asked, "What did he do?"

They ignored her. She wasn't their concern. They focused on taking God into their custody. Charlie could only watch as they escorted her man away and shoved him into the back of an unmarked police car. He would be going to trial soon on the gun charge he'd picked up almost a year back. But the cops wanted to harass him. They hadn't forgotten about the death of their fellow officer on that fateful New Year's Day. His murder was still unsolved and it left a bad taste in the NYPD's mouth. God and Fingers were their primary suspects, but there wasn't enough evidence to charge them.

Charlie fumed as she watched them haul God away. The thought crossed her mind again that it was like a curse—an omen of worse to come since they robbed her sister and shot Mateo. God was back in jail, Fingers was dead, and Mateo was still alive.

The only thing she could do was continue to keep her mouth shut and, yet again, see what the charges were against God and try to get him out of jail.

Fortunately for God, there were no new charges against him. He was only brought to the precinct for questioning. They kept him in a room for nearly twenty-four hours and interrogated him. But God was a rock, and since they had nothing on him, he was free to go.

The moment God walked out of the precinct, his cell phone rang. He answered, and it was Tonya.

"Yo listen, God, I'm gonna need you to drop off some more money so I can get ahead of my bills, you feel me?"

God was taken aback by the blatant request. "What—?" He stopped short of calling her a bitch. And in a stern voice, he replied, "Yo Tonya, I ain't your man or your son. If you need money, then I suggest you get a fuckin' job. I don't owe you shit. My nigga just got murdered and I gotta deal wit' that."

"How *you* gotta deal wit' *my* son getting murdered? How the fuck you sound, God? How the fuck you come up wit' that shit? He was my son and you couldn't stick around for his funeral."

"Tonya, I said I can't fuckin' help you."

"So, it's like that?"

"Yeah! It's like that!" God wasn't about to be forced to pay anyone anything.

"Okay, so maybe Chanel can help me out, then. You think Charlie's sister can help wit' that, huh? Or maybe the police?"

God's stomach dropped. She was threatening him with information she could have gotten only from her son. The nigga done snitched to his moms when what they did was only supposed to remain between the three of them.

His bitter tone suddenly changed. "Nah, I feel you. You right, Tonya. A'ight, lemme see what I can do."

"I bet you will, muthafucka. Shit done changed real quickly, I see. Don't fuckin' disappoint me, God, cuz I treated you like a son too," she said.

She ended the call, and God was left furious. He hated to be blackmailed.

Chapter Thirty-Three

Chanel would spend ten-hour days at Jacobi Medical Center in the Bronx with her comatose fiancé. Each morning she prayed for Mateo in the hospital chapel, and her nights were spent in her mother's bedroom, with Bacardi by her side in her bed. She was afraid of God. She hated him being inside their apartment. She hated that she had to see him almost every day. Seeing those scratches across his back, she suspected he was the monster that raped her. But she wasn't sure. She did everything in her power to try to avoid him, but with it being a small apartment, it was nearly impossible. So, during the day, the hospital became her safe haven.

Chanel would take the train from Brooklyn to the Bronx, and back to Brooklyn late at night. Surprisingly, Bacardi and Butch would meet her at the station and walk her home safely. There had been a silver-lining behind the tragic incident; she had become closer to her parents and they were finally there for her.

One evening at the hospital, she ran into Pyro outside Mateo's room. He could see that Chanel was still distraught over the incident. It had been a month, but to Chanel, it would always feel like it was yesterday.

When Pyro went to go hug her, she cringed and shied away from him. He understood. She had gone through a very traumatic experience. But to give her some kind of comfort, he leaned closer to her and said, "One down, and now one to go."

They locked eyes, and Chanel instantly knew that he was talking about Fingers.

"So, it *was* them?" she said softly. "How do you know?"

"Mateo knew he needed to get you outta that spot once your sisters came through. And he was right. I did some digging around after what went down wit' y'all, and those fools are known for violent home invasions. They kill people, Chanel. They did it, and your sister is on my list too. She set you up," he said.

Chanel didn't want to believe it. Not Charlie. "No, you can't. I won't let you."

Her response was surprising to him. Why would she protect that bitch? He kicked himself for telling her about Charlie. He should have just done it without telling her anything—but the sad look on Chanel's face got to him and he'd hoped the news would give her strength.

"Okay, I promise I won't touch her. I just thought—never mind what I thought. You okay, though? Do you need money or anything? I should have looked out sooner, but I've been busy."

She looked away and replied, "I'm okay."

"Nah, you ain't, Chanel. Not when you're in the same place as that bitch and her nigga. Do me a favor. When you leave here, I want you to go straight to the Manhattan Hotel in the city. I'll have a room already paid for and it will be in your name. Stay there for a month," he said.

Chanel didn't know what to think. It was a lot to process.

Pyro reached into his pocket and pulled out a wad of hundred-dollar bills. "Here, take this—for food, cab rides, and any incidentals."

Chanel feebly accepted the cash. Pyro then took her phone and programmed his number into it.

"Keep in touch. You need anything, Chanel, just hit me up," he said.

Chanel nodded and walked back into the room to be with Mateo. Pyro truly felt sorry for the innocent girl. Had it been his baby mama,

Mateo would have definitely looked out for her—killed those fools and not thought twice about it. They were brothers from a different mother. They loved each other and always looked out for each other. But what God and Fingers did to the couple a few days before their wedding date, it was deplorable and unforgivable, and Pyro could see the remnants of the tragedy in Chanel's body language. She would probably never be the same again.

That night, Chanel checked into the Manhattan Hotel on the west side. Like Pyro had promised, the arrangements had already been made, and the only thing she had to do was go to the hotel clerk and get her keycard to the room.

The luxury hotel room was a one-bedroom suite with a king size bed, a pull out sofa, a large flat screen, plush carpet, and a beautiful view of the city that stretched across the Hudson River and toward New Jersey. The suite was nearly bigger than her entire apartment.

Chanel was grateful. Finally, she could sleep peacefully without God being in the next room.

She called Bacardi and told her where she was so she wouldn't worry.

"I'll bring you some clothes in the morning," said Bacardi.

"Okay. And, Ma, please don't tell my sisters where I'm at, especially Charlie."

Bacardi paused. She wanted to ask why, but deep down inside, she felt that she already knew the answer. The revelation came quickly, only after Chanel's remark. She agreed to keep Chanel's location a secret.

The following morning, Bacardi packed a few of Chanel's things, including a few things for herself, panties, bras, toiletries, and some comfortable clothing, and she kissed her husband goodbye and told him to hold the household down until she came back.

"I'm glad you goin' to be wit' her, Bernice. She needs you. Make sure you tell her that Daddy loves his baby girl."

"She knows."

Butch earnestly asked, "Does she?"

Bacardi drank in the question. It stopped her in her tracks. She and Butch had been terrible parents to Chanel. "Well, Butch, she will know now and that's all that matters."

Bacardi decided to put all of her energy into helping her daughter.

Chapter Thirty-Four

God sat parked outside the somewhat dilapidated brownstone in Bed-Stuy, Brooklyn and smoked his cigarette. He kept a keen eye on the residence. He hated that it had to come to this, but he didn't have a choice. His head was on a constant swivel watching his surroundings. It was late at night on a summer day, and there were folks lingering on the block, but he felt that now was the time.

He dowsed his cigarette in the ashtray and once again looked around the block. When he was comfortable it was clear, he stuffed the .45 into his waistband and climbed out of the vehicle. He coolly strolled to the door and rang the bell. He had an envelope filled with cash for Tonya.

There was movement behind the door, the foyer light turned on, and he heard, "Who is it?"

"It's God, Tonya. Open the door. I got ya money."

Hearing "money," she unlocked the door and swung it open. Tonya stood in front of God dressed in a blue housecoat and slippers, indicating that she was about to go to bed. She was an average looking woman in her early forties with her hair styled in a flat twist crown and she was slightly thick in the hips and the chest area.

"You got some money for me?"

He held up the bulky envelope and Tonya's eyes smiled. It was what she wanted to see.

"Can I come in? Can we talk?" he asked.

After a brief hesitation, she stepped to the side and allowed God into her home and closed the door behind him. God handed her the cash and Tonya quickly went through the hundred-dollar bills.

"We good?" he asked.

Her eyes shot up at him, and they told him yes. She smiled and said, "I deserve this money, you know. I lost my son."

"Yeah, I know."

"And where were you when Fingers was killed? He trusted you, God. You were like a brother to him," she fussed.

"I know, Tonya. I'm still fucked-up about it. But best believe I'm out there lookin' for who did it. They gonna pay for what they did to him."

It was music to Tonya's ears. She believed him.

"But look, can I use your bathroom? I gotta take a mean piss," he said.

She nodded toward the bathroom.

God went down the hallway and shouldered the door open, making sure he didn't touch anything. Once inside the bathroom, he removed a pair of black latex gloves from his pocket and stretched them on. He glanced at his image in the bathroom mirror, and a twinge of guilt hit him. He was about to do the unthinkable to Fingers' mother, someone he had known for years. But she left him no choice. She threatened to tell his secret—to go to the cops. God couldn't afford to have that happen. He couldn't leave that bitch around as a loose end that could get him locked up or killed.

He breathed out, knowing what had to be done.

He made his way out the bathroom and joined Tonya in the disheveled living room. Tonya had always been an unorganized and cluttered woman. The disorderly ambiance of her home matched her life.

She still had the money in her hand. God moved closer to her. His smile was awkward toward her when they locked eyes. And then, out of the blue, he reached up and wrapped his gloved hands around her slim neck.

Tonya was caught off guard. The envelope fell from her hands as fighting for her life became more important. She desperately grasped at God's wrists, trying to break free from the powerful grip he had around her neck. He squeezed and squeezed, and she could feel her neck almost breaking and her breathing becoming restricted.

God stared deeply into her eyes as he strangled the life out of her. She gasped and continued to fight him until he squeezed the final breath from her lungs and her body fell limp in his hands. God had watched the life gradually fade from her eyes. He huffed and puffed while doing so.

"You blackmail me, bitch!" he growled.

This murder was personal, so he took his time and savored the moment. He could have killed her quickly with a gun, but God wanted that bitch to have time to process what was going on—that he was going to squeeze the life out of her with his bare hands and he wasn't going to be fucked with. He was a monster—a killer, a rapist. Pure evil.

He didn't care that it was Fingers' moms. What mattered to him the most was survival.

God left her body on the floor. He picked up his money and headed out. Tonya lived alone, so either her body would lay there and rot for days, or maybe someone would find her corpse before the maggots got to it.

God calmly walked to his car and climbed in. Tonya was one problem gone, but there were other problems that he needed to solve. No way would Chanel or anyone else be the end of him. It was about survival—by any means necessary.

Chapter Thirty-Five

Bacardi couldn't believe her eyes when she first entered the luxury suite in the city. She was impressed. Mateo was in a coma, yet Chanel was still coming up, and she still had people looking out for her. She continued to see Chanel as her golden goose—her lucky child, the one who was coming up somehow. She started to care more and more for the girl, with them having long talks and quality time together while enjoying the suite.

The soaking tub was huge and the marble bathroom was well appointed—and Bacardi made sure to take long, hot baths and sip on some wine. The moment Bacardi arrived, Chanel had hit her off with some cash and Bacardi, like always, stuffed the money into her bra. She never complained about getting money, no matter who it was from.

They ordered room service, took in the picturesque view that the suite had to offer, and although the suite had a pull-out sofa, Chanel wanted her mother to sleep with her in the king size bed. Bacardi didn't have a problem with that. To her, it was like she was on a vacation—a paid one.

The next morning, mother and daughter had a nice breakfast from room service, and out the blue, Bacardi asked, "Why didn't you want me to tell your sisters that you were staying here?"

Chanel sat there in silence, wanting to brush off the question. She didn't want to say the words out loud, but Bacardi continued to push.

"You can talk to me, Chanel. You can talk to me 'bout anything," she said. "I'm here for you now, and I know I've been a terrible mother to you, but I'm tryin' to make up for it."

Chanel remained quiet. It was still hard for her to open up about that night.

Bacardi read into her daughter's concerns and fears, and she was able to put two and two together. "Was it God and Fingers who hurt you?"

Hearing those two names made tears leak from Chanel's eyes, and a stream moved down her face. She nodded. *Yes.* She knew it was them. She felt it deep inside her gut. It was so embarrassing and degrading that she couldn't say the words out loud.

Bacardi's face changed from gentle to absolute anger and rage. She jumped from the table upset and exclaimed, "I'm gonna kill that nigga!"

"Ma, please . . ." Chanel faintly uttered.

"This nigga thinks he can rape and assault my youngest daughter and fuck my oldest, and stay inside my home, smiling in my face after what he did to you!"

"Please, don't mention it," Chanel pleaded.

But how could Bacardi not mention it? She wasn't one to let shit go, especially not this. The nigga was a monster—he was two-faced, and she wanted to make him pay.

"He hurt you, I fuckin' wanna hurt him."

"I just want to focus on helping Mateo get better right now, that's all."

"He needs to fuckin' pay for this, Chanel."

"And he will. But not now. I-I just want him gone from the apartment."

"Oh, he's gone, all right. I can promise you that, Chanel."

It was good to hear. But Chanel knew that with God gone, she wasn't out of the woods yet. She continued to confide in her mother. She was worrying about Mateo, and she worried whether he would still want her if he survived this—would he still want to be with her after finding out it was her fault? She allowed Charlie to come over when he'd forbidden it. She was an emotional wreck and she blamed herself for everything—the shooting, the home invasion, even her own rape.

Bacardi saw that Chanel was truly a wreck and that she would need some counseling in the future. Bacardi was familiar with her daughter's horror. Having been an ACS employee for several years, she'd done seen it all—the nightmares that some of these young girls go through—rapes, molestation, abuse, abandonment, starvation, some even committed suicide. She was familiar with counseling.

"Until you get through this, Chanel, I'm right here," she said sincerely. Chanel smiled.

"You think I could stay here with you till the time's up? I don't trust myself not to go after that muthafucka with a knife and butcher that son of a bitch from head to toe—cut off his dick and balls and carve him up like a fuckin' jack-o'-lantern."

Bacardi also questioned her parenting skills. How could she raise a daughter that would be okay with this? *Who was Charlie? And why would she do this to her own sister?*

Day after day, Chanel, and sometimes Bacardi, would go visit Mateo. He had been transferred from ICU and placed in a private room. Chanel would sit by his bedside for hours and take his hand into hers and kiss it. Sometimes she would climb into bed with him and kiss his face, and she would whisper loving things into his ear, play music for him, read to him, and, most important, she would pray for him.

Pyro continued to pay for the hotel room, and he managed their drug empire alone. He knew about the apartment Mateo had bought for them, but he figured that Mateo would want to be the one to take his new bride there if he ever woke up from his coma and fully recovered. It was supposed to be a surprise for Chanel, and he didn't want to take that away from them.

In the meantime, what he could do for his friend was execute his revenge. It was taking longer to kill God than he had expected. When Pyro would drive to the Glenwood Housing Projects to spy on the apartment, it seemed that the local police were watching God too.

.

Chapter Thirty-Six

August

You ou sure these fools got paper like that?" God asked Charlie.

"I'm sure, God. These fools are fuckin' paid," Charlie assured him.

God nodded. "A'ight, cuz you know we need this fuckin' money. We gotta leave town fo' a while."

Charlie nodded. "I'm wit' you, baby, fo' real. Let's get this money."

The two were like fireworks ready to go off—a bit edgy and less prepared than with their previous licks. They were hungry for another payday, and Charlie felt that this was it. The couple was like two crack fiends parked outside the Queens residence. The home invasion had become addictive to them. The money was good, but it was the rush of kicking in doors and committing murders that got them high and excited.

Charlie had found another mark for them to rob. However, doing a lick without Fingers around was an odd feeling.

In a Brooklyn nightclub, Charlie had found some bitch from Queens who was fucking with a grimy Brownsville dude. Charlie noticed the woman's Hermes bags, the Rolex watch, earrings—the whole nine yards. She just knew they had paper. Charlie had befriended the woman and gotten close to her, close enough to get her address. Now it was action time—mayhem and murder.

God handed Charlie a .45, and he cocked back a 9mm. The home looked average—nothing spectacular about it. There was a Ford Explorer in the driveway and a lawnmower left out in the yard.

Watching the place from across the street in the dark, God and Charlie felt they were ready to go. They saw their opening when another car pulled into the driveway. It was going to be as simple as 1, 2, and 3—push their way into the home and take over shit. They'd done it countless times.

A woman got out of the Chrysler 300. She was dressed nicely and carried a different color Hermes bag. Charlie had her eye on that bag. She ached to snatch it from that bitch's hand.

"Let's go!" God said.

God threw the black hoodie over his head, somewhat masking his face. Charlie did the same. Both wearing all black and black latex gloves, they promptly exited the vehicle and darted across the street in the shadows toward the unsuspecting victim. But unbeknownst to them, they were also being watched from a short distance.

The moment the woman stepped foot on her porch and put her key in the door, God and Charlie lunged at her from behind. Charlie thrust the barrel of her gun in the frightened woman's face and they pushed their way into the home. Before she could even scream, Charlie was all over her, violently pistol whipping her. God hurried through the house and caught the boyfriend completely off guard in the kitchen. He aimed his 9mm at him and told him to get down on his knees. The man complied.

The couple was duct taped and restrained in the kitchen, and God and Charlie started to ransack their house. Charlie immediately went to their bedroom to find those designer Hermes bags that she always saw that bitch with. She came across half a dozen of them in the closet. But Charlie had an eye for fashion and she spotted the difference in stitching and material. They were fake. All of them. And the jewelry was fake too.

"What the fuck!" she cursed.

God and Charlie vehemently went through the entire house, tearing things apart, turning things over, tearing down pictures and cutting up the couches and chairs. Where was the safe? The money? The clothes? There was nothing inside the house worth taking.

God looked fiercely at Charlie and shouted, "You told me they had fuckin' money!"

"I thought they did!"

All the couple had combined in the house was $97.00. Furious, God marched into the kitchen and went for the boyfriend, angrily pistol whipping him until his face turned bloody and there were several gashes across his forehead. Blood ran from his hair and forehead into his eyes and down his face.

"Where the fuck is everything?" God shouted at the boyfriend.

The boyfriend didn't respond. He had been badly beaten. He was a bloody mess. God had injured his hand during the attack and cross contaminated his DNA with the victim's. He wasn't thinking straight. He wanted cash, jewelry, drugs—anything.

"You fuckin' heard him!" Charlie shouted at the female.

She viciously assaulted the female while she was restrained. She kicked and pistol whipped the girl. Her face became puffy and swollen, a result of several hard blows to the face.

"They ain't got shit here worth taking!" God shouted.

"We need to go."

There was no payday. The couple had been fronting around town like they were ballers. But they weren't. It was only a gimmick. God felt that they'd left him with no choice. He lifted the barrel of the gun to the man's head and fired—*Bak!*

He coldly walked toward the girlfriend and repeated the same action, firing a bullet into her face at close range. Her body dropped face-down against the kitchen floor.

They hurried out the front door, God with the smoking gun still in his hand, and moved for their car parked across the street. They left the house with less than a hundred dollars, and God didn't plan on sharing it with Charlie.

Pyro watched the couple leave the Queens home in urgency. He bolted from his car with a .50 Cal Desert Eagle in his hand, a gun strong enough to bring down a charging elephant. The weapon wasn't meant to leave anyone alive.

Although he'd given Chanel his word not to harm her sister, this was his only opportunity to avenge Mateo's shooting, and he was going to take it. He charged toward the couple and started to cut loose the cannon in his hands—*Boom! Boom! Boom! Boom! Boom!*

The gunshots echoed through the streets like thunder, the rounds shattered car windows, and one bullet dangerously grazed God's ribcage. He stumbled and went down near the car. Charlie immediately ducked to the ground and was dumbfounded by the sudden attack, but she was miraculously spared. She had no idea who was shooting at them or why.

"Oh shit! Oh shit, what the fuck! Shit, I'm fuckin' hit!" God cried out in a panic. He could feel the warm blood against his skin and his adrenaline pumping.

Charlie provided him some cover when she fired back at Pyro, causing him to take cover behind a parked car. The distraction gave God and her just enough time to thrust themselves into the car they came in. God hurried to start it, and they peeled away from the scene, tires screeching and speeding away from Pyro trying to kill them both.

"Shit!" Pyro shouted. He'd missed his shot.

God felt like he had been hit with a large brick that came at him lightening speed. He was hit, but when Charlie inspected the wound, she told him that all he needed was a few stitches and a maybe a band-aid. The bullet had only grazed him, and the wound wasn't too deep.

"That muthafucka was from your sister's man—his friend," God exclaimed. "She fuckin' sent him."

"How do you know?"

"I got a good look at him."

"What beef does he have wit' you?"

God didn't reply right away. He had to think about things. "I don't know!"

"What do you mean you don't know?"

"I said I don't fuckin' know! It fuckin' looked like him—you know all them spics look alike."

"What the fuck is goin' on, God!"

"Dude must think we robbed his man!"

"You did!"

"*We* did, bitch, and don't you ever fuckin' forget that shit."

Charlie cringed at hearing her affiliation out loud. "Anyway, how would he know? I ain't talking. Chanel's scary ass don't know shit and Mateo has one foot in the grave."

"Well somebody's snitching, and it's either you or you told Claire and she's talking. I swear on my life I'll kill y'all bitches if I get jammed up!"

"Snitchin'!" The word offended Charlie. She rejected the insult. "Are you dumb?"

Things got heated inside the car. Their last lick was a flop, God was slightly injured, and they were still broke. Charlie was willing to stick by her man, but she knew he was lying to her. Since she'd set her sister up, their luck had been changing and things were going downhill.

"I know this is your fault, bitch!" God cursed.

"What? My fault? Fuck you! Fuck you, nigga!" she yelled.

Charlie couldn't control herself. While God was trying to drive the car, she put her hands on him, smacking him in the face and punching him everywhere. The car swerved on the road and God had to pull to the side to keep from crashing. Charlie was going off. God reacted and punched her in the face. It felt like he had broken her nose. The blood became thick over her mouth.

"You fuckin' bastard!" she shouted.

"Get the fuck out, Charlie!"

Charlie refused to leave. So, God irritably got out of the driver's seat, and even though shot and injured, he forcefully removed Charlie from the passenger seat. She tried to resist, but God threw her to the pavement, kicked her in her side, and left her there.

"Walk back to the projects, bitch!" he chided.

Coldly, he climbed back into the car and sped away, leaving Charlie stranded in Queens. With little cash on her and blood trickling from her nose, Charlie fussed, cursed, screamed, and had no choice but to go somewhere to clean herself up and try to get home.

She had to call an Uber and finally arrived home two hours later. Charlie walked through the front door looking a hot mess, and Claire, who was still up because she couldn't sleep, became concerned for her sister.

"What the fuck happened to you?"

Charlie snapped, "Mind ya fuckin' business," and she marched by Claire and stormed into her room, slamming the door behind her. It was one thing to be in love with a womanizer, but it was another ballgame to be in love with a violent and abusive man like God.

Claire wanted to help, but she knew Charlie wouldn't allow her into her business. She could only sit and watch from the sidelines while her older sister's life was spiraling out of control. She knew whatever it was Charlie and God were into wasn't pretty at all.

Claire was really trying to make amends for her wrong. She was trying to change her ways, and this time she was studying hard and wanted to give college another shot. The environment at home wasn't the best, but she tried to work with what she had. Bacardi was away with Chanel, Butch was being Butch, and Charlie was too busy chasing behind God. Being the middle child, Claire had to make do on her own.

Claire couldn't sit back and watch her sister crumble. *Fuck it*, she said to herself. She marched into Charlie's room to aid her.

"You need help, and I love you and I ain't taking no for an answer," said Claire gruffly.

Charlie was taken aback by Claire's sudden entry and snippy tone.

Claire gave her sister a bath and cleaned her wounds before feeding her and helping her to bed. Both her sisters were going through critical drama, and to think, Claire thought she had it bad.

Chapter Thirty-Seven

After the attempted murder on God, he decided to leave town right away, but first he made a quick stop to see his side chick, Kym. He needed her help. Kym left town with God for a few weeks. Her parents had a place in Syracuse, New York. It was a cabin on the lake where he could chill out and think and not look over his shoulder. The area was isolated and quiet, any neighbors were miles away, and the local road seemed to be longer than that. It was nothing but trees, grass, animals, and Mother Nature. God had to get used to the new and strange surroundings. He was a city boy, and the country was an entirely different world for him.

God watched Kym move around the place like a natural. She knew where everything was and how to operate things he had no idea what they were for.

"My parents used to bring me up here almost every summer when I was young. My father had a thing for the outdoors. He liked to get away for weeks at a time," said Kym.

What she said was irrelevant to God. He just needed a hideout. Brooklyn had gotten too dangerous and hot for him. He felt that the cops were coming down on him. That last lick was really sloppy, and there was no telling what kind of evidence they'd left behind. He'd assaulted Charlie and left her on the street like she was road kill. Would she be mad enough to come after him? God wasn't sure.

God watched Kym try to make the cabin a home for him. She was a nice girl, and God felt that he could really fall in love with Kym, if she wasn't so boring. She was so vanilla, just one flavor all the time. But she was useful, and that's what he needed right now—someone he could trust.

"We'll be okay here, God. It's just takes some time to get used to."

Yeah, getting used to. It was easier said than done.

By day three, God felt like he was going stir-crazy, but he couldn't leave because he had to sort some things out. He needed to get some cash together, and he wanted go after Pyro—plot to kill that fool.

Kym had become his liaison to the outside world. She would go back and forth for him, bring him food, clothes, entertainment, including pussy, and some comfort. Being alone in the woods in the middle of nowhere could change a man. God knew that he couldn't last for too long in Syracuse, and he was desperate.

He watched Kym in the kitchen cooking a meal for them. He knew her family had money and he needed Kym to do him a huge favor. Knowing what mood to put her in, God went to her and romantically grabbed her from behind and kissed the side of her neck. Kym smiled, loving his affection.

"You know I love you, right?" he said.

"I know."

"And I would do anything for you. I don't know what I would do without you," he said.

God squeezed her lovingly and continued to tenderly kiss the side of her neck. He turned her around in his arms and they came face to face with each other. She was a pretty woman, but far from a ride-or-die bitch like Charlie, he believed. God passionately tongued her down and his hands roamed across her breasts and grabbed her butt. She was becoming hot and bothered.

It was then that he said, "Can you do me a favor?"

"What is it?"

"I need a small loan." He kissed her lips.

"How much?"

"Not too much, just five stacks."

"Five stacks?"

"Five thousand dollars."

She was quite taken aback by the amount. Five thousand was nothing to sneeze at.

"That's a lot, baby."

"I know, but I promise I'll pay you back. I really need this. I got lawyers to take care of," he lied.

She heaved a sigh and relented. "Okay. I'll give it to you. But with one condition."

"What's that?" he asked.

"I need for you to sign a promissory note," she said.

A promissory note? Inside, he was cracking the fuck up. What the fuck good was a piece of paper? He didn't have a job or credit, and he never planned on going legit. If he lived a long life then it would be a jobless life.

"I promise," he said.

She smiled.

He was now hungry for something else. God kissed Kym fervently and threw her against the kitchen table, turned her around, ripped away her panties, and thrust his hard dick inside of her from the back. Kym gasped as God fucked her. The feeling of his big dick inside her, filling and stretching her, it was the way she liked it.

"You like this dick?" he teased. "Tell me you love this dick."

"I love your dick," Kym panted.

He entangled his fist around her hair and grabbed her side and continued to fuck the pretty bitch doggy-style. Their sexual movement forcibly shook the table. She could feel his muscles clench and release inside of her as he continued to thrust. It wasn't long before she came, and he—breathing hard and excited—came too.

It was what he needed, sex—something to get his mind off the troubles in the city. And Kym happily gave him whatever he wanted.

Later that week, after another long and hard fuck, God was showering while Kym was tidying up. God's cell phone rang in the bedroom. He couldn't hear it due to the running water, but Kym heard it ring several times and curiosity got the better of her. A picture of a pretty, light-skinned female with red hair popped up and the name read: Charlie B.

She gladly answered his phone.

Charlie was stunned to hear a bitch on the phone. "Bitch, who the fuck is this?" Charlie bickered.

"Bitch, who the fuck is this calling my man's phone?" Kym retorted.

"*Your* man?"

"Yes, my man," Kym repeated sternly.

The two women started to argue, and Kym made it a point to tell Charlie how God had just gotten finished eating her pussy and fucking her sideways, and now he was taking a shower.

The information infuriated Charlie. "Bitch, you don't fuckin' know who ya fuckin' wit'! I'll fuckin' kill you, bitch!"

"Fuck you, bitch!" Kym retorted.

But Kym, coming to her senses after briefly allowing Charlie to bring her out of her character, went on to explain how she would never fight over a man. She indicated that Charlie must have a low IQ to match her low self-esteem to fight over a man. The remark was a low blow toward Charlie, and it started to fuck with her head. Where she was from, everyone fought over their dudes.

"Kym, where you at?" she heard God calling her from the shower.

Kym smirked, and said, "You hear that, bitch? That's him calling me right now to join him in the shower. Bye bitch."

Kym hung up, leaving Charlie dumbfounded by the entire ordeal.

Charlie was devastated. She was slowly watching her world do a 180. She was no longer the apple of anyone's eye—not her parents, not her man.

When God finally called her weeks later, Charlie had mixed emotions. She didn't mention to him that she knew he had been staying with a girl named Kym. Despite everything he put her through, Charlie was still in love with him and she was happy to finally hear from him. It had been too long. She wanted to see him again.

"I got a place for us, baby," said God. "I want you to come over."

She was ready to run back to him with open arms. She missed him.

God had rented an apartment with the money Kym had given him. It was a decent place in New Jersey, a low-key neighborhood. He was tired of Brooklyn and tired of being harassed by detectives. He still had to watch his back, and New Jersey was close to home, but still far enough away to keep a low profile.

Charlie came to see him with extreme eagerness and some concern. The moment she walked into his new place, she hugged him and kissed him, already forgiving him for his past sins. They fucked everywhere from the bedroom, to the floor, to the shower, and back to the bedroom. Charlie was showing him how much she really missed him.

After the sex, Charlie's good pussy knocked God out cold as she knew it would. She took the opportunity to go through his cell phone and see what her unfaithful man was up to. God was a simple man and Charlie knew she'd crack his code. On the fourth try she got it. It was his building number: 89715. Once in, Charlie read all the texts between God and

Kym and a couple other jump-off bitches. She scrolled through his stored photos to see a myriad of pussy pics and ass shots from random hoes. Then there were a number of pictures from a prim and proper looking skank. Charlie knew this was her—the slick talking bougie bitch who answered his phone. Stupidly, God had stored her address and Charlie was salivating. This bitch was going to get her ass whooped.

When God woke up, Charlie resumed catering to him. She was willing to cook for him, and after feeding her man, she started with the questions.

Where did the money come from? She thought he was broke. The apartment was small, but it was cute and cozy. God made it clear to Charlie that he wasn't for the questions. He just wanted to have a good time and enjoy her. He was adamant that she "Shut the fuck up!" about everything.

"Don't ruin the moment, Charlie," he warned her.

To ease things between them, they started to drink and smoke weed. God was a heavy smoker and took a blunt of Amnesia to the face. Mixed with the alcohol, he became a very chill and laid-back individual. He no longer looked ruthless and malicious, but like a stoner high off of mushrooms. He was ready to talk about anything.

Unbeknownst to him, Charlie had drugged the liquor and laced the weed.

"You okay, God?" asked Charlie.

"Baby, I'm fine," he coolly replied.

Charlie started her line of questioning again, now that he was in a more relaxed and open state of mind.

"You know you can always keep it a hundred wit' me, right, God?"

"I know, baby . . . always one-hundred wit' you."

"So, who gave you the money for this new place?"

He smiled at her and said, "I got this new bitch I'm fuckin' wit' . . . Kym—good-ass pussy and shit, and if she wasn't a boring bitch, that bitch would be my ride-or-die. She's rich and she takes care of me."

The information was a lot for Charlie to take in and she frowned. But she continued with the questioning and the conversation transitioned to Chanel. Charlie needed to know the truth. She needed to hear him say it.

"What happened to my sister, Chanel?"

He finally came clean and said, "I didn't plan for it to happen. It just happened that one time. And the way your sister used to flaunt that sweet dark pussy around the place, I had to sample that shit. But that bitch wanted it. I ain't rape that bitch . . . and that pussy was too good. She got better pussy than you, baby." He had a dopey looking smile on his face.

Charlie's stomach started to do all kinds of flips and it was churning like a NutriBullet. She tried to fight the tears back. It felt like she was about to detonate from the anger that was swelling inside of her.

The drug she used was working far too well. God continued to dig his own grave. "I used people, Charlie, that's what I do, baby. I fuck bitches, kill people, and keep it moving . . . make this money. That's all I care about, is fuckin' money, baby. Money is my bitch."

"Do you love me?" she asked.

God laughed. "Bitch, I love what you can do for me."

The reply deeply hurt Charlie. She loved him with all her heart, but he continued to use her and disrespect her.

When he was done confessing, he lay back on the couch, legs cocked open and he continued to smoke his blunt and drink his liquor, not knowing he'd done fucked up. Charlie coolly got up from her seat to go into the kitchen.

God looked at her with his glassy eyes and said, "Babe, bring me some snacks back from the kitchen."

Charlie simply nodded her head. She soon returned looking like she was in a trance. She walked toward God and abruptly plunged the serrated steak knife into his chest. God jolted suddenly from the stabbing, jumping to his feet in absolute shock, but quickly he fell to his knees, becoming dizzy and weak. Charlie quickly pulled the knife out of his chest and she stabbed him again in the neck. His blood gushed out of him like a fountain. Charlie stood there like a woman possessed. She was shocked about her impulsive action. A part of her wanted to help save his life, but there wasn't much she could do for him now. From all the blood spewing from him, she knew that she'd probably struck an artery.

God held his hand over his neck wound and tried to reach for his cell phone on the coffee table, but Charlie grabbed it first and took a few steps back and stood there, watching the man die in agony.

"Please . . . please help me, babe. Call an ambulance . . . call . . ." he stammered as he was choking on his own blood. "I-I . . . I'm dyin'. . ."

Charlie stared at him. His eyes feared death and he uttered, "I-I love you, Charlie . . ."

He was crawling to her, leaving a trail of his blood behind. He definitely was a tough son of a bitch. He refused to die right away.

"Don't do me like this," he pleaded.

But it was already too late. He soon stopped moving and his eyes closed. He lay there unconscious and face-down on the floor, and then his heart eventually stopped. God was finally dead.

Charlie stayed in the apartment for several days with the body. She was completely shell-shocked. She had killed him. She had brutally stabbed him to death. Her days were spent crying and her nights were spent being terrified. She didn't want to go to jail for the rest of her life.

God's body had started to decay and it was leaving behind an awful stench that Charlie tried to mask daily. She would spray the place with Lysol and open all the windows, but it being a warm September with little breeze, it didn't help much.

Charlie desperately wrapped the body in blankets and moved it to the front door. She wanted to load him inside the trunk of her car, but God's carcass damn near weighed a ton to her. He was dead weight. How would she get him to the trunk of her car without being noticed?

She needed help. But from who?

She thought about calling Claire for help, but she didn't want to get her sister into any trouble. This was her mess, and she needed to clean it up. The fewer people who knew about this, the better. Charlie needed to take action, and sitting around the apartment twiddling her thumbs wasn't going to help her. The only thing she was capable of doing was using bleach to drench the body and wipe the entire area clean of her DNA. She loaded a plastic bag with the sheets, deleted her name and all her text messages from his phone, and finally left the apartment.

Kym arrived at the New Jersey rental and was extremely upset and frustrated with God. She had been calling his number for days with no response, and he wasn't returning her phone calls. God owed her a lot of money and she was there to collect. He needed to know who buttered his bread. Kym was ready to let God know that she wasn't some random bum bitch that he could fuck and use. She demanded respect.

Just as she was pulling up to the building, Kym saw a familiar looking woman. It had to be Charlie B. leaving the building. She fumed. God had some explaining to do.

Meanwhile, Charlie was making her exit from the lobby and saw Kym from afar, knowing that bitch was there to see God. She pulled out her phone and anonymously dialed 911 just as Kym was marching into the building. She told the dispatcher that she'd heard arguing coming from a certain apartment and subsequently a gunshot.

"Please hurry," Charlie cried out.

The police were on their way.

Inside the apartment, several uniformed officers burst through the door to see a grief-stricken Kym wailing and cradling a very dead God in her arms. "I know she did it! She did it! She killed him! She killed him!"

The cops forcefully pulled Kym from the body and placed the iron bracelets on her dainty wrists. She was arrested for murder.

Epilogue

Hawaii was a paradise—Heaven's artwork as far as the eye could see. It had beautiful sunsets, a rich blue ocean and clean, sprawling beaches. The weather was perfect. Romance and paradise went hand-in-hand for couples in Hawaii, where they could take advantage of moonlit walks on the pristine, sandy beaches, and where only the palm trees could hear their whispers. There were clear ocean views from the balconies of many suites. The sun and the moon seemed to glow brighter in paradise. Hawaii was peace of mind for newlyweds and everyone else. The melodious rush of warm Pacific waters surged at folks' ankles as their feet would pleasantly sink into the moist white sand.

The rich blue ocean was therapeutic, and as the ocean gently crashed against the white sands, it sounded like the beach was singing a tune—a melody that harmonized beauty and love and put a joyous spell over everyone.

She held Mateo's hand and stared lovingly in his eyes, as they walked barefoot across the beach, allowing the waves to wash against their feet. Chanel wanted to stay in paradise forever. She didn't want to go back home. She felt there was nothing there for her. Being with Mateo in bliss like this, it was all she wanted.

Hawaii was heaven. It was how she dreamed it to be—even better.

But that's all it was. A dream.

Chanel woke up by Mateo's side and immediately was thrust into a chaotic situation. Mateo's vitals had dropped dangerously low and he was about to flat-line. The machines sounded with alarms, and several doctors and nurses frantically rushed into the room to try and save Mateo's life.

"What's going on?" Chanel cried out.

"Ma'am, we need you to step outside," said the nurse.

"No! What's happening?"

"He's crashing. We need you to step outside!" the nurse exclaimed. She attempted to shove Chanel from the room so the staff could do their job at trying to save Mateo's life.

Chanel was overwhelmed with worry and grief. She tried to peek into the room to see what was happening, but there was a crowd of staff surrounding Mateo's bed. Equipment was being rushed into the room, and Chanel had no idea what they were trying to do. It all looked frenzied to her. But she couldn't lose him. Not now—not ever.

"Please, don't let him die! Don't let him die! Come back to me, Mateo. Ohmygod, come back to me. You promised that you wouldn't leave me," Chanel cried out.

The only thing she could do was drop to her knees and pray for him. Her eyes were coated with tears and grief. She prayed and prayed, and the medical staff was doing the best they could.

Mateo's heart stopped and he went flat-line.

A few hours later, Chanel stood by his bedside while Mateo gazed up at her beautiful face. He was silent, but she was all smiles.

"You came back to me," she said.

Mateo stared at Chanel dispassionately, almost like he didn't know who she was.

"I love you, baby. I do. I thought I was going to lose you," she said.

Mateo lay there quiet, almost like he was a vegetable. Chanel took his hand into hers and leaned forward and kissed him. But he didn't kiss her back. Chanel figured that he was still recovering, probably still in shock about what happened. His body had gone through a very traumatic experience and he'd been in a coma for quite some time.

"I love you, baby. We have a wedding, right? And a trip to Hawaii, Mateo. Okay? I'm here every day by your side until you get better, and I'm gonna become your wife."

Chanel then erupted into tears. "I'm sorry, baby. I'm so sorry. Can you please forgive me? I never should have invited them over. I'm sorry."

Mateo blinked a few times and stared at her with no reply. It was as if the lights were on, but no one was home.

Putting Out Fires

Charlie Brown, known in the streets as Red Charlie, has burned more bridges and started more fires than she can put out. Rehabilitation isn't high on her priority list, so when the smoke clears, she delves deeper into Brooklyn's underworld.

Soon Red Charlie becomes a miracle worker for a notorious organization, and her rise to the top is swift. Still, she's lost the one thing she yearns for: respect. The streets whisper words like grimy and trifling behind her back, but not out of earshot. This ding in her reputation compels her to seek revenge on her baby sister and regain her street cred.

IT'S ABOUT TO GET DIRTY

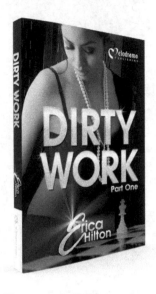 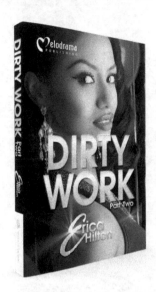

Poisoned Pawn

Harlem brothers, Kip and Kid Kane, are like night and day. While Kip is with his stick-up crew hitting ballers and shot-callers, the wheelchair-bound Kid is busy winning chess tournaments and being a genius.

Kip's ex, Eshon, and her girls, Jessica and Brandy, put in work for Kip's crew as the E and J Brandy bitches. Eshon wants Kip, but Kip is always focused on the next heist—the next big come-up.

When given an assignment by the quirky Egyptian kingpin, Maserati Meek, Kip jumps at the chance to level up to bigger scores. While doing Maserati Meek's Dirty Work, Kip and his crew find that doing business with crazy pays handsomely. But at what cost? Insanity leads to widespread warfare, and the last man standing will have to take down the warlord.

DON'T CALL IT A COMEBACK.